TRUST the PUSH

NEW YORK TIMES BESTSELLING AUTHOR

KAYLEE RYAN

Cover Design: Sommer Stein, Perfect Pear Creative Covers
Cover Photography: Sara Eirew
Editing: Hot Tree Editing
Formatting: Integrity Formatting
Proofreading: Deaton Author Services

CHAPTER One

Aubree

CLICKING SAVE ON THE PATIENT'S file, I glance at the clock. It's after seven on Wednesday night. My last patient left over an hour ago, and my ass has been glued to this chair ever since, getting caught up on the charting that I didn't have time to do today. Not that it matters. There's not anyone waiting at home for me.

I moved to Knoxville, Tennessee, the same day I graduated high school. I lived in a small rural town in Northern Tennessee with my father, well, if you can call him that. I like to refer to him as my sperm donor; that's about the only thing he's ever done for me. Yeah, he put a roof over my head and food on the table, but the roof leaked and the food was in short supply. I can't ever remember a time when things were good at home. As the story goes, or so I'm told, my mom ran off before my first birthday. Turns out she was only with my dad because of me; she wanted to make it work but couldn't. She turned to drugs, and well, you can take it from there.

My father resented me for her leaving. Hated is a better term. He blamed me, but to hear my Uncle Bobby tell it, Mom would have left a hell of a lot sooner had it not been for me. Uncle Bobby was the one person in my life I could count on, always… no matter what. I spent more time with him than I did with Dad. When I was eleven, I begged my father to let me live with him. That was the first and last time he ever hit me. I never asked again. He never brought it up.

That was my life.

I planned to move in with my uncle as soon as I turned eighteen. Dad would stop getting assistance from the state, so he would no longer care what I did. At least that was my thought. Turns out I never got to test that theory. Two days before my eighteenth birthday, just two months before I graduated from high school, Uncle Bobby passed away from a massive heart attack.

That put things in motion, plans changed, new ones were made, and here I am. Living in Knoxville on my own, working as a massage therapist. I love my job though it's not what I wanted to do. I always wanted to be a physical therapist, but life happens and you alter plans. I'm happy with my career choice, and the life I've created for myself. What else could a girl ask for?

After shutting down my computer, I pack up my bag to head home. Just as I'm walking out of my office door, I run into Jackie, my boss. "Hey, sorry, I didn't hear you coming."

She waves me off. "I thought maybe you might still be here. Hoping is more like it."

"What? No lecture on how I work too hard? How I'm working my life away? You do know you're my boss, right?" I tease. She's the absolute best person to work for. She's fair, understanding, and she acknowledges those of us who go above and beyond, even by making us block out time to go home early when she sees we're burning the candle at both ends. Like I said, she's amazing.

"No," she says with a laugh. "Not tonight. I did have something I wanted to talk to you about. Can we sit?"

"Sure." Turning around, I head back in my office. Instead of taking the chair behind my desk, I sit in one of the two chairs I have for visitors or patient consults. Jackie takes the seat next to me. "Is everything okay?"

"Oh, yes. Sorry, I didn't mean to alarm you. It's just been a long day, and then I just received a call from Jonah."

"It's never good when the CEO calls you this late in the day. Patient complaint?" I guess.

"No, actually a request. Did you know that Knoxville Health Partners sponsors a racing team?"

"No, but then again, this organization is so large it's hard to keep up with all the ventures. Not to mention, I'm not much of a racing fan. I mean, I guess I can't say I'm not a fan. I've never watched it."

"My husband loves it. We've gone a few times. It's dirt track racing. When we first started sponsoring the team, I volunteered to represent KHP and we got all-access passes. He was in heaven."

"I bet." I smile at her. She always gets this sparkle in her eye when she talks about her husband or her kids. "So, what does KHP sponsoring a racing team have to do with me?"

"Well, we got a call from the crew chief of the car we sponsor. I guess one of the crew members was trying to be Hercules and pulled a muscle in his back. He wanted to know if our sponsorship involved treatment for the crew."

"Okay, so put him on my schedule." Seems easy enough to me.

"Well, that's the thing. They leave first thing in the morning for a race. So, they were hoping that someone could work on him tonight."

"I can stay," I tell her. "What time will they be here? If I have time, I'll run down to the cafeteria for a sandwich. I'm starving," I say, just as my stomach decides to let me know it's empty. This causes us to laugh.

"That's sweet of you, but Jonah kind of told them that we would go to them."

Sighing, I sit back in my chair. "Okay, when and where?" I'm just going home to an empty apartment. I'll just consider this a part of my 'get out more' plan.

"I can't thank you enough for this, Aubree."

"It's fine. I'm off tomorrow since I work Saturday, so I'll be able to sleep in."

"Here's the address." She hands me the yellow Post-it note. "The guy you need to ask for is Kevin."

"Kevin. Got it. Anything else I should know?"

"That's really all the information that I have. Other than the fact that Jonah was adamant that we take care of whatever it is they need."

"We already sponsor them. I wonder what the big deal is?"

"Public image is my presumption. This goes above and beyond sponsorship. My guess is that this driver is a big deal since we're sponsoring him. I assume Jonah is hoping for a shout-out in victory lane."

"Isn't that a NASCAR thing?"

She laughs. "Honey, that's a racing thing."

I nod. "I've got this. I'll go meet this Kevin guy, work on whoever it is that needs me, and be gone. I don't really need the details of the track."

"No, you really don't. Thank you again, Aubree. I'll be sure that you are well compensated for this."

"No problem." I wave her off. "I'll see you on Friday." With a smile, she stands and leaves my office. After pulling a Knoxville Health Partners bag out of my bottom desk drawer, I head to one of my two treatment rooms to grab some supplies. I don't really know what I'm up against, so I grab a few different lotions and oils, as well as a few massage aids. That's the best I can do with the information that I have.

Back in my office, I snag my bag and purse and lock up. My first stop is a drive-thru, for some food. I park in the grocery store parking lot next door while I scarf down my burger and fries. Plugging my phone into the charger, I pull up my GPS app and type in the address that Jackie gave me. "And we're off," I say aloud.

Thirty minutes later, I'm pulling up to a mailbox with the right numbers, but I can't see anything but a driveway and woods. Slowly, my car creeps along the gravel path lined with trees. I'm starting to worry, thinking maybe I should turn around, when the trees disappear and the most beautiful log cabin I've ever seen presents itself. Scanning the property, I see there is a massive building that sits off to the right. There is a huge trailer and lots of trucks. My guess is that is where I should be. I point my car toward the shop even though the house is calling to me. It's gorgeous. Maybe I can ask to see it before I leave.

Once I've pulled my Impala between two trucks, I turn off the ignition and reach for my phone. I scream when someone knocks on my window.

"Sorry," the guy says, holding his hands up in surrender. "Are you from KHP?"

Rolling down the window, just enough so he can hear me better, I reply, "Yes." I give him a shaky smile. "I'm Aubree."

"Thank you for coming on such short notice. Rick thinks he's Hercules and pulled out his back. We leave for the track in the morning and we need him better." He steps back so I can climb out of my car.

"I'll do my best. Sometimes these things take time and more than one session. It all depends on what he can handle as far as pain tolerance." I offer him my hand. "Aubree Chance, nice to meet you…"

"Kevin, Kevin Henderson. I'm the crew chief for Bishop

Racing."

"So, where's my patient?" My heart has finally slowed back to a normal rhythm. This guy seems nice; his eyes are kind. Not the best way to judge a stranger, but from my life experiences, kind eyes usually never steer you wrong.

"He's in the lounge." He points to the large building. "Follow me. Do you have anything I need to carry for you?"

"No, the facility doesn't have a travel table, so we will just have to work with what we have."

"He's desperate, so I'm sure he'll do whatever you tell him to do." He opens the door and motions for me to go in before him.

Kevin referred to this as the lounge, and it looks just like that. There is a small kitchen area off to the side, and a small living area with a huge sectional couch and the largest television I've ever seen mounted on the wall. There are three doors on the far wall. The floors are a mix of gray, black, and white paint flecks. It's much nicer than I would have imagined a race shop to be.

"That door…" Kevin points to the first door on the left. "…is the bunks. That's where we crash when we're too exhausted to drive home after we get back from being on the road. The middle door leads to the shop, and the third door is the bathroom. It's more like a locker room of sorts."

"Got it. So where do you think we should try this?"

"Actually, I'm not sure. I guess on the couch? That would be more comfortable for you than the bunks."

"Yeah." I laugh. "The couch it is. I can just have him switch directions if I can't reach both sides."

"Great. He's lying down. My wife, Ashley, told him to lie down with a heating pad. She also gave him… Advil, I think." He pulls out his phone, hits a few buttons, and places it to his ear. "Hey, babe. I have Aubree here. She's from KHP. What did you give Rick?" He waits for her to answer. "Okay, thanks. Yeah, that's fine." Again, he pauses. "Love you too." He's grinning when he hangs up. "So, yeah, Ashley gave him Advil."

"Thank you. Where's my patient?" I ask again.

"Right. I'll be right back." He strolls to the left-hand door and disappears behind it.

I get to work, setting the items I brought with me out on the table. Looking down at the couch, I worry about the oils and lotions leaking through. I'll have to ask Kevin for a blanket or sheet if they have one. The chaise lounge section should work for what we need. It might be a bit awkward, but possible. I didn't even think to run home and get my portable table. Oh, well, nothing I can do about it now. I'll remember this for next time. If there ever is a next time.

"So, he's asleep," Kevin says from behind me.

Turning to face him, I nod. "The Advil more than likely helped with the pain and relaxed him enough to sleep."

"Yeah, I tried waking him, but he's dead to the world."

"Okay, we'll let him sleep a little longer. I have my e-reader with me. I can just sit here and read for a while, and we can see if he wakes up. Oh, and do you have a sheet or a blanket or something we can put down on the couch? I don't want the oils or lotions to soak through."

"This is a shop couch," he counters.

"Still, I'd hate for it to be stained. Do you have something that might work?"

"Sure, we have extras in the bunk room. I'll go get one and try to shake Rick again while I'm in there." He winks and turns back to the bunk room.

"Any luck?" I ask a few minutes later when I hear the door open.

"Blanket, yes, Rick, no." He hands me the extra blanket.

"Okay, well thankfully, I'm off work tomorrow, so I'll just hang out for a bit unless you think he's okay and I should go?" I know the answer before he opens his mouth, but I wanted to throw that out there just in case. My bed is calling my name.

"No, he's still going to need to be worked on. You're a

massage therapist, right? That's what we asked for. Ashley, my wife, thought that would help him the most."

"Yes, I'm a massage therapist." Looking around the room, I point to the couch. "I'll get everything set up over there and wait for a bit."

"Thank you, Aubree. We leave tomorrow early for the track, and we have a limited crew, so we need Rick in working order."

"I'll do my best, but like I said, sometimes one session isn't enough."

"We'll take what we can get."

I chuckle at that. "All right then."

"My wife will be here in a little while. She's bringing dinner. There will be plenty for you as well."

"Thank you, but I hit a drive-thru on my way here. I came straight from the office."

"And his dumb ass is asleep," Kevin mumbles, but I can still hear him. "Right, I'll give him another hour or so. Is that okay? Then I'll dump cold water on him if I have to."

"Sure," I concede. "I'll just be over here on the couch." I get to work setting the blanket on the chaise lounge and then settle in to read for a while. I could have thrown a fit and said I wouldn't stay, but really, nothing is waiting for me at home, and Jackie acted as though this was important. I'd hate for her to catch the fallout from Jonah, the CEO of KHP, because I up and decided to be a diva. I would be reading at home too, so this works.

"Who the hell are you?" a deep booming voice demands.

I startle and open my eyes. Getting my bearings, I realize where I am and that I fell asleep reading. Blinking, I focus on the man standing before me, arms crossed over his chest, glaring at me. "I'm sorry?"

"Who the hell are you?" he repeats.

I sit up straighter to address him. "My name is Aubree, I—"

"I don't care. What are you doing here? Who let you in here?" He fires off questions. "This is not a fucking hangout for groupies," he spits.

"Hold up," Kevin says, appearing at his side. "This is the massage therapist I told you about."

"Really? You did a bang-up job picking this one. What the hell is she doing sleeping on the job?"

"I-I'm sorry." I stand and come face-to-face with him. "I was waiting on Rick." I look at Kevin for reassurance. "I was reading and must have fallen asleep."

"Relax, man," Kevin says. He's looking at this new guy, whoever he is, but the new guy still has his eyes locked on me. "Rick took some Advil and fell asleep. Aubree was nice enough to wait to let him sleep it off a little. Take it easy. She's doing us a favor."

He turns to look at Kevin. "Where is he?"

"Sleeping."

"Jesus. Does anyone work around here?" He turns on his heel and stomps toward the door of the bunk room. He's not quiet when he storms into the room, flips on the light, and yells for Rick to "wake his ass up." There are some muffled words before he turns and heads back toward us. Instead of stopping, he keeps walking past and right out the shop doors.

"Sorry about that. He's a little worked up," Kevin says. "This race tomorrow. He's leading the points, and we've had some issues with the car, and now Rick. He's stressed."

"What's his issue?" A tall guy with dark hair, who I assume is Rick, joins us.

"No issue," Kevin says. "Rick, this is Aubree. Aubree, this is Rick. She's a massage therapist from KHP here to work on you."

"You think it will help?" he asks me.

"Not really knowing much about your pain and condition, I'm not sure. Let's get started and see what we can do." I turn around and hit Play on my soothing playlist on my phone. It's more for me than for him. I usually don't play music in my treatment rooms. However, right now I need something to calm my nerves. I spend the next fifteen minutes or so talking with Rick about his injury and where the pain is, what makes it better or worse, and then have him lie on his belly on the chaise lounge. Time to get to work.

CHAPTER Two

BLAINE

COULD ANYTHING ELSE GO WRONG with this day? When we went to load the car this afternoon, I could tell something was off. After a few practice runs around our track here at the house, we figured the rear bearings needed to be replaced. Not a huge issue, but before race day, it sucks balls. Shit isn't supposed to go wrong the day before we leave. On top of that, the hauler needed to be stocked with food and drinks, which required me to go to the grocery store. Normally, this too is not an issue, but they had two lanes open for fifty shoppers. I stood in line for thirty minutes, which of course, put me in a bad mood. Who has time for that? Normally, this is something my mom would help out with. She's retired now and says she enjoys it, that it gives her something to do. However, she and my father are on vacation in Aruba. Thanks to yours truly. What in the hell was I thinking when I booked it midseason? Oh, right, I wasn't thinking. I just called the travel agent and told her to make it happen.

Rookie mistake.

Then, I walk in the shop and find a sexy-as-sin redhead asleep on the couch. My first thought was she was a groupie who'd somehow snuck her way in. I admit that I looked my fill of her before demanding to know who she was. Her big green eyes, sleepy and confused, and those full pouty lips. Fuck, she's a looker. With a glance I could tell she wasn't the groupie type, which means she's not for me. Not that I'm against settling down, but this life... it's hard. Traveling the majority of the week, being away from friends and family. I've been fortunate enough that my closest friends are my crew, and my parents, who are both technically retired if you don't count the work they do for me, travel with us most of the time as well.

I see the strain it puts on the other drivers and their significant others. I hear their kids crying that they miss them on the days they do make it to the track. Why would I want to put my wife and kids through that? I'm at a point in my life where relationships of that nature are a low priority. I'm the youngest driver to win two championships. I'm the youngest driver to win back-to-back championships. This year, I want to break both of those records.

My focus is racing.

I have zero time for a relationship. So, I don't do it. I have the occasional random hookup—one night, no strings—and it works for me. I have everything I need. Besides, it's hard to know who you can really trust in this business. Most women see your fame or your fortune and look at you as a way for them to further their careers, or hell, even just a meal ticket. I have no interest in either one, no matter how hot she is.

Double checking that I have everything loaded in the hauler, I head back to the shop for the same reason I was there earlier. I need to grab some more tear-offs for my helmet. I got distracted by the auburn-haired beauty.

Aubree.

Her name fits her. She distracted me, so here I am retracing my steps. As soon as I enter the room, I hear a low deep moan.

"Right there, oh, that's it," Rick moans loudly.

I freeze, stopping in my tracks. If he's fucking her on the couch, I'm going to kick his ass. The pulled muscle in his back will be the last thing he has to worry about. Moving toward the couch, I stop and take in what's happening. Aubree is sitting on Rick's back, straddling him, right over his ass, as she has both hands massaging and working his back. He moans again, as if what she's doing to him is better than sex.

"This how you work on all your patients?" I ask, crossing my arms over my chest. I'm fully aware my stance and the tone of my voice makes me sound like a dick. I'm good with that. There is just something about this girl that rubs me the wrong way.

Her head pops up, and those green eyes look alarmed and... angry. This little redhead definitely has fire inside of her. "This is not normal working conditions," she snips. "Normally, I would have a table."

"So, where is it? Where's your table?"

She huffs out a breath, causing the hair hanging over her eyes to blow out then fall right back where it was. "I came straight from the office. We don't have portable tables there. I didn't want to waste time going home to get mine, so we are working with what we have."

"Right." I give a derisive laugh. "You didn't want to waste time going home to get yours, yet you had plenty of time to fall asleep on my couch."

"Your couch?"

"That's right. Who do you think owns this place?"

"That's irrelevant. I'm here to do a job. That's what I'm trying to do."

"Come on, man, let her finish. I never would have believed this would help. Ash was onto something," Rick says, his words muffled as he speaks into the couch.

"Ash? What does she have to do with her?" Just my luck she and Ash are friends, and the sexy temptress will be hanging around more. I don't need the distraction or the temptation, not with a girl like her. Without a doubt, she would want nothing to do with my one-night stand mantra.

"This was her idea. She suggested massage," Rick tells me.

"Make sure you don't get that shit on the couch."

"What the fuck, Blaine? It's the shop couch. We sit on it with way worse on our clothes," Rick says, lifting his head as much as he can to be heard.

"I don't want to sit down and get up smelling like a bitch."

"Excuse me?" She stops and looks up at me, blazing fire in those green eyes of hers.

"You know, the smell of that shit. Smells like a woman, or one of those stores in the mall."

"It's menthol," she says, deadpan.

"Well, whatever it is, I don't want to smell like it." I turn and walk off. In the shop, I gather the extra tear-offs before I forget them for a second time and take a look around, making sure there is nothing that we've forgotten.

"Ash just pulled up," Kevin says, walking toward me. "She picked up some pizza."

"She coming with us this go 'round?" I ask him. His wife, Ashley, is a receptionist at a law office here in Knoxville. She only works part-time, but her schedule does not always coincide with her being able to travel with us. Much to her husband's dismay.

"Nah, not this time," he tells me.

Kevin Henderson has been my best friend since the sixth grade. We bonded over our love of racing—both of us equally surprised that the other knew what dirt track racing was. Our fathers were big fans and passed that on to us. Kev and I took our love for the sport to a whole new level. I love the thrill of being behind the wheel of a car, going into the turns, never lifting, the adrenaline. Kev, his love is the mechanical side. Making the car purr as he likes to call it. I can tell him what I'm feeling and together, we make it the best car on the track. We work well together. I'm lucky to have him on my team.

"Next time," I console.

"Yeah, we're gonna start trying," he says with a grin. "Fucking stoked and scared all at the same time."

"That's gonna be hard, man." I could not imagine having a baby and being gone as much as we are. It's selfish but I hope he stays with me on the team as my crew chief. I wouldn't hold it against him if he decided not to. I just can't see being away from your family like that.

"I know, but it'll be worth it. You know you can't stay a bachelor forever."

"Says who?"

"You're an only child. You really going to deprive your momma of grandkids?"

I run my fingers through my hair. "Fine," I concede. "Maybe one day, but right now, I want this championship." That's the goal. Eyes on the prize.

His phone dings. "She's here. Let's eat." With a slap to my shoulder, he quickens his strides as he makes his way into what we like to call the lounge or living area of the shop to meet his wife.

I take my time, taking one last look, slowly going through my mental checklist to make sure that we have everything we need this weekend. Once I'm satisfied, tear-offs in hand, I join them in the lounge.

"Guys, I'm telling you. You need a massage," Rick says, standing from the couch. He turns this way and that, testing out the muscles in his back. "You're a miracle worker." He picks Aubree up and spins her around. Her laughter rings out throughout the room. It's almost if she has this sweet yet innocent air about her. What game is she playing?

"You done playing?" I call out to him.

"Blaine, don't knock it until you try it."

My eyes move to her, to Aubree, to find her already watching me. "That what you want, sweetheart? For me to give you a try?" I smirk. "Ouch," I say when I feel a not-so-hard punch to my arm.

"Be nice," Ashley scolds me. "Aubree, thank you for coming last minute. Come eat with us."

"You're welcome, and thank you, but I grabbed a sandwich on my way here."

"That was hours ago. Eat," Kevin encourages.

"Really, I should get going. It's been a long day." She turns her attention to Rick. "You should drink plenty of water to help wash out the toxins. I would suggest another in a week or so. You might be sore tomorrow, but it will be better than the pain," she explains.

"Thank you, Aubree. I feel better already."

"I bet you do," I mumble under my breath. Forcing myself to turn away from her, I grab a couple of slices and toss them on a paper plate. On their own accord, my feet carry me to the couch, where I plop down and put my feet up on the table. I ignore her while I shovel bite after bite of the greasy pizza into my mouth. It's not until I'm finished with my first slice that I realize I haven't eaten all day.

"Excuse me," she says, standing beside me. She has her bag full of whatever it was she was using that's smelling up the place on her arm.

I contemplate making her step over, but decide against it. Instead, I drop one leg then the other, allowing her space to pass. I check her out as she walks away, and I can't help but wonder what she looks like out of those scrubs. Pity I'll never know.

"How much do I owe you?" I ask Ash once the pizzas have been devoured.

"Nothing."

"Really, tell me how much. I appreciate you taking care of me this week."

"It wasn't just for you." She shakes her head.

"I know that, but you know what I mean."

"I do, and it was Little Caesars so it was inexpensive. You

don't owe me anything."

Reaching into my wallet, I pull out a fifty-dollar bill and shove it into her purse that's hanging off her shoulder. "I appreciate it." I wink and then rush out the door knowing she'd try to fight me on it. As soon as I exit, I see red hair crouching next to a red Impala.

Aubree.

She's petting my boxer, Camber, and the traitor is lapping up the attention like she never gets any. She's the most spoiled dog on the planet. "Camber!" I yell out for her. Her ears perk up, and she turns her head but makes zero effort to move away from the back scratch that Aubree is giving her. I walk toward them, and neither my traitor of a dog or the gorgeous redhead seem to care. "Thought you left," I say when I'm just a few feet away.

"That was the plan," she says, all her focus remaining on my dog.

"What stopped you?"

She points to her back left-side tire that's completely flat. "That."

"You don't know how to change a tire?" I ask. "Isn't that something that all dads teach their daughters?"

"I wouldn't know. Mine hated me, so...." She shrugs, hurt crossing her face.

I'm taken aback at her bluntness of the situation. I also feel like a piece of shit for obviously upsetting her. "So, you just going to sit out here all night and pet my dog?" I reach out and scratch Camber behind the ears.

"I called AAA."

I raise my eyebrows at her. "You did what?"

"I called AAA. They should be here soon. I'm sorry if I'm in the way."

"You called AAA, when you're in the driveway of a race shop?"

"Yeah, I mean, I know you're not happy I'm here, and it's not any of your responsibilities to take care of me. I can do it on my own."

"With AAA?"

"I pay them for this exact reason."

"Call them back. Tell them it's taken care of." I'm already walking around to the back of her car. "Pop the trunk."

"What? No, it's fine. They should be here any minute."

"I call bullshit. They always take forever. Pop the trunk and cancel them. I'll have you fixed up in no time."

"Really, you don't have to do this."

Crossing my arms over my chest, I glare at her. "Aubree. Pop the damn trunk."

"Fine," she grumbles, reaching in through the driver's side window and hitting the button.

There is a blanket and an auto emergency kit, you know the kind with flares and jumper cables. I smile because even though she has it, I can almost guarantee that she has no clue how to use them. At least she's prepared for the worst. Lifting the bottom, I verify that she does indeed have a spare. I shut the trunk and head toward the shop.

"That's it? All that pop the trunk"—she tries to make her voice deep—"and you walk away."

Stopping in my tracks, I turn on my heel and face her. "I'm going to get the portable air compressor."

"Um, I have a flat," she says slowly, like she needs to be as clear as possible for me to understand.

"I know that, smartass. I'm going to put air in your tire so you can drive around to the garage doors. I'm going to put it on the lift to change it. If you drive on it like it is now, you'll destroy your wheels."

"Sounds like a lot of trouble. Really, AAA will be here soon."

"Cancel," I say again before turning back around and heading toward the garage for the portable air compressor.

CHAPTER Three

Aubree

I WATCH HIM WALK AWAY. His jeans are tight in all the right places, worn and faded from hours in the shop I'm sure. He may be an asshole, but his ass is fine. I'm tempted to pull out my cell phone and snap a picture for Maria, my best friend. Then I remind myself I'm a professional and I'm here for a professional matter. In all honesty, he walks too damn fast, and I knew he would be too far away if not already inside the garage by the time I had the camera ready.

Leaning in through the window, I grab my phone and call AAA. "Hi, I need to cancel a call I put in about thirty minutes ago. My name is Aubree Chance." I wait while they pull up my account.

"Ms. Chance, we're running behind and it will be at least another hour."

Gah. Thankfully, Blaine is willing to help. "I need to cancel," I tell her again.

"I'm truly sorry for your delay. I've got your appointment canceled in our system."

"Thank you." Once I end the call, I toss my phone back through the window and it lands on the seat with a thud.

"You get through?" His deep voice comes from behind me, causing me to jump.

"Yeah, it was going to be another hour before they could get here. Thank you. For helping me. I appreciate it."

He doesn't acknowledge my thank you; instead, he gets to work putting air into my tires. I watch him as he works, all the while petting Camber—at least I think that's what he called her. Not that she's giving me a choice. She touches her nose to my hand every time that I stop. She's such a sweet dog. Nothing like her owner.

"All right, give me the keys." He stands and holds his hand out.

"I can drive," I insist. It's a shame his good looks have been wasted on such an arrogant asshole.

"Suit yourself. Drive around back. Put her in bay three." He picks up the portable air compressor and heads back toward the garage.

Opening my door with a huff, I'm almost knocked over when Camber jumps inside. "You want to go for a ride?" She barks and I have my answer. "Okay, well, you have to move over." I wave my hand to get her to jump over the console into the passenger seat. Once I'm settled behind the wheel, I reach over and scratch behind her ears. "Good girl."

Doing as he said, I drive around to the back of the building and realize there are four bays. Did he mean third from the left or third from the right? I'm going with third from the left, that's the most logical with the third from the right, which is the second door in my eyes.

"I said third door," he calls out.

"This is the third door," I call back out the window. Backing up, I start to pull into bay two and realize he wants me to drive it on the lift contraption. "I don't want to wreck," I say, hanging my head out the window to look at where I'm going.

"I told you to let me drive."

"You didn't tell me I'd have to drive it up on this thing," I point to the lift.

"Climb out." He opens my door. I do as he says, not because he can boss me around, but because I don't want to wreck my car. Furthermore, I don't want to hit anything or cause any damage to his shop either. It's best if I sit this one out.

Camber barks when Blaine climbs in, making him laugh. I watch as a smile lights up his face. He really is handsome. Dark hair, hazel eyes that make you feel as if he can see right through you. He's sporting a few days of stubble on his face, not quite a beard, but in another couple of days, it would be. Then there's his muscles. His black T-shirt is stretched tight around his arms. I'm envisioning a story where my favorite author referred to it as arm porn. I totally get the appeal after meeting Blaine.

I stand by and watch as he pulls my car onto the lift and begins to jack it up. Camber keeps me company, and before I realize it, he's lowering the lift and backing my car out of the garage. It took no time at all. "Thank you," I say when he steps out.

"That donut will get you home, but you really need to take this and get it repaired or buy a new one." He's straight to the point once again with no acknowledgment of my thank-you. I'm not sure what his deal is, but he's maddening.

"I'll take care of it. I really appreciate you helping me."

He nods and walks back into the garage. I wait, not sure what he's doing, but when the garage door closes, I realize I've been dismissed. Looking down at Camber, who is still attached to my side, I give her another rub behind the ears. "How do you put up with him?" She doesn't reply, not that I expected her to. I say goodbye to Camber, before climbing in my car and driving home on my spare. Looks like I'll be spending my day off in the tire shop.

Walking into work Friday morning, I'm still off-kilter. As soon as I got home on Wednesday night, I started searching the internet for him… Blaine. My search was fruitful as I discovered his name is Blaine Bishop of Bishop Racing Enterprises. I also learned that they call him Checkmate. Apparently, he's a force to be reckoned with on the track. He's won back-to-back championships, and if he wins this year—and by what my research tells me, he's on the right path—he will be the youngest Dirt Late Model driver to not only win three championships, but win them consecutively.

He's kind of a big deal.

I guess that explains his attitude on Wednesday night. I get it. I was a strange girl in his shop or headquarters… whatever in the hell I'm supposed to call it. However, that doesn't give him a free pass to be a dick. Mr. Checkmate seems to have a chip on his shoulder. Maybe he was just nervous about the race? I think about it and then quickly dismiss the idea. It wasn't nerves that had him acting that way. It was just him. Blaine "Checkmate" Bishop in his full glory. I guess it could have been worse. I could have had to work on him instead of Rick. At least *he* was grateful.

I can't seem to figure him out. What's worse than that, is that I want to. I've done nothing but think about him and his contradictory mood swings. There has to be some good in him somewhere; he did help me with my tire. Then again, he probably just wanted me off of his property, and the fastest way to do that was to help me. I can't seem to figure him out. He's nice, and then he's a jerk. He's contradicting himself at every turn. The tire was irreparable, per the man at the tire shop. I have a feeling he just wanted to sell me a new tire, but what do I know? He knew that I had no clue, and I'm sure he took advantage of the situation. It's not like I have anyone to call or go with me who would know about these things. I probably could have asked Isaac, my best friend Maria's husband, to help me out, but I hate asking him. I feel like I lean on them, especially

Maria, more than I should. They're really all that I have.

"How did it go?" Jackie asks from the doorway of my office.

"It was fine. He was pretty stiff. He'll need another session." There is no point in telling her about Blaine. Besides what would I say… his sexy boss was an asshole. Then he was nice and fixed my tire, then went back to being an asshole? I confuse myself just thinking about it. I can only imagine how it would sound if I spoke the words aloud.

"Yeah, it must have been bad for them to call in a favor from a sponsor."

"Definitely," I say, glancing at my laptop screen to see my patient schedule for the day.

"I'll let you get to it. I just wanted to stop in and see how it went and to thank you again."

I stop and look up. "Sorry." I realize I was being rude. "Just getting ready for the day. You're welcome." With a nod, she leaves my office, and I go set up my treatment rooms for the day. There is a receptionist who checks the clients in, but I take care of bringing them back and cleaning my own rooms. It's not a huge deal as a clinical hour is fifty minutes and a clinical half hour is twenty minutes. I have plenty of time to clean one room, while my next patient is getting ready in the room next door. I've done this so many times over the last few years, I have it down to a science. I feel like I could prepare the rooms, and maybe even massage, in my sleep.

The day moves on at a steady pace. I have a full schedule, but I like it that way. It keeps me busy. Sitting in my office, I'm watching my computer screen, waiting to see if my last patient for the day has arrived. A quick glance at the clock, I see that they are already four minutes past their appointment time. The screen turns to "no show" status just as the phone on my desk rings.

"Hey, Aubree, this is Angie in reception. Your four o'clock just called to cancel. I explained the no show policy and marked them as a no show," she explains.

"Thanks, Angie. Did they mention why they were not coming?"

She laughs. "Yeah, something about a race tonight that he forgot about."

"Thank you." Hanging up the phone, I lean back in my chair. How is it that I've worked here for over four years now and this is the first I've heard of this racing epidemic? Shaking out of my thoughts, I finish up my charting for the day and am actually out the door at five, which is a rare occurrence for me.

Once I'm in my car and on the way home, I call Maria to see what she and Isaac are getting into tonight.

"What's wrong?" she asks in greeting.

"Um, nothing. Why?"

"Because you're supposed to be at work."

My best friend is a worrier. I met Maria at the coffee shop just around the corner from where I attended massage therapy school. We were standing in a long line waiting for our caffeine fix and started chatting. She invited me to sit with her and we hit it off. I was new to town, didn't know a soul, too busy working retail at the mall and going to school to make new friends. It was just me. Now I have Maria and, by extension, her husband, Isaac. They're my family.

"I'm fine." I chuckle. "My last patient canceled. Something about a race."

"Oh, I wonder if it's the same race we're going to?"

"You go to the races? How did I not know this about you?"

"I've been to a few dirt track races here and there. Isaac gets pit passes through his work. They're a big sponsor for this weekend's event."

"Weekend? How many races are there?"

"One big race, but there's qualifying and things like that."

"Huh. I guess this racing thing is a big deal." I want to tell her about my Wednesday night adventure, but with privacy rules and all that, I keep it to myself.

"It really is. You've never been, I assume?"

"Nope."

"You want to come with us? Isaac has four tickets. He's bringing his brother, Chris, but we have an extra."

"Thank you, but no. I have some laundry to catch up on." What I don't tell her is that I've had my fill of racing for the week.

"Come on, Aubs. It's been forever since we've hung out."

"I was just at your place last weekend."

"I mean, when we're not at my house or yours," she amends.

"Thank you. Maybe next time." I don't know why but the thought of running into Blaine has me on edge. I'm not positive that he'll be there. I'm assuming since it's dirt late model racing, he will be. It's not like I can't handle myself around him, that is if I don't let myself get lost in how good-looking he is.

"I'm going to hold you to that," she warns.

"I promise. Next time. It's been a long week. I'm ready to just go home and chill."

"All right. I'll call you later. We'll be at the track all weekend. It's a three-day event. If you change your mind, you can drive up and meet us. It's only, like an hour away from here."

"Thank you, really, but I'm good. Promise."

"Fine," she grumbles. "Next time I'm not taking no for an answer."

"Deal." I end the call as I pull into my apartment complex. It's nothing special, just a small one-bedroom, about seven hundred square feet total. It's plenty for me. However, I do wish I could have a dog. Unfortunately, this complex is no pets allowed, and really, I work so much it wouldn't be fair to keep a dog cooped up and alone all day. My mind immediately goes to Camber. It's hard to believe blistery Blaine is her owner.

Walking into my quiet apartment, I almost regret not taking Maria up on her offer. Almost. I know that I need to get out more. I know that I work too much and that Maria and her husband are all that I have. The day I turned eighteen, I couldn't get out of town fast enough. I left that small town in northern Tennessee and never looked back. Shaking out of my thoughts, I kick off my shoes and head for the shower. I always feel like I have oil all over me at the end of the day.

Refreshed from my shower, I find myself standing in the kitchen, staring into the fridge. It's hard to cook for one and really not much fun. I settle on a box of instant macaroni and cheese. This is my life. It may not be exciting and full of fun and laughter, but it's safe. I've created a home for myself when I had nothing. My little one-bedroom apartment isn't grand, but it's safe and warm and all mine. I've worked hard to get where I am. Working two jobs to make ends meet, putting myself through school. I'm proud of that. I'm content in my life, and I have everything I need.

CHAPTER four

BLAINE

STEPPING OUT OF THE LIVING quarters of our hauler, I look around. All is quiet right now. Yesterday when we got here, it was a flurry of activity getting ready for last night's qualifying race. It was only an hour's drive for us to get here, so the crew and I were well rested and raring to go. It's nice when we race close to home; it's less time we actually have to spend away. Closing the door to the hauler, I call for Camber, and we walk down to take a look at the track. Volunteer Speedway is 4/10 of a mile of red dirt and clay. It's known as the world's fastest dirt track. I don't disagree. I've had some good racing here and hope that this weekend is no different. I'm aiming to win a points championship after all.

Crouching down, I dig my hand into the red dirt and let it fall through my fingers. We set a fast time last night, which puts us with a mark on our back this weekend. We're the team to beat. I was three seconds off from breaking the record and setting fast time for this track. I guess you can't win them all. This is a special holiday weekend race, three nights. Normally, they don't drag it out like this unless it's a big money race, and often times they still condense it into two days. This, however, is not only a sanctioned race for the Outlaws, but a benefit for a fellow racer. Camber nudges me with her nose, and I laugh. "What do you think, girl? We going to bring home the win?" She licks my hand where the dirt used to be. "Come on, let's go help unload the car."

"I see how it is," Rick calls out as I approach the back of the hauler. "You sneak away while all the work is getting done."

"You caught me," I say, stopping to stand next to him. "Looks like you guys got it all worked out."

"Yeah," he says, twisting and turning.

"How's the back?"

"Good. Aubree is a damn miracle worker. I'm sore, but the pain is gone."

I can see it on his face that he's in much better shape than he was this time two days ago. Looks like she's more than just a pretty face and a rocking body. "Good." I clap him on the shoulder and step inside the hauler to find Kevin.

"There he is." He beams. "Blaine 'Checkmate' Bishop, Mr. Fast Time for this weekend's festivities," he says in his best announcer voice.

"How in the hell did I get branded with that nickname anyway?" I ask, already knowing the answer. My first year that I decided to run with the Outlaws instead of just hopping from track to track on my own, I came up the ranks quick. I was racking up points fast. I was the new guy, a young punk, and somewhere along the way, I was branded with the nickname Checkmate. All the drivers have nicknames, and the announcers love to draw them out during driver introductions.

Kevin holds his fist out for me. "They can't escape you, brother."

I bump my fist with his, trying to contain my smile. When it comes to nicknames, it could be worse. I am a force to be reckoned with out on the track. "They can't escape me because

I'm always out front."

"Modest as always." He grins.

"Hey, I'm just being real. I have the championship trophies to prove it." He nods, unable to argue the fact. "What's left to do?"

"Nothing, man. Setup is on point, tires are good. Fluids are being topped off. You were fast, so we're not changing anything. Now it's up to you to not tear anything up during the heat races."

"Like I said," I point to my chest, "out front. Kinda hard to tear anything up when they can't catch you."

"This is true," he says with a laugh.

"We're all set," Jacob, another member of the crew, tells us as he joins us in the hauler. "Just topped off the fluids."

"Now we wait," Kevin sighs. "This is the worst part. I mean, I'm glad the car is good and we're not racing with the clock to get it where it needs to be, but all this downtime sucks ass."

"Go call your wife," I tell him. His entire demeanor changes at the mention of Ashley.

"Yeah, she's at work, but a quick hello is exactly what I need." He steps out of the hauler, I'm sure headed to the motor home, which we refer to as a "toter" home since it serves dual purposes, to call her. It's the same midnight black as our hauler, they're a matching set, and it's where we all stay when we're on the road. Well, except for my parents. They claim to be too old to sleep on a pull-out couch, so they get a hotel room. I try to tell them it's a waste of money and that they should be using that money to travel. They counter with "we are traveling." I've always had their support 110 percent. I wouldn't be where I am today without them.

"I'm starving," Rick says, bringing me out of my thoughts.

I reach into my pocket and pull out some money. "I'll stay here with the car, you go grab us some burgers or something. Whatever it is, get a lot of it." He snatches the money out of my hand and practically runs toward the infield concession stand.

Hopping up on the counter, I rest my head back against the cabinets. It's quiet without my parents here to tag along. Mom not fussing over us, feeding us. We have food we could have made, but I know Kevin is in there talking to Ash, and even though I'm not married, or hell even attached, I can hedge a bet that if that were me talking to my wife, I wouldn't want all of the guys hanging around. No, in fact, I would want her here with me, and that is precisely why I'm not married. Well, part of it. The other part is that I don't really have time for the distraction. I'm bound and determined to win the championship this year and make history. I'm so close. I'm not going to let anything get in the way of that.

Finally, it's go time. Untying my racing suit at my waist, I then slip my arms into the sleeves and zip it up. With practiced ease, I slide into the car through the hole where the window should be. Kevin hands me my helmet and helps me connect my HANS device. Wearing it is second nature to me. One thing my parents insisted on growing up was safety was number one. I started racing go-karts when I was five. Dad likes to tell the story that in my first race I was fearless and never lifted while Mom claims I took ten years off her life that day. I don't remember my first race. I do remember working out in the garage with my dad on our kart, and he and Mom driving me to local tracks on the weekends.

I skipped my junior and senior prom because I was in the middle of the season and leading the points. Priorities and all that. Besides, why dress up to go out on some fancy date when I have girls ready and available for me at the track? Mom hated it, Dad gave me the speech about being safe. I was selective but not innocent. That's my routine, and it works for me.

"Don't tear anything up!" Kevin yells, tapping the roof of the car with a grin and walking away.

Locking the steering wheel in place, I grip it and wait to be called out into the track. I'm fast time, but they chose an invert for the heat races, which means that I'll be starting at the back of the pack. That's fine by me. It doesn't mean as much if I don't earn it. The top three winners from each of the six heat races will advance to the feature race tomorrow night. That's the big money race. Tonight, is just proving you're good enough to make the show.

Kevin waves, giving me the signal to go, and I follow the pack of twenty out onto the track. Ten laps. I have ten laps to make it back to the front. No problem. When the green flag drops, so does my foot. I press the accelerator to the floor and never lift. Weaving in and out of lapped traffic, throwing the car into the corners, it's a rush like nothing else I've ever known. I live for this. The thrill, the excitement, the adrenaline that courses through my veins. Merging in and out of traffic, passing car after car as I make my way to the front. When the checkered flag drops, I'm leading the pack across the finish line.

My crew greets me in the pits as I drive my car back to the hauler. "You fucking killed it!" Jacob cheers as I hand him my helmet and climb out of the car.

"All in a day's work." Kevin laughs. "Check-fucking-mate." He holds his fist out for me and I bump his knuckles with mine. "How's the car? Any changes?"

"Perfect."

"You heard the man," Kevin tells Jacob and Rick. "Let's get her cleaned up, top off the fluids, and loaded for the night."

Inside the hauler, I grab two bottles of water and down them, before jumping in to help my crew. I'm more than just a driver. This car being right is a top priority, and I keep myself involved as much as possible. I'll be driving this thing at upwards of 120 miles per hour. I want to know every bolt has been tightened, and every hose is anchored down. I seek the thrill, but I'm not crazy. Safety comes first.

"Checkmate?" a sultry voice asks. Turning, I see a blonde, big tits, short shorts, and her T-shirt, the one with my car and number on it, is tied, showing off her flat belly. "Can I have your autograph?"

I give her a panty-dropping smile that I perfected years ago and grab a towel, wiping off my hands. "Sure." I hold my hand out for whatever it is she wants me to sign. She bats her long ridiculously fake eyelashes at me. Who wears fake eyelashes to a race track?

"Um, here." She pulls down the neck of her T-shirt. Low enough to show the swell of her breasts.

I'm a man. I like tits, all shapes, all sizes. I'm gonna look if you show them to me, no question. However, you showing that shit for all to see is not gonna get you where you think it will. I've met her kind before. Show some skin, bat those eyelashes, and get the guy to fall at your feet. She doesn't want Blaine; she wants Checkmate. Girls like her are good for a night of fun, but then you pay for it when they turn into stage-five clingers. No thanks.

"Checkmate," she purrs, bringing me out of my thoughts.

"Sure." I take the Sharpie she offers and step closer. She arches her back, shoving her tits, that I'm sure are also fake in my face. I scribble my name, adding my number 1B next to it. When I back away, she steps closer.

"I thought maybe we could hang out tonight." Reaching out, she runs the long pointy nail of her index finger down my chest.

I take another step back. "Sorry, lots of work to do on the car. Thanks for coming out to watch the event." With that, I turn my back to her, picking up a wrench that I don't need and pretend to be working on the car. I hear her huff and if I'm not mistaken, stomp her foot before walking off.

"Dodged a bullet with that one." Jacob laughs.

"You seem to be able to spot them a mile away. She's off to latch herself to the next unsuspecting schmuck."

"She's a clinger," I agree.

"She looks like she'd be fun." Rick holds his hands out in front of his chest, to insinuate her large breasts.

"You can still catch her."

He turns to look in the direction I'm guessing she walked away. "Nah, she'd want to hang around to get to you and I'm not in the mood for games."

"Wise decision," I tell him.

We spend the next couple of hours going over everything on the car, tightening bolts, checking tires, brakes. You name it, we have our hands on it.

"Man…" Rick stands and bends, stretching his back. "I'm going to call and see if I can get in with Aubree next week before we leave again."

"Ash swears by massage. She keeps trying to get me to get one," Kevin says.

"You should schedule with Aubree. I'm telling you, she's a miracle worker. I was ready to drop to my knees and propose marriage," he says, laughing.

"She's cute," Kevin agrees.

"Hell, yes she is, but those hands," Rick moans, causing Kevin and Jacob to laugh.

"I'm starving," I say, changing the subject. I don't need to spend anymore time thinking about that gorgeous creature that is Aubree, the massage therapist.

"Me too," all three say at the same time.

"I'm grilling those steaks." Jacob rubs his stomach.

"My man!" Rick gives him a high-five. "I'll see what else I can whip up."

"I'm hitting the shower first," I tell them. They wave me off. While we've all been working in the heat, I'm by far the one who needs a shower the most. My flame-resistant driver's suit, helmet, and HANS device are hot as fuck. So much so that I have three drivers' suits. Trust me, putting that sweaty, smelly thing on again the next time at an event like this is not a good time. Some drivers do it, those who are on a racing budget. I'm lucky I'm not, and even if I was, I'd find a way. Eat Ramen for a month, whatever. There is nothing worse than racing a hundred-lap race with a fuck ton of cautions smelling ass the entire time. You would think the fuel smell or oil, even the dirt would overpower it. Not so much.

After a shower, the guys and I eat our steaks, a salad, and baked beans, drink a cold beer, and call it a night. Tomorrow is race day, and we all want to be ready. I'm fortunate that my team, my friends are just as invested in me meeting my goals as I am. They don't fuck off when we're here. This is their job, how they put a roof over their heads and food on their table. Some of the crews party it up, but not us. Not before a race. Now, after a win, sure we celebrate, but never before. My team and I we're determined, and we all want to break this record.

"The car's good. You're starting on the pole, so stay out front," Kevin jokes. He's crouched down looking through the window of my car with my helmet in his hands.

"That is the idea." I can't help but smile as I shake my head.

"There." He hands me my helmet. "Got you to lighten up a bit. Stay safe, brother." He stands and helps me connect my HANS device. Two taps on my shoulder and he's gone.

Time to get this party started.

The official motions for us to take the track. The first couple of laps are leisurely. I move the steering wheel from left to right making sure the tires are clean and warmed up. When the green flag drops, I mash the accelerator to the floor. I shoot out to the head of the pack, exactly where I like to be. For several laps, I hold the lead and then a caution comes out. I immediately slow, not sure what caused the caution—the last thing I want to do is drive up on a wreck with nowhere to go but into the accident. I've seen it happen; it's not good for anyone involved.

There are another four laps before the green flag drops again. I shoot out in front of the pack, setting my pace. I eye Jacob, who is my spotter, and his arms are wide open, telling me that I'm pretty far out front. Looking ahead, I can see the end of the pack which means someone is about to get lapped. It's nothing personal; it's racing.

My hands grip the wheel. My hold tight as I work my way through lap traffic. This is where things get hectic. I'm leading the race, but I'm also in the back. As a spectator, you have to really watch what's going on to keep up. My spotter has his hands full as well, keeping track of those on the lead lap that are behind me. It's times like this I wish for a caution. I want out of this lap traffic and back out front. Clean air, nothing in my way.

Unfortunately, that doesn't happen as we race, lap after lap. When the white flag drops letting us know that we're on our final lap, I don't worry about my spotter or the leader board. I know I'm still out front. I've kept my eye on who I've passed and who has made their way past me. I'm the leader bringing this show across the finish line. Coming into turn four, I see smoke from beside me, but I don't pay it much attention as I cross the finish line. Slowing my pace, I take another lap and this time, I look at the leader board. My number one sits proudly in the first spot.

Another win.

Another step closer to breaking the record.

Stopping at the flag stand, I accept the checkered flag and make a lap the opposite direction of the race, my victory lap. The crowd is in on their feet cheering me on. When I reach the flag stand, I spin my car in circles throwing red dirt and clay all over the flag stand and those there to greet me. Not that they care. Making my way to the scales, I drive over and wait for the green light. There is nothing worse than winning the race, and then your car being light causing you to be disqualified. I've seen it happen to some of the best in the business. When I park my car and climb out, they are smiles all around. For me. For the win.

Kevin and the guys are there. Rick hands me a Bishop Racing hat, Kevin takes my helmet, and Rick hands me an energy drink that tastes like a sweet tart, sour as hell, but it's one of my sponsors and I have to play the dog and pony show to keep their money coming in. It's worth it.

"I'm here with Blaine 'Checkmate' Bishop. Congrats on the win, Blaine."

"Thank you," I say, taking a swig of the sweet-tart concoction.

"You dominated the track tonight. Something we're used to seeing from you. What were you feeling when you took that checkered flag?"

"My team should be proud," I tell him. "They got me here. Without the help of my sponsors," I hold up my energy drink, "we wouldn't be where we are today."

"I heard your crew had some health issues this week," the announcer asks.

I'm not surprised by his question. Kevin, as the crew chief, filled him in while I was taking my victory lap, giving him some talking points. It helps keep the focus on the team, and not drama that can often surround the racing industry. We control the media that way. It works. Other teams use this same tactic and some just don't give a fuck. They just want the win. "Yeah, thanks to our sponsor, Knoxville Health Partners, a member of the crew received the medical attention they needed and was able to be here with me tonight."

"Great job out there. We'll see you next week at Eldora for the Dream."

"Thank you." I take another swig of my sugary drink and smile for the camera. The cameraman yells cut, and I keep the grin but lose the drink. Jacob hands me a bottle of water knowing I hate that shit. The Dream is a big money race. It's not for points, but bragging rights are good enough. Not to mention it's one of the biggest races of the season and adding a win to my resume is always a plus.

"Now," Kevin says, clapping his hands together, "we celebrate."

We load the car, not bothering to clean it or look it over. We can do that when we get back to the shop. Tonight, we kick back around a fire and drink a few beers, celebrating yet another win for Bishop Racing, another step forward to the championship.

CHAPTER five

Aubree

AFTER A LONG, LONELY WEEKEND, I'm ready for today. Three-day weekends are great, but spending them holed up in your apartment is not such a good idea. I could have called Maria, but I feel like I always tag along with her and Isaac. I cleaned, got caught up on laundry, did a little online shopping, and watched a lot of Netflix. Such an exciting life for a twenty-three-year-old.

I love what I do, so going to work is not something I dread like so many others in the world. I remember a teacher I had in high school who said: "Do something you love, and it will never feel like work." I didn't believe her then, but now, I get it. I enjoy my job and the people I get to meet and help.

Firing up my laptop, I log into the system and look at my schedule for the day. We like to leave some spots open at various times throughout the week for those who call and have an issue that needs to be treated right away. Here at KHP we focus on the medicinal side of massage more so than the relaxing. The majority of our patients are auto accidents, Bell's Palsy diagnosis, stroke patients, and many other medical diagnosis. They're here for treatment of medical conditions. Although many say it relaxes them as well, we're not here for that. We have some of the same elements, the relaxing music if they want it, but we treat multiple conditions working in alliance with physical therapists, primary care, and a multitude of other specialists to get our patients where they need to be in their recovery.

When the status of my first patient changes to arrive, I lock my laptop screen and head out to the waiting room to call them back. I have four one-hour appointments this morning and two for this afternoon. I have ten minutes at the end of each hour to clean the room and chart. It's also when I rush to the restroom if needed. It's going to be a busy day for sure. "Mr. Mayer," I call out.

"Aubree, sweet girl, I have something for you," Mr. Mayer tells me. He's a sweet, older gentleman who suffered a stroke about a year ago. He has function in his left arm, but it tends to go numb on him. We use massage to relax the muscles and stimulate the nerves, giving him relief from the tingling sensations. "The wife said to make sure you heat it up first. Swears it's better that way." He hands me a plate covered in plastic wrap.

"What exactly am I heating up?" I ask as I follow him down the hall. "Treatment room one," I tell him.

"Homemade bread. Add a little honey after you heat it up. Hell, I add it when I don't, but the wife swears it's better warm," he says again.

"Please thank her for me, and I promise to warm it up first. Go ahead and get undressed. We're going to start with you on your belly today. I'm just going to run this to my office."

"You got it. I even wore my American flag boxers. I know the holiday is over, but hey, the wife bought them for me, so what can I say?" He shrugs. I smile at him before closing the door.

Mr. Mayer is in his late seventies and has suffered from muscle spasms in his back for years after a bad car accident in addition to the stroke he had last year. Massage seems to help him. I see him faithfully every week for a one-hour visit. His wife is always sending goodies with him to give to me. They're a sweet couple.

My morning flies by with a full schedule of regular patients. That's another thing I love about my job. I get the opportunity to really get to know my patients. Some think of massage as quiet and calm, and that can sometimes be the case, but most of my regulars are rather chatty. I spend a lot of time alone when not at work, so it's a nice change of pace for me.

"Knock, knock." I look up to see Jackie standing in my office door. "Got a minute?"

"Sure, I just finished with my last patient of the morning. Just working on getting caught up on some notes. What's up?"

Jackie has a look on her face, one I can't quite place. When she steps into my office, I'm surprised to see Jonah, the CEO of KHP, following along behind her. I immediately break out in a sweat. I love this job, and I've worked here since I was nineteen. Never, not once, has Jonah been in my office. My mind races with why he could be here and then it hits me.

Blaine Bishop.

Surely, he didn't call and complain about me. Did he? Sure, I was snarky with him, but he was an asshole and deserved it. I made sure to thank him for changing my tire.

"Aubree," Jackie says, pulling me out of my internal panic.

"Hi." I walk around my desk and offer Jonah my hand. He takes it and gives me a warm smile.

"Aubree, I've been hearing good things," he says.

My shoulders relax, and by the look on Jackie's face, it was visible as well. "That's a good thing," I manage to say. Jonah is young, early thirties maybe, but that doesn't make him any less intimidating. He is the CEO after all.

"It is. We've been inundated with calls this morning. Your schedule is full this afternoon."

I can't hide my surprise. "Okay, well, we leave those spots open for this reason. Although we usually have at least one that goes unused. I haven't had a chance to look at the afternoon schedule, but it's all good," I offer them a bright "I've got this" smile.

"Good indeed. Have a seat, Aubree." Jonah points to the chair behind my desk. On shaky legs, I do as he says while he and Jackie take the two open seats facing me. "Let me start by saying thank you for going to the Bishop Racing headquarters and taking care of their crew member who was injured."

"You're welcome. I was just doing my job."

"No. You went above and beyond your job description. Your visit has had a positive outcome for KHP. Seems Blaine Bishop won his race on Saturday night. It was a local track of sorts, just an hour away. How familiar are you with the racing circuit?"

"Not very," I admit.

He nods. "The drivers who win, usually the first through third place winners, are interviewed. Like any other sport, they mention their sponsors. Apparently, Mr. Bishop has a big following in the dirt racing community. His team must have mentioned how they were down a crew member. When the interviewer asked him about it, he gave a shout-out to KHP. Hence, the influx of appointments."

"Really?" I ask, surprised. "His mention of our facility caused that?"

"Indeed. There is power in marketing when it comes to celebrity status."

"He's hardly a celebrity," I counter.

"Maybe not to you or me, but in the racing community, he's just that."

Jackie must see the confusion on my face. I don't understand why I'm having this meeting with both of them. This could have easily been an email. "Jonah has an idea, a proposal of sorts that he wants to run past you."

"O-kay," I say slowly, looking at Jonah, giving him my attention.

"When it comes to marketing, you can spend thousands of dollars and still never find that one niche that brings in your customers, in our case, patients. We sponsor the race team so that thousands of fans can see our name, our logo every Saturday night. We do see return on our investment, but nothing like this. I've been brainstorming with Jackie as well as the marketing team this morning, and I think I've come up with something."

"Okay. I'm happy to help if I can."

"I'm glad to hear you say that."

"Hear him out before you make your decision," Jackie chimes in.

"What I would like to propose is to have a staff member, namely you, travel with the Bishop Racing team. The driver, Blaine, especially, could greatly benefit from this, according to his crew chief, Kevin."

Did I hear him right? He wants me to travel with them? That means I'll be spending more time with Blaine, the asshole. I guess there are worse things. I could be losing my job. My hands begin to sweat. Can I do that? Can I travel with a race team? I don't know anything about racing. "I met Kevin when I was there," I finally say. What else do I say to this crazy outlandish idea of his? He's my boss. I can't tell him I think it's certifiably nuts.

"Yes, well, he's agreed to have you travel with them and basically be there to work on any member of the Bishop Racing team as needed."

"Are any of them injured?"

"No. However, working on the race car can be very physical. Long hours, some heavy lifting, bending, and reaching. Then you have the driver. Hands clasped on the steering wheel at high rates of speed, he too could benefit from your services."

"Why me?" I ask him. I wipe my sweaty palms on my scrub pants, hoping that they are unable to hear the beat of my racing heart. Blood whooshes through my ears as I try to block it out and focus. I'm content with my life. I have a routine; this is uprooting that routine.

"Well, you already know them and to be honest, you're our best. If we want these guys, Blaine specifically, to keep singing KHP praises, we need to send our best."

"Also," Jackie adds, "it's a lot of travel. It would be more difficult for someone with small children to take on this role."

"So, because I'm single and have no family, I get this... extreme job offer?" Okay, maybe not exactly extreme, but to me it is. I'm sure most would enjoy getting out of our three-story medical services building and spending time outdoors. I should be honored they're asking me. Instead, I'm freaking out. At least on the inside. Never let them see you sweat, right?

"No." Jackie's voice is firm. "You are our best, and I've told you this before. Jonah asked me who our best was, and I said you. No questions asked. It's a bonus that you do not have small children."

I admit that I took the "no small children" as a dig that I have no family to mention. It's a sensitive subject for me. One that I've learned to deal with but I can still get edgy when I let myself think about how alone I really am.

"The job, of course, comes with perks. You work when they travel, and you are off the remainder of the week, during racing season. You will also receive an increase in pay as the job responsibilities have changed," Jonah explains. "Twelve thousand dollars a year increase. I know it's a lot to ask, and is unorthodox, but I truly believe this is a good move for KHP."

"What about my patients? I have regulars." I point to the bread on the corner of my desk. "They're counting on me."

"So are we. We'll make sure they are well taken care of. When you come back during the off-season, they can resume seeing you for their care."

"This is… a lot. I mean, do they really need a massage therapist with them all the time?"

"No, they don't. However, this will keep us at the forefront of spectators' minds. You will have a uniform that represents both Bishop Racing and KHP clearly. As you are at the track, it will be a walking promotion. In return, Blaine will mention our partnership every time he's interviewed."

"What makes you think this guy will win often enough to make that happen?"

"He's the youngest driver to win a championship. The youngest to ever win back-to-back, and he's well on his way to winning his third consecutive. Trust me, he's the real deal."

"I'm just a little shocked with all of this. I mean, I don't know anything about racing."

"You don't have to know about racing to do your job, Aubree," Jonah says gently. "You just have to accept the position. Be there if the crew needs to be worked on, injury or not, and we'll pay you to do it."

"You'll get to travel," Jackie adds. "The team travels all over the United States for the races. I know that's something you've always wanted to do." Her voice is soft as if she too is thinking of the fact that I have limited family. I've not told Jackie about my life growing up, just that things at home were not good and that it's just me.

"Can I think about this?"

"Of course, you can. They are off this weekend, then heading out of town for Northern Ohio the following weekend. I would need to know this week so that we can organize acceptable accommodations as well as arrange a uniform." Jonah stands from his chair and offers me his hand. "I look forward to your decision."

I watch as he walks out of my office, then turn to Jackie. "I don't get it. Is this a thing? Sponsors sending people to be with the race team?"

"No, not usually, but this is different. That one mention has brought an influx of patients not just for massage, but to the facility as a whole."

"So, we have him give a shout-out every week. Easy."

"Not really. It was more than just a thank-you mention. It was details about how we helped his crew member and that because of us, because of you, they were able to be at the races with him."

"Why me?" I sound like a broken record, but I just can't seem to wrap my head around it. I've always lived in the shadows. I work hard and keep to myself. It's not that I don't appreciate the opportunity, this is just… overwhelming, and nothing like this has ever happened to me before.

"Like we said, you're our best, and you don't have small kids who you would be leaving at home. You also already have a relationship established with Bishop Racing."

"Right." I laugh humorlessly. "Blaine was pissed that I was there."

"Really? When we talked to Kevin, his crew chief, he said you got along well with everyone."

"Tell me, Jackie. Am I going to lose my job if I say no?"

"No, you won't lose your job, but my guess is that you'll be looked over for future promotions. Jonah has it in his head that this is the future of marketing and sponsorships for KHP. He's convinced this will work. That having you there, to offer massages to Blaine and his crew will get more shout-outs and thus, more exposure for KHP."

"Do you hear how ridiculous this sounds?"

She shrugs. "It's not my area of expertise. I'm a physical therapist who runs the rehab department. I know shit about marketing."

"What would you do?"

"I'd take it. You get to travel, for free I might add. It gets you out of the office."

"But my patients."

"Will see you when the season is over."

I have a gut feeling that turning this down is not going to be a good thing for me. But can I do it? Can I travel with Blaine, the guy who so obviously can't stand me to be in his presence, or anyone really? I won't be able to escape his cranky ass. "I need to process this, to think about it." Can I give up my patients? The ones who treat me like a member of their family? Can I give up that feeling of... belonging?

"That's fine, just don't take too long." Jackie stands and walks out of my office.

I don't go out to lunch like I had planned. Instead, I find a granola bar in my desk and eat that staring at my now full afternoon schedule. When my next patient's status changes to say arrived, I grab my phone and send off a quick text to Maria.

Me: Hey, I need some advice. Can I stop by after work?

Tossing my phone on my desk, I turn my focus to my patients and getting through the remainder of the day.

Four hours later, I drop into my chair and close my eyes. I'm mentally exhausted. My new patients were not as chatty, so my mind was able to wander and worry and process this new predicament I've found myself in. I don't know why, but this feels like a punishment if I go, and possibly an even bigger one if I don't. Grabbing my phone, I check to see if Maria got back with me.

Maria: I'll make dinner. See you when you get here.

Me: I'm on my way.

God, I love my best friend. I'm so grateful to have met her my first day here in town. I'm not sure how I got so lucky, but I'm keeping her. As fast as I can, without being negligent, I wrap up my afternoon charting, close down my laptop, but leave it sitting on my desk. Work is the last thing I want to do tonight. Locking up my office, I head to Maria's house. I really need her to help me work through this.

When I pull up into Maria's driveway she's already standing

on the front porch holding two wineglasses. "Thought you could use this," she calls out, holding the wineglass up in the air, as I climb out of my car.

"You have no idea," I say, approaching her. She hands me the wineglass, and I take a big gulp.

"What's up?"

I spend the next ten minutes telling her about what happened at work today. I also fill her in on what happened when I went to the Bishop Racing shop, something I've not divulged up to this point.

"Wait, why am I just now hearing about this?"

"I don't know. I guess I figured it was a one-time deal."

She nods. "So, what are you going to do?"

"I don't know," I sigh and rest my head back against the rocking chair. "What would you do?"

"Do you want my honest opinion, or do you want me to tell you what you want to hear?"

"Honest. Always, honest."

"I think you're scared. You're comfortable in your job, with your patients, you've started over, busted your ass to get where you are, but now that you're settled you're… complacent."

"Complacent?" Is that what I am? My mind races with the possibilities this new assignment can bring me. Jackie's right. I've always wanted to travel and see the world. Anything outside of my home state of Tennessee. *Complacent.* I'm comfortable, stable in life. Is that so wrong?

"Yeah. You're okay with sitting home alone on the weekends. I get it, Aubs, I do. I understand that your life growing up sucked hairy donkey balls, but your life is what you make it. You didn't let your childhood bring you down. You fought, left that small town, and came here. Worked two part-time jobs while putting yourself through school. You got a good job, and you became satisfied because it's more than you've ever had."

Tears prick my eyes. "I've worked so hard," I say, fighting

back the tears. "I am happy where I am. I have a good reliable job, food on the table, a nice apartment, you and Isaac."

"I know, sweetie," she says, reaching over and resting her hand on my knee. "But you can be happier. Open your heart. Fall in love. Travel. One day get married, have babies. There is so much more waiting for you in this world to conquer. You just have to have the guts to take it."

"I got here on my own," I remind her.

"You did. I'm damn proud of all you've accomplished. However, you close yourself off. I just happened to meet you when you were down on your luck and had no one. You let me in, but you've kept everyone else at arm's length." She removes her hand, and sits back in her rocking chair. "I think you should take it. Who cares how Blaine feels? So, what if the guy doesn't like you. All the others did. This is a great chance for you to travel and see the world."

"I'll be working, and it's not like it's Europe."

"You're right, but it's not just Tennessee either."

"I'll be working," I say again. "Not like I'll have time or the money to sightsee."

"They drive, Aubs. They travel together, and you will get to see so many new cities and add some states to your visited list. Maybe you won't be able to go out and explore, but it's more… you know. It's more than being here in Tennessee having dinner alone, spending the weekends *alone.* Consider it training for you too. To open yourself to the possibility of more. It's a few months."

"She's right, you know," Isaac says.

"Where did you come from?" I ask, looking up at him.

"Came to tell you dinner is ready. Look, Aubree, we're here for you. We always will be. If something happens and you want to come home, I'll come and get you. I know you've never flown on a plane, you big chicken." He smiles.

"I can't ask you to do that."

"You didn't ask. I volunteered. You're family to us, Aubree. We—" He steps up on the porch and stands beside Maria, placing his hand on her shoulder. "—want you to be happy."

"Fine, I admit that it's out of my comfort zone."

They both laugh. "We'll come and get you. Just say the word."

"Right, but if I go and then leave before the season is over, chances are I lose my job."

"So, you find another one." Isaac shrugs. "Don't let the fear of the unknown or the what-ifs keep you from living life."

"We want you to find what we have. One day our kids are going to be playing together, right out there." She points to their huge front yard. "I'm not saying you'll meet someone on this adventure, but you just might learn to live a little, and that, my friend, is a good first step."

I take a minute to let their words sink in. They're right, even though I hate to admit it. I've never been a risk taker, never been one to step out of line. I've made a life for myself here, and I am comfortable, something I wasn't sure I would ever have. I never want to lose that.

"Besides," Maria says, "it's a raise, twelve thousand dollars a year. That's a thousand dollars a month before taxes, my friend."

"Umm, why are we discussing this?" Isaac laughs. "Take the money, promotion, and trip. Enjoy yourself for once."

I shake my head at them. "I love you guys."

"We love you too."

"Let's eat." Isaac holds a hand out for each of us and pulls us out of our chairs. We follow him to the back deck and have dinner. There is no more talk of what I will or won't decide, but I know what I'm going to do. I'm going to say yes. It's time to start living. They're right, and they promised to come and get me. That's my comfort of home coming with me.

CHAPTER Six

BLAINE

"You want to run that by me one more time?" I ask Kevin.

"You heard me," he says, grinning.

"Why in the hell would you agree to that?"

"I have multiple reasons. One, they increased their sponsorship. Two, it would be nice to have her around. You're bitching and moaning all the time about your neck being tight, and look what she did for Rick."

"Why her?"

He shrugs. "She's familiar with us already, and apparently she's their best."

"Why would they send their best out in the field? Sounds to me like she's a fucking train wreck and instead of firing her, they are shipping her off with us."

Kevin throws his head back and laughs. "You really think a corporation as large as KHP would go to those lengths to not fire someone? Come on, man, what's your deal?"

"She rubs me the wrong way. Not to mention, we don't have

time to cater to her. We've got a goal set, and we're going to meet it."

"She's not going to hinder that. If anything, she's going to help. Keep the crew relaxed and healthy."

"What does Ash think about this?" Surely his wife will have an issue with the sexy but irritating Aubree coming on the road with us to every race.

"She thinks it's a great idea."

"Really?" Surprise pitches my voice.

"Yep," he says, popping the *p,* wearing a huge-ass grin.

"Call them back. Tell them no."

"No can do, man. She's coming with us to Eldora this week."

"What?" I say louder than I intended to.

"Blaine, the hauler sleeps eight. The master, the four bunks, the table, and the couch. We have room for her."

"Right, and all of her girly shit lying all over the hauler. Fuck me, I can't believe you agreed to this."

"Get used to it. It's a done deal. I sent your mom to the bank with the sponsorship check an hour ago."

"Fuck." I run my fingers through my hair. "This is on you, Henderson," I tell him. "You keep her out of my way. We're not changing a damn thing to accommodate her."

"Wasn't my intention."

"I've never heard of this before in my life. Am I being punked?" I look around the garage waiting for a camera crew to jump out and surprise me. I'm not that lucky.

"Apparently, your last interview resulted in lots of new appointments for them. They want to see how far they can get with this reach."

"But we're going to be traveling all over. KHP is based here in Knoxville."

"They are, but they have facilities all over Tennessee. Not to mention, you can watch the races online, and some are even televised. They're branching out with their marketing, which I think is a good move on their part. You have to do what works, right?"

"Keep her out of my way, Kevin, I mean it."

He salutes me. "You won't even notice she's here. That is unless she needs to work on you."

"I doubt that," I mumble under my breath. "Fine, we leave tomorrow morning seven sharp."

"She's already been notified. She'll be here. Don't worry."

"I'm not worried, hopeful is more like it."

He looks down at his watch. "I gotta get home and pack."

I wave over my shoulder as I feel a nudge against my leg. Looking down, I see Camber, peering up at me. "It's all good, girl. I'm not sure what the hell these people are thinking, but I'll deal. How bad can it be, right?" I scratch her right behind her ears, causing her to lean into me. She's such a big baby and will give you all her love for a good scratch behind the ears.

I spend the next couple of hours walking through the shop and the hauler making sure we haven't forgotten anything. Mom and Dad have an RV they'll be driving to pull the T-shirt trailer. They don't take it to all events, but with an event like the Dream, if you have an RV you take it. The closest hotels are at least twenty minutes or more away. Maybe I can put Aubree there with my parents, out of the way. Yeah, that's a perfect idea. She'll be out of the pits, and out of the way. Satisfied with my plan, I shut down the lights, lock the shop, and head into the house.

"Camber!" I yell, tapping my leg, and she comes running. I open the door for her, and we head to bed.

The next morning, I throw some essentials—jeans, T-shirts, underwear, and socks—into a duffel bag. I have a toothbrush that I leave in the toter home, as well as shower supplies so I just need clothes and food, which Mom took care of yesterday.

Camber has a tote of food, and a few toys underneath the toter, so we're good to go. "Come on, girl," I say, calling her toward the door. I stop and grab my cell phone and the charger before locking the door behind me. When I turn to face the driveway, she's there.

Aubree.

She's in her red Impala. I can't help but notice that the donut is no longer there. At least she listened and didn't try to keep driving on it. "Let's go," I tell Camber, but I didn't need to, she's right on my heels. As we approach Aubree's car, she climbs out, and Camber takes off running. "Camber!" I yell out for her, but it's as if she doesn't even hear me. She has one goal: getting to Aubree.

"Hello, pretty girl." Aubree crouches down and lets Camber lick her face. "It's good to see you too." She laughs, a sound that washes over me just as sweet as honey.

"Camber." This time my voice is stern. My dog stops, and turns to look at me, then turns right back around waiting on more affection from her new friend.

"Where should I park my car?" Aubree asks, standing back to her full height.

"Pull it up to the shop. That way it will be on camera."

"Uh, should I be worried about it being stolen?"

"No. However, when in the public eye, everyone knows your schedule. We don't take unnecessary risks."

"Got it." Without another word, she climbs back into her car and pulls up next to the shop where I instructed.

"Come on, girl." I tap my leg, and Camber follows dutifully. "Pop the trunk and I'll get your bags." I'm sure she has a shit ton, so I might as well get them loaded now.

"Oh, I can get it." Opening the back door of her car, she reaches in and pulls out a duffel bag much like mine. She reaches in again and comes back with a small messenger bag.

"Step back and I'll get the rest," I tell her.

"This is it."

I watch as she slings one bag over each shoulder, hits the lock on her remote which sounds the horn, letting us know her car is now locked. "You got everything you need?"

"Yeah, I mean, it's a race track, right? I brought shorts, jeans, a hoodie. They gave me new shirts to wear with our logo and your name and number on them. Should I have brought something to dress up in?" She bites down on her plump bottom lip.

I can see the worry and… what might be fear on her face. "No, you're good. I guess I just expected you to have more."

"I think I have what I need. Enough clothes for the week, cell charger, bathroom essentials. My laptop and e-reader. Money." She verbally goes through her mental checklist as if I'm not even standing here.

"Aubree." She stops and looks up at me. "Are you done? We need to get loaded so we can roll out when the rest of the crew get here."

"Oh." Her face turns an adorable light shade of pink. "Sorry." Since when do I notice adorable? Not just that, but my body reacts to her. I have to shift my stance to make room for my cock and his appreciation for that exact light shade of pink on her cheeks.

She hitches her duffel higher on her shoulder, causing her pink tank top to stretch over her breasts. *Nope, can't go there.* Shutting down that train of thought, I turn and head toward the toter home. I can hear her following along behind me.

"Wow," she breathes as we step into the living quarters. "This is… not what I expected."

"No?"

"No, I mean, I don't really know what I was expecting but not… this." Her eyes travel over our surroundings, taking it in. Black leather captains' chairs for whoever happens to be up front. State of the art GPS and a sound system sits in the dash. There's a leather couch that turns into a bed, as well as a booth that also has black leather seats that turn into a bed. "It's all close together," she comments, still taking it all in.

"These are slide outs. You push that button on either side and the room expands. It's actually a lot of space once that happens."

"This kitchen, I'm impressed."

"You cook?"

"Yeah, I mean a little. It's not so much fun cooking for one. I know enough not to starve."

With a nod in her direction, I head back to the master bedroom. Full-size bed with a slide out on each side.

"This is you?" she asks from behind me.

"Yep. My domain." I say it so she knows she won't be spending any time in my bed. No way am I going there if she's going to be traveling with us. That's a disaster in the making. She'll think it's more and it's not. It would never be more.

"Got it. Uh, where will I sleep?"

"There are four bunks. You can take one of them or the couch or table. Ash is coming this trip, so she and Kevin usually take one of the two. If you prefer to not have a bunk, you can work it out with the two of them." I hear a truck pull up and know everyone is starting to get here. Stepping toward her, I turn sideways to move past her. Her breasts brush against my chest, her breath hitches, and my cock twitches. Her scent, something sweet and flowery assaults my senses, but I don't stop. I continue on as if she's just another stranger on the street and step out of the toter home.

"There you are." My mom smiles. "We saw Camber so we knew you were out here somewhere. All set?" Something catches her eye as she looks over my shoulder. I close mine and take a deep breath. "Oh, hello," Mom says, way too damn chipper for this time in the morning. It's her "I'm excited and trying not to show it" greeting. She assumes Aubree is here with me.

"Hi," a soft voice greets her.

"Mom, this is Aubree. Aubree, this is my mother, Robin

Bishop. Mom, Aubree is from KHP. Apparently, Kevin agreed to have her travel with us this year as a part of our sponsorship."

"How wonderful. It will be nice to have another woman around. I usually only get that when Ashley comes with us."

"Don't mind me. I'll just be over here on my own." Dad chuckles.

"Dad, this is Aubree, Aubree, my dad, Brian Bishop."

"Nice to meet you." Dad offers her his hand and she shakes it.

"You as well."

"So, what it is that you do, Aubree?"

"Well, I—"

"Mom, can we do this later? We have a long drive ahead of us for the two of you to get acquainted."

"Well, that's nonsense. She's not riding with us, and I was just being polite, something you apparently forgot how to be."

I have to refrain from rolling my eyes. It's a feat, trust me. "Fine, but I've got shit to do today."

"Blaine Bishop, you're not too old for me to wash your mouth out with soap," she calls after me as I stalk off toward the shop. I need to take one last look, just to be certain everything is loaded and ready to go. We're going to Eldora this week, and it's a six-hour drive if we don't stop. That never happens. We always stop to eat and to fuel up. The toter home is badass. It's matte black and with blacked-out windows, but it sucks the diesel.

By the time I make it back outside, everyone is there. Mom and Ashley are laughing with Aubree, while Dad and the guys are shooting the shit. "We ready?" I ask, stalking past them.

"What crawled up your ass?" Kevin asks as I pass them.

"We need to get on the road," I say, not bothering to stop. Instead, I climb on the toter and get behind the wheel. I fire up the engine and take a deep breath. So, what if this hot, little number is tagging along for the remainder of the season? She's just another pretty face and hot body. I won't let her get under my skin. Her sweet and innocent act is not going to work on me. One by one, they pile on while my parents head to their RV that's pulling the T-shirt trailer.

"Just have a seat anywhere," Rick says. "We just kind of spread out. The four of us take turns driving this beast, the rest of the time we just enjoy the ride."

"Okay. Thank you. I don't want to be in the way."

"Too late," I mumble under my breath, but it must not have been low enough because I get smacked in the back of the head. Turning to see who it was, I find Ashley glaring at me with her hands on her hips. Then a grin breaks across her face. That can only mean trouble.

"Aubree, have you ever ridden in a toter home or RV?" she asks.

"No. We, uh, didn't travel when I was a kid."

"Well, then you have to experience it. It's so weird sitting up high and being king, or should I say queen of the road. Take the passenger seat. You and I can switch off when Kev takes his leg of the driving."

"I don't know...." She hesitates.

What is with this girl? "Come on if you're going to. We need to get on the road," I snap. I feel another smack to the back of my head and wince. "Damnit, Ash."

"Be nice," she whispers harshly.

"Come on, Aubree. Just for a bit. It's fine. Blaine is just a grumpy bear. Get used to it. That's his normal MO."

"If you're sure," she says, and I know she's asking me, but I don't bother to reply. I pretend to be messing with the navigation.

"Definitely. Let me know if you want to switch or get tired of sitting next to Mr. Moody Pants."

Ash steps back, and Aubree takes her place. She climbs into the passenger seat, straps her seat belt, and folds her hands on her lap. She keeps her stare straight ahead as I pull out onto the road. Everyone is quiet. It's still early in the morning and we have a long way to go. I turn on the radio, to a country station. It's something I know everyone will enjoy. Well, everyone but Aubree, I don't know her preference. Not that it matters. She's outnumbered.

When we reach the Kentucky state line, she pulls out her cell phone and snaps a picture. Her eyes are wide as she takes in the scenery as it passes by. "You act like you've never been to Kentucky before," I comment.

"I haven't."

"Really? We're what, forty-five minutes from the state line. You've never been here?"

"No." Her voice is soft. Glancing over, I see her staring out the passenger window. "I've never been out of the state of Tennessee."

I let her words sink in. How is it possible she's never been out of the state of Tennessee? "How old are you?" It's a simple question, but it comes out harsh.

She turns to look at me. "I'm twenty-three. How old are you?" she asks, crossing her arms over her chest.

Pulling my attention back to the highway, I answer her. "Twenty-five." We're quiet for a few minutes. I can hear murmurs of the others' conversations but can't quite make them out. "You've really never been out of Tennessee?" I ask her. This time my voice is calm.

"No." One word is spoken so that I know this conversation is over.

Over the next couple of hours, I watch her from the corner of my eye as she snaps pictures of scenery. Her eyes light up as we pass the many horse farms of Lexington. It really is beautiful to see: huge houses, bigger barns, and fields of white painted fence for miles. I want to ask her what she's thinking, but I don't. I let her enjoy it, the newness of it all while I ponder why she's never left Tennessee.

CHAPTER Seven

Aubree

IF I WASN'T SO EXCITED to be seeing new places, I would be embarrassed. I'm sure Blaine thinks I'm acting like a kid, but I can't seem to help myself. I've always wanted to travel, see what else was out there past my little home state of Tennessee. Growing up, that wasn't an option, and now that I'm on my own, well... I don't really have a reason. Not unless you count fear and change as excuses. The fear of change to be more specific. Maria and Isaac were right. I've found my little piece of comfort. I make a good living and can provide for myself and whatever I might need. That's more than I've ever had. When the majority of your childhood you grow up without those things, it's only natural that when you finally get them, you hold on tight.

"Hey, man." Kevin appears between Blaine and me. "You ready for a break?"

"Yeah, we need to stop and fuel up. I need to tell Mom and

Dad." He reaches for his phone, but I stop him.

"What are you doing? You can't drive this monstrosity and text at the same time."

He throws his head back in laughter. "I can, but I'm not going to." He hits a button in his phone and presses it to his ear. "Hey, we're stopping just up ahead." He listens, says goodbye, and places his phone back in the cup holder between us. "Happy?" His smile is smug.

"Yes." I turn my attention back out the window, not wanting to miss anything and to avoid any further conversation with him. First impression, he was an asshole. Second impression, he's still an asshole.

Once we're at the gas station, I rush inside to use the restroom. After, I grab a bottle of water and also pick up a few snacks. The others seem to be doing the same.

"He's not a bad guy," Ashley says from beside me.

"No?"

She throws her head back and laughs. "No. I promise. He's not much for change, especially when it comes to racing season. Blaine is focused. Determined to win this championship."

"Then why agree to this?" That's what I can't seem to figure out. If he's so pissed off that I'm here, then why am I here?

"You can thank my husband for that. Kevin agreed to the deal with KHP. Your boss I assume?"

"My boss's boss."

She nods. "It'll be nice to have you around. These guys work hard, and as a fan of massage, they don't know what they're missing."

"Speak for yourself. I know, and I can't wait for my next visit," Rick says, reaching around me to grab a Snickers bar.

"You're good," I tell him. "Two sessions, and on our second you were much better."

"Do I have to be injured to use your services?" He wags his eyebrows.

"Yes." Blaine's deep voice appears from behind us, causing us all to jump. "Get what you need. We gotta go." He stalks off toward the register to pay for whatever it is he's buying.

I look at Ashley with a "see" expression, and she laughs. "He'll warm up to you. Give him time."

"I'm not here for him to warm up to me. I just need to stay out of his way, and it will be fine."

"Come on." She tugs on my arm, and I follow her to the checkout.

We each pay for our items and head back to the toter home. "I'll sit up front with Kevin. Take a seat anywhere," she tells me as we climb back inside. I take a look around. Blaine and Jacob are sitting at the table, a notebook between them, deep in conversation. Rick is sitting on one end of the couch on his phone. Deciding Rick is the safer bet, I take the other side of the couch and settle in. Grabbing my phone out of my pocket, I sift through all the pictures I've taken this far. Turning sideways, I open the blind so I can see out. The view is not nearly as good as the one I had up front, but it's still better than the walls that seem to be closing in on me. It's a tight space without the slide outs extended. Cramped.

"Whatcha looking at?" Rick asks.

"Just taking it all in."

He looks out the window. "You travel much?"

"No, never been outside of Tennessee actually."

"I heard you mention that."

"Yeah, my mom left when I was young. On my first birthday, actually." I don't know why I just told him all of that. I'm usually a closed book. Rick is so laid-back he's easy to talk to, I guess.

"Tough break."

"Dad blamed me. Life was hard growing up."

"That sucks, Aubs."

"Yes. Yes, it does. But things are better now." I take a sip of my water. "What are you doing over there?" I point to his phone.

"Oh, I was just playing poker."

"Big gambler, are you?" I tease.

"Nah, just something to pass the time. You play?"

"Um, that would be a no."

"Slide over. I'll teach you." He pats the center couch cushion next to him.

Doing as he says, I move over. He slants his phone so that we can both see the screen. "Okay, so we're playing Texas Hold'em." He goes on to explain the combination of cards, and it's going through one ear and out the other.

"You expect me to learn all this? I need to be taking notes," I say with a laugh.

"It takes practice." He grins. "Now, this is what I call a royal flush." He points to his cards.

"I take it that's good?"

"Yeah, Aubs, that's good. Girl, I've got my work cut out with you." He goes back to playing and I watch. I'm not really retaining it, but it's something to pass the time. Uncle Bobby tried to teach me to play poker once. Dad found out and threw a fit. I have no desire to learn now, didn't really then either, but it made Uncle Bobby happy. He was doing the best he could with a teenage girl who was hated and scared to death of her father.

When I yawn for the fourth time, Rick chuckles. "Use me as your pillow. I'm too hyped up about this race to sleep."

"No, I can—"

"Aubree, it's fine. Take a catnap. We still have about two hours or so to go."

"Okay." I relent and cautiously lay my head on his shoulder and let the lull of the tires against the road send me off to sleep.

"What the fuck are you doing?" a deep voice asks. I know that voice; it's Blaine. I keep my eyes closed, not wanting to be on the receiving end of his bad attitude yet again today. I've met my quota.

"What?" Rick whispers.

"She's here to work, just like you. Not for you to hit on her and… this… whatever this is," Blaine sneers.

"This is me being nice. She kept yawning so I told her to use me as a pillow and take a nap. It's not exactly the Hilton on this thing all cramped up like this."

"There's a full-size bed back there."

"Right? And you would have been okay with me sending her to your bed?"

Blaine releases a heavy sigh. "She's not here for you, or you"—I assume he's talking to Jacob—"to hit on, or fuck or whatever it is you might have brewing in your mind. She's an employee of our sponsor here to represent them. End of."

"Chill out," this from Kevin. "Go take a walk."

Heavy footsteps and a slamming door I assume courtesy of Blaine. Slowly I open my eyes. I find Rick, Ashley, Kevin, and Jacob all watching me. "I'm so sorry. I just meant to shut my eyes. I didn't mean to fall asleep."

Rick stands when I sit up. "Don't worry about him. He has a shifter up his ass," he mumbles before stepping out of the toter home as well. Kevin and Jacob trail behind him, leaving me alone with Ashley.

I bury my face in my hands, barely able to fight back the tears. "I knew this was a bad idea." My gut clenches and nausea washes over me. This is my first trip with them and I'm already screwing up. I didn't mean to fall asleep.

"What are you talking about?" she asks, placing her arm over my shoulders.

"Being here. I knew he hated me, and this… this is a disaster in the making."

"Aubree, you didn't do anything wrong. You fell asleep on a long-ass car ride. There is no wrongdoing there."

"I don't think I can do this. He's not my biggest fan and has made it clear that he doesn't want me here."

She nods. "I can see how you would see it that way. Want to know how I see it?"

"There is no other way, Ashley."

"Oh, but you're wrong. I've known Blaine for years and never seen him be this... prickly."

"It's me. I'm telling you, he hates me."

"Maybe," she muses. "Maybe he doesn't. Maybe he's attracted to you?"

"Right." I laugh. "Thanks for trying to make this better, but you're way off base. You don't see the way he looks at me." Although I don't believe her, it's still nice to hear that maybe he really doesn't hate me like I think he does.

"That's just it. I do see it. I see how he looks at you when you're not looking."

"Like he wants to strangle me?"

She laughs. "Nope. Like he wants to kiss the hell out of you."

"Are we talking about the same person? Tall, dark hair, scruff on his face to accompany his permanent scowl? That guy?"

"One and the same. You'll see. I know these things."

This causes laughter to burst free. "Thank you for cheering me up. I needed that. I still think I should go back home." My stomach quivers at the thought. What will Jonah say if I leave? Will I lose my job?

"It's been a few hours we've been cooped up in here." She looks around. "Give it time. Trust me."

"As mad as he was, I won't be surprised if he tells me to go, at the very least that I'm relieved of my duties when we get back."

"Come on, we'll help Robin set up the T-shirt trailer."

"I'm not familiar with any of this. I'm like a fish out of water."

"Stick with me. I'll have you up to speed in no time. I'm glad we'll get this week to hang out. I can show you the ropes, that way, when it's just you and the guys, you'll be more prepared."

"Ugh, can we not talk about me and just the guys."

She laughs. "Come on." She stands and, reluctantly, I follow her. It's a better option than sticking around for the wrath of Blaine. We walk past the guys standing at the end of the trailer. I keep my head down and keep on walking. Lay low, that's my new motto. Robin and Brian greet us with open arms, and we spend the next couple of hours setting up the T-shirt trailer.

"Do you sell a lot of these?" I ask as I'm wiping down the counter.

"We usually sell out at big events like this," Brian tells me.

I look around the trailer and all the T-shirts we just organized in bins by size. "There must be five thousand shirts here."

"Close." Robin grins. "We brought seven thousand this year."

"And you sell out?"

"Blaine's kind of a big deal," Ashley says with a smile.

"That explains the ego," I mumble.

"Oh, he's always been that way. Focused that one is." Robin laughs when she sees the pink in my cheeks from being overheard. "No need to be embarrassed. We know how he is. But I'll let you in on a little secret." She leans in close. "His bark is bigger than his bite."

"Exactly!" Ashley says. "I've been trying to tell her that. He's been not so... nice to her in their limited encounters. He's really not that bad. He just has to warm up to you, that's all."

"If he becomes too big of an ass, you let me know," Brian says. "I'll talk to him."

"No." I rush to get the words out. "Please don't. That will just make it worse. I get it. I'm a stranger tagging along for the season, an outsider in his world. I plan to just lay low, be here if any of you need me, and watch the days and the miles tick by. You won't even notice I'm here."

"Nonsense. You're here and you've been a big help to us today."

"Then I'll hang out with you and he won't even notice I'm around."

"I doubt that," Brian and Ashley say at the same time.

"Come on, let's go round up the crew and have some dinner. We're all set here," Robin suggests.

I want to argue and tell her that I'll just hang out here in the Blaine-free zone, but I know I can't do that. Instead, I help them close up shop and follow along behind them.

"Hey." Ashley bumps her shoulder with mine. "Relax. Just be you. Don't worry about Blaine. He's stressed about this race. Well, all races really. He wants to win this championship. He wants to make history."

"Thanks, Ashley." I offer her a smile. She links her arm through mine and begins to tell me how this event works. Qualifying and hot laps, heat races. It's a blur, but I'm determined to learn it all, to fit in with them. I make a mental note to google Dirt Late Model Racing later tonight.

CHAPTER Eight

BLAINE

I'VE MANAGED TO AVOID HER most of the afternoon. Mom and Dad have her and Ashley helping out in the T-shirt trailer. Not that I was checking up on them. Kevin told me. I don't know what it is about her that has me so on edge. Little Miss Aubree gets under my skin like no one ever has.

"Ash just texted me. They're done and ready to eat. I think we're all good too," Kevin says, wiping his hands on a shop towel.

"Yeah, the car's good."

"Have you decided if you are going to run in the event Wednesday night?"

"Nah, I know the fans love it, but no way am I risking tearing something up."

"This isn't a points race, Blaine."

"Regardless, it's not worth the wear and tear on the car or the engine."

"Then why in the hell are we here on Monday?"

"To get a good pit spot. You know how this place fills up. I thought we could all kick back and enjoy the racing Wednesday night. Be fans for once."

"Checkmate, you being nice to us?" He smirks.

"Don't get used to it." I toss a rag at him, which he catches easily.

"Speaking of being nice, you know you could ease up on Aubree."

"What? I am nice." I'm not, I know this. I've been a dick, but I can't seem to keep it in check around her.

"Right. Try a little harder." I roll my eyes, but don't have time to reply as they approach us.

"We're all set," Mom says.

"Thank you." I lean in and kiss her cheek.

"Now we're starving."

"I'll fire up the grill," Dad says, giving her shoulder a gentle squeeze and heading for the outdoor kitchen that's in the toter home.

"Wow," Aubree says when she opens the door that conceals the kitchen. She walks over toward Dad. "This is really cool."

"You act like you've never seen an outdoor kitchen before," I smart off, unable to control it.

"That's because I haven't." She doesn't look at me as she watches Dad fire up the grill.

"How is that possible?"

"Well…" She turns to face me, crossing her arms over her chest, pushing her tits up and on display for me in that tank top of hers. "I've never been camping."

"Never?" Rick asks.

"Nope, we, uh… didn't really do much when I was a kid. Like I said, never been out of the state of Tennessee."

"Well," Dad says, "how about you be my sidekick and I'll show you how this thing works?"

She turns sideways to look at him. "I'd love to, Brian. Thank you." Her smile is wide, and her green eyes seem to sparkle when she smiles like that.

Instead of sticking around to watch the show, I head inside and wash up. After I grab a couple of cans of baked beans and throw them in a pan, and collect a couple of bags of chips, I head back outside. Mom is already setting up the table with plates, napkins, and condiments from the outdoor fridge. "Here's some chips. I'm going to take these beans over to Dad."

"Got some room for baked beans?" I ask, walking up behind my dad and Aubree.

"You know it." Dad takes the pan from me and lights the side burner. "Aubree was just telling me she's never been to a race."

"Don't get out much, huh?" I ask dryly.

She shrugs. "I work a lot, and when I'm not working, I'm at home. I've worked hard to have a nice place and I enjoy spending time there."

"Nothing wrong with that, darlin'," Dad tells her. "Working hard for something makes you appreciate it more. Kind of like Blaine and racing. He knows how much work it is to win week after week. He stays focused, sometimes too focused. It's like winning that race is all he can see."

"I'm standing right here," I remind them.

"Oh, I know that. But when I remind you to live a little, you don't listen, so I figured you wouldn't be now either." He smirks.

"I'm doing just fine, Dad. I just happen to be focused on my career."

"Too focused if you ask me," Mom chimes in. "All work and no play isn't good for anyone. Both of you" — she points at me and then to Aubree — "should remember that."

"My work is play," I say in defense.

"Uh-huh," she says with a chuckle. "How long until we eat? I'm starving to death, and poor Aubree looks like she might just keel over from starvation."

"Me too!" Rick yells out.

"Order up!" Dad hollers, handing Mom a disposable aluminum pan of grilled burgers and hot dogs. "Just another minute or so on these beans and I'll bring them over."

"What can I do?" Aubree asks.

"You can head on over and make yourself a plate. I've got this," Dad says.

I watch her as she hesitates then makes her way over to the table. Her long auburn hair is blowing in the wind, and she laughs as it tickles her nose before she can remove the offending strands from her face.

"She's a looker." Dad bumps his elbow into mine.

"Really, Dad?" I can't help but shake my head at him.

"What? Just because I'm happily married doesn't mean I can't appreciate a beautiful woman."

"What would Mom think?" I goad him.

"Pfft. Have you heard her talk about those books she reads, and the covers? Son, we love each other, and we both have trust... you know that feeling deep in your gut that the other will never stray."

"Trust." I try the word out. "Seems like too big of a risk."

"Listen to you." He grins. "You drive that car around in a circle at high rates of speed with a dozen and often more other drivers just like you. You trust that you have the skill to keep it on the track and make it to the front. That son of mine is a risk taker."

"It's my job," I remind him.

He nods. "I get that. But what you don't understand, Blaine, is that loving your mother, that's my job."

"Love shouldn't feel like a job."

He lowers his head, giving it a gentle shake before looking back up at me. "Blaine, until you open yourself up and let someone in, you're never going to understand what I'm talking about. Loving your mother is my job, but, son, it's not work. It's the greatest gift I've ever been given. One day, you'll understand."

"Dad, come on. You're not making any sense."

"I get it, Blaine. You love racing. It's in your blood. Since you were a little boy from go-karts on up, you were hooked. However, racing can't give you what the love of a good woman can."

"Sure it can. I'm happy. My life is good. I'm healthy. What more could I ask for?"

"How about someone to warm your bed at night?"

"Come on, Dad, we both know that's not an issue."

"What about someone to come home to?"

"I like my space."

"I don't know where these... barriers came from, the ones that you keep built around your heart, but, son, I'm telling you it will be a lonely existence if you don't lower them."

"Dad..." I place my hand on his shoulder. "I'm happy. This is what I want, racing the circuit. You and I both know that it's hard to make relationships work living this lifestyle. I want racing more."

"Let me ask you something. When you're out on the track, let's say you're in turn three and the car starts heading toward the wall, what do you do?"

"I cut the wheel and trust that we're going to make it through the corner."

"Do you slow down? Do you lift your foot from the accelerator even the slightest bit?"

"No. You know I don't."

He nods. "Exactly. You trust that even though the car is pushing that you're going to make it around that track. So, why not do the same when it comes to the walls you've built around you? When the right woman comes knocking, I want you to do something for me. I want you to trust the push, Blaine. Take a chance. You risk your life daily out on the track. Why not risk a little pain to find happiness?"

"Dad, I get it, but not everyone finds what you and Mom have. I'm not unhappy."

"I get that, I do. I also know what the love of a good woman can bring into your life." He turns and grabs the pan of beans and shuts off the burner. "Trust the push, son." With that, he walks over to the table, sets the beans down, and kisses Mom on her temple.

I think about everything he just said, and I don't have walls. I'm realistic. Traveling is hard. I see how miserable Kevin is when Ashley can't travel with us. I've seen other guys' marriages crash and burn from the strain. Why would I put myself through that? This is what I want. I'm focused on becoming the youngest driver to win three back-to-back championships. One day, once I've met my career goals, sure I'd like to settle down, but right now, this is what I want.

I wait until everyone has a plate before making my way over and grabbing one for myself. I've just finished piling it high with a burger, hot dog, chips, and baked beans when I sense her next to me. Out of the corner of my eye, I see her. She reaches in front of me to grab a napkin.

"Sorry," she says softly. She quickly grabs the napkin and scurries away back to her seat.

She acts as if she's afraid of me. Sure, I've not been the nicest, but afraid? That's crazy. I'm just about to call her out on it when Jacob asks her what she does for fun. I can tell he's interested. That shit is not happening. We all need to stay focused. We are winning this championship, even if I have to tell KHP to kiss my ass.

CHAPTER Nine

Aubree

TINGLES RACE UP MY SPINE when I reach in front of him. Why? Why now? I've gone all this time doing just fine on my own, and my body decided that now is the time to be attracted to someone. Not just someone, but Blaine "Checkmate" Bishop. He's egotistical, smug, and he's an asshole. Well, at least he's all that to me. I don't know what it is about me that he doesn't like, but my body doesn't seem to notice. Nope, traitor breaks out in goose bumps when it's eighty-eight degrees outside. Just because I was close to him.

Just my luck.

I make it back to my chair and keep my head down, that is until Jacob asks me what I do for fun. I hate to be rude, and everyone has been so nice and welcoming, all of them except for Blaine. "Uh, not much really. I work a lot."

"Yeah, but fun, girl, what do you do for fun?"

"My best friend, Maria, she and her husband have me over

for dinner at least once per week."

"That's it?" Jacob asks.

"Like I said, I work a lot."

"Don't mind him," Ashley says. "He wouldn't know fun if it hit him upside the head. Some friends and I do this thing each month, we have a few drinks and just catch up. You have to come with us next week."

"Oh, I don't want to impose." She seems sincere, but the last thing I want is an invite because she feels sorry for me. I'm in a good place. I have everything I need, and that's saying a lot considering where I come from.

"Never," Ashley says adamantly. "The more, the merrier. You'll get along great with Beth, Susanne, and Lisa."

"We'll see," I concede.

"So, you don't go to bars or anything like that?" Jacob asks.

"Did you not hear her the first time?" Blaine asks him.

"Oh, I heard her. I'm just baffled that a young, gorgeous girl like her sits at home all alone."

"She never said she was alone. Drop it. It's her life. If she wants to sit alone, let her sit alone." Blaine stands and tosses his plate and water bottle in the trash. "I'm going to go check out the track."

"Good idea, son. Aubree," Brian says, "why don't you go with him? You've never been to a race before, and this place will be crazy tomorrow with all the racers coming in and the fans too. Blaine can give you a tour so to speak."

"No, really I'm fine." I'm quick to shoot down the idea. Blaine doesn't want to spend time alone with me anymore than I want to spend time alone with him.

"Great idea, honey," Robin says. "Make sure you take her through the tunnel." She grins.

"Tunnel?" My brows dip in confusion.

"The Love Tunnel," Rick chimes in.

"Uh...." I'm not sure what to say to that. Luckily Brian helps me out.

"There's a story there, and not what you're thinking, at least not at first," he says with a laugh. "Blaine can fill you in. He knows the story."

I'm ready to decline yet again, but Blaine beats me to it. "You coming?" His voice is gruff and I can tell he wants me to say no.

"I should help clean up."

"Nope. We've got it. Go on. You're going to be with us for the season. It'll do you good to learn some of the history and the ins and outs of what goes on behind the scenes," Brian encourages.

"It's up to you, but I'm not waiting around." Blaine turns to walk away.

"Go!" Ashley nudges my arm.

Reluctantly, I climb out of my chair and follow after him. As if he can sense me behind him, Blaine slows his pace, allowing me to catch up, which surprises me. We walk in silence until we reach a turn in the track.

"This is turn four." He points to the corner.

"How are the turns determined?" I ask, my voice is strong, even though my insides are shaking. Why does he make me so nervous?

"That's the flag stand, the starting line, and the finish line all in one." He then points to each corner naming them off one by one. "We always go in the same direction, so the turns and their numbers never change."

"Your dad said you go over one hundred miles an hour."

He nods. "Yeah, this track is short and fast."

"That's scary."

"I guess to some. To, me, well, it's who I am."

We both grow quiet as he stares at the track. I wish I knew what he was thinking. Is he strategizing how to win the race? Does he even need to do that? This is a whole new world for me. "I'm sorry that my being here upsets you," I say when I can no longer take the silence.

He heaves a heavy sigh and turns to face me. "It's not you, as much as it's the change. I have goals, Aubree. I want this championship. I want to make Dirt Late Model Racing history, and this is my chance to do that. I need my team zoned in and focused."

"You think my being here will prevent that?"

"I don't know. I know the guys, and even Ashley and my parents are enamored with you."

"But not you?" I don't know why I say it, and as soon as those three words leave my mouth, I can feel my face heat with embarrassment.

"Your beauty is hard to miss."

I'm shocked, embarrassed, and elated all at the same time. Biting down on my bottom lip I fight to keep my smile from showing through. "I'll stay out of your way, and I promise you, nothing will happen with me and your crew. I'm here to do a job. If any of you need me, let me know. Otherwise, I'll wear my required Bishop Racing and KHP apparel and smile for the cameras."

His eyes are trained on my lips, which makes me think about kissing him. I lick my lips, and he takes a step closer. My heart is beating so fast I'm sure he can hear it. I want him to lean in and kiss me. I want to taste his lips, for them to press against mine. Instead, I do the right thing, which is take a step back. "So…" I clear my throat. "Where is this tunnel?"

He blinks rapidly before focusing his gaze back on me. "The Love Tunnel." His voice is husky and sexy.

"Y-yeah, that. Where is that?"

"Turn three."

"So, there." I point to turn three.

"Yep. You wanna check it out?"

"Are we allowed?" The last thing I want to do is get caught doing something illegal. Jonah would fire me for sure.

"Yeah, it takes us to the infield." He points back to where we just were.

"So, why the tunnel if we can walk there the way we just did?"

We begin to walk toward the tunnel. "The story goes that Earl, he used to be the owner, built this place to what it is today. Anyway, when it would rain, the track would be muddy as hell and getting from the stands to the infield" — he points to where we are parked — "was a challenge. I've seen some pictures where people would form a chain, linking hands to keep from falling just to cross the track. So, Earl decided to build the tunnel."

"And the name?" My mind is coming up with all kinds of scenarios of why it's called the Love Tunnel.

"Ah, the name. Not what you're thinking." He laughs, causing my breath to stall in my chest. He's gorgeous when he's not pissed off. "Once the tunnel was done, people would yell out as they saw him, "Hey, Earl, love the tunnel," so that's how it got its name. At least that's the story I've heard countless times over the years. Who really knows if that's the real reason or history behind it. However, I'm certain there's an alternate story that would be guaranteed to make a girl like you blush."

"A girl like me?"

"Yeah, innocent. Or is that just a front?"

"Wow, from nice guy to asshole in two seconds flat. You're good at that. If this racing gig ever goes south and you can find a use for that particular skill, you'll have more money than you know what to do with." I don't wait for him; instead, I quicken my pace and head for the tunnel. I can't help but smile when I see the sign that hangs above the entrance labeling it The Love Tunnel. I take one step then two until I'm inside. It's dark and dingy and smells like dirt. There are dim lights near the ceiling as well as the fading sunlight at the entrance and exit. Leaning my back against the wall, I close my eyes and take a deep breath.

"You okay?" his deep voice asks.

My eyes flutter open, and there he is standing way too close for comfort. "Fine."

He steps even closer, so close that our toes are touching and if he or I either one of us were to lean in just a little, our bodies would be aligned. Suddenly, it's hot as hell in this tunnel. "Don't do that."

"What?" I manage to ask.

"Don't sugarcoat it for me with *fine*. I know you're pissed."

"You know what? I am pissed. One minute you're this nice, charming guy, and then next you act as if I have some rare communicable disease." He surprises me when he reaches out and moves my bangs out of my eyes.

"I'm sorry," he says softly. "I don't mean to be an asshole, but you being here, it messes with me."

"Then call my boss and tell him that you don't need me."

"I can't do that, Bree." The nickname rolls off his tongue effortlessly, as if he's called me that for years. Truth is no one has ever called me Bree; it's always Aubree or Aubs.

"Then we have to find a way to work together."

"That's the problem," he admits. "When you're this close to me, I want to do more than just work with you. You're under my skin, like no other woman has ever been." Slowly, his index finger traces the line of my jaw. "You feel it, right?"

"No." *Lie. Lie. Lie.* I'm lying through my teeth and he can see right through me.

"Hmm," he says, his thumb landing on my pulse at the base of my neck. "This says otherwise."

"Fine."

He chuckles. "There's that word again. *Fine.*"

"Yes, *fine*. I feel something, but then you open your mouth, and it all goes away. It's a physical attraction. We're both adults. We're smart enough not to act on it."

"Are we?" He leans in and whispers, his lips next to my ear, "I'm not so sure I am."

As soon as his hot breath hits my skin, I close my eyes and fight like hell to not let him see what it does to me. What *he* does to me. I've never been this attracted to someone. It's running hot through my veins, and it's a bad idea. A very bad idea.

"Doesn't matter," I murmur.

"We can figure this out," he urges. "As long as you know up front that this thing between us will never be more than a fling, a way to scratch this itch, to eliminate this burning attraction between us. It will be a good time."

"No." Placing my hands on his chest, I push him back. "No. There will be no fling, no scratching of any itch, no good times, not in the way you're thinking." I take a deep breath and slowly exhale. Before either of us can say a word, his cell rings.

"Hello." He listens. "Yeah, we're in the tunnel now." Again, he listens to whoever is on the other end. "Good." Even though it's dimly lit in this tunnel, I can see the fire burning in his hazel eyes. "Aubree can get the full experience." Another pause. "Yeah, we'll head back soon." He slides his phone back into his pocket just as a rounding sound of an engine sounds above us.

"What?" I ask.

"Seems a few of the drivers are taking their cars out on the track."

"Now? Is it safe to be here?" I ask, moving from my perch against the wall, to head out of the tunnel. Blaine stops me by grabbing my hand.

"Relax, Bree. It's safe. Come here." He gives my hand a gentle tug and pulls me into him. He moves us so that our backs are against the wall, his hand remaining laced through mine. The roaring starts again, and the walls vibrate behind us. It's loud, so loud I can feel the vibration as if it's a part of me. "Feel it," he asks, his lips are once again next to my ear so that I can hear him. "Let it roll through you. The vibration, the thrill. There is nothing like it. This place is special." He places a featherlight kiss just below my ear. Pulling away, he rests his head back against the wall, his hand still holding tightly to mine as the cars race above us. When the noise fades away and the walls are no longer shaking, he releases his hold on me. "We better get back."

He doesn't wait for me. No, he's back to asshole Blaine as he walks out of the tunnel. It takes me a few minutes to get my feet to move, overwhelmed with this entire interaction between the two of us. When I exit the tunnel, I have to run to catch up with him. Neither of us says a word as we approach his hauler. Ashley pulls me to the side and begins asking about what he showed me. I give short answers, but she doesn't seem to notice. Looking around, I try to find Blaine, but he's nowhere in sight. It's better that way. I don't want him to see me flustered by what happened. I'll be better prepared for him next time around.

If there is a next time.

CHAPTER Ten

BLAINE

IT'S JUST AFTER MIDNIGHT AND I've had enough. I can't sit here any longer and listen to her soft laughter or see her bright smile over the fire. She's driving me fucking insane just for breathing. Living. It's time for me to call it a night. Standing from the lawn chair, I stretch and toss my water bottle into the trash can that we keep outside. "See you all in the morning. Come on, girl," I say to Camber, not stopping to talk to any of them. Instead, I walk right on past my family and friends, not making eye contact. In the toter home, I head to the bedroom and fall face first into the bed. I'm almost asleep when I hear voices.

"Kev and I usually take the sofa bed," Ashley whispers. "Are you claustrophobic?"

"No," Aubree replies.

"Great. You can take either of the bunks on the right side. Rick and Jacob are on the left."

"Which one does Kevin usually sleep in when you're not here?"

"He usually takes the top."

"Then I'll take the bottom. You won't even know I'm here," Aubree tells her.

If only that were true. I've done nothing but think about her since the first night she stepped into my shop. Even though I am dead tired, I'm all too aware of the fact that she's going to be sleeping just mere feet away from me. I blame Kevin. He should have asked me before he agreed to let her tag along. She's a distraction, a big one. One that I don't want or need in my life right now.

I hear rustling around, and then their voices grow softer. A murmur that I can't quite make out. I'm both relieved and angry by this, which pisses me off even more. I don't care what they're saying. Sure, I like the sound of her soft southern voice, but she's bad news. Very bad news.

After tossing and turning for what feels like hours, I'm finally drifting off to sleep when I hear feet hit the floor. Camber jumps off the bed to go investigate. I left the door cracked, and she was able to wiggle her nose to get out of my room. Lesson learned. I can tell from the soft pad of feet that it's her, Aubree. None of the guys are that light-footed, and Ashley is sleeping up front so I wouldn't have heard her climb out of bed. Using Camber as an excuse, I climb out of bed and softly call for her. Not wanting to wake anyone, but loud enough for those who are already awake to hear me.

"Sorry," Aubree says.

I look down to see her crouched to the floor, petting Camber. Of course my dog, man's supposed best friend, is loving every minute of it.

"I had to use the restroom. I didn't mean to wake either of you," she whispers.

I watch her as she nuzzles close to Camber, showing her the kind of affection only a dog's owner shows them. That owner being me. Camber doesn't care. She just wants the attention. Traitor.

"Camber," I say, stern yet soft. "Come." I pat my leg for her to come to me. She whimpers, licks Aubree's hand, and then slowly makes her way to me. "Back to bed," I tell her. Like a child who has been scolded, she hangs her head and heads toward the bedroom.

"She's smart," Aubree comments.

"She is," I say, looking her in the eyes. I'm trying really hard to not rake my eyes over her toned, little body. She's wearing a tank top with thin straps and a tiny pair of shorts. So tiny that they should be illegal. Giving in, my eyes drop to her bare feet. Light pink polish adorns her toenails, soft and subtle. Her toned, tanned legs lead up to those tiny cream-colored shorts that mold to her body as if they were a second skin. Her tank top has ridden up so I can see a small slither of skin. Just enough for my cock to wonder what else she's hiding from me. I keep going, my eyes raking over her chest. Not small, not outrageously large. Just about a handful if I had to guess, which is perfect. She's wearing a bra, much to my disappointment, but I'm a man of many talents, and I can imagine her pert nipples as I suck them into my mouth. My eyes roam over the column of her long, slender neck, and I lick my lips, my mouth watering, wondering what it would be like to trace it with my tongue.

"Sorry." Her soft, plump lips move. "I didn't mean to wake you."

Her green eyes, bright even in the dim light, are boring into me. "I'm going back to bed." I turn on my heel and head back to the bedroom. My feet carry me as fast as they can go, my only defense mechanism from pulling her into my arms and kissing the hell out of her. Then finally I could feel her plump lips pressed to mine; I wouldn't have to wonder about their softness. I could use my tongue to trace the long, slender column of her neck, making sure to cover every inch. Lying down on my bed, Camber hops up next to me and settles in. My cock is hard, and I can't do a damn thing about it. Not with a trailer full of my friends and… her. Instead, I grab my phone and my headphones and turn on some music. I don't know how long I lie here, but I do know that thoughts of Aubree are in the forefront of my mind when I drift off to sleep.

When I wake what feels like minutes later, the sun is shining through the windows. Camber is no longer at my side, which means I'm probably the last one up. I left the door cracked again, but this time not by accident. Climbing out of bed, I pass the bunks and notice the curtain is pulled on Aubree's. Slowly, I peel it back and reveal her there, sleeping peacefully. I take her in, the gentle rise and fall of her chest, the softness of her features. She's breathtaking. I stare at her a little longer, tempting myself with the forbidden fruit I can never have. I will admit, I'm surprised she turned me down, but in the end, it's what needed to happen. She's indirectly an employee of Bishop Racing. I need to remain professional. Not to mention, if we took things farther, that's sure to be a complicated mess. A very pleasurable mess, but complicated all the same. One that I don't need. I need to keep my focus on my career.

Stepping back, I close the curtain and head to the bathroom, to take care of business, and turn on the water. I'm excited to be a spectator today for the sport I love. It's not often I get to watch a race. Climbing out of the shower, I grab a towel and dry off. Reaching for my clothes, I realize my mistake. I was so consumed with Aubree, I didn't bring any with me. Tying the towel around my waist, I brush my teeth and head to my room. Aubree is bending over, pulling clothes out of her bag, and the asshole that I am, even though I see her, I keep walking so that we bump into one another. My hands grip her hips to keep her from falling over.

"Ahh," she screeches. Her hands reach for the bunk to steady herself.

"I've got you." My voice is a husky whisper in her ear as I pull her ass into me. My cock twitches from beneath the towel. I know she can feel it.

She stands to her full height and steps out of my hold. Reluctantly, I let her go. "You scared the hell...." Her voice trails off as her eyes rake over my naked chest.

I watch her closely as her eyes follow along my abs until they reach the towel, and the obvious bulge hiding just beneath the surface. "That's not helping," I tell her.

"Uh, wh-what?" She shakes her head and looks up at me. Her pupils are dilated and her breathing is rapid as she bites down on her bottom lip. I wonder if she realizes what that small action does to me? Does she know she's making me hard? Does she realize how fucking sexy she is when she does that?

"Your eyes, Bree. The way you're staring at my cock. That's not helping."

"I wasn't, I mean, I—" She closes her eyes as her cheeks turn the slightest shade of pink.

I step toward her. "You were. Do you like what you see?"

Slowly her eyes open, liquid pools of green filled with desire stare up at me. "Doesn't matter," she croaks out. "I'm not playing this game with you." She stands tall, squaring her shoulders. "Excuse me, I need to take a shower."

I don't move, making her press her tight, little body against mine as she passes by me to get to the shower. It's wrong, I know this, but the feeling of her pressed against me was worth it. Getting involved with her would be a disaster, I know this too. She would be a major distraction because I'm almost certain that one taste of her would never be enough. Moving to my room, I hurry through getting dressed and go in search of some food. I find everyone sitting outside.

"'Bout time you got up," Dad says.

"Didn't sleep well," I tell him.

"Is Aubree still sleeping?" Ashley asks. I can tell from the sugary sweetness of her voice she's prying.

"She must be in the shower. I heard it running when I walked by." I don't make eye contact, because sure as shit as soon as I do, she's going to see right through me.

"I made both of you a plate." Dad points to the outdoor kitchen where two plates covered in foil are waiting.

"Thanks, I'm starving."

"Maybe you should wait on Aubree, you know, so she doesn't have to eat alone," Mom suggests.

"She's a big girl," I say, pulling the foil from my plate, grabbing a plastic fork and digging in. Bacon, eggs, and biscuits are piled high, and I'm starving.

I feel a slap on the back of my head just as I'm taking a huge bite of bacon. "I raised you better than that," Mom says.

"It's okay, Robin. I'd hate to be a further inconvenience."

"Nonsense," Mom tells her.

Slowly, I turn to face Aubree. She's dressed in a pair of short cut-off jean shorts and a T-shirt. This time it's just me and my number that adorns the front. "What happened to your uniform?" I ask her, taking another big bite. I don't comment on the fact that she took the world's fastest shower. I didn't know it was possible for a woman to get ready that fast.

"Technically you're not racing today, right? So, I'm off the clock. However, I still feel like it's important to support the team. This is more comfortable than the polos they had made." She shrugs as if it's not a big deal that my name and number are stretched tight across her chest.

I don't reply; instead, I shovel in my food while Dad hands her a plate and offers to get her something to drink. I have to make an effort to not look at her. It's like she's this... force and is constantly pulling me to her. I have to find a way to eliminate it. To form a shield to keep her out of my head. I need to distance myself from her today. Keep my eye on the prize. That's the goal, that's what I need to do. Aubree who? That's my new motto.

"So, today there's a race, but Blaine isn't racing? Why?" Aubree asks.

"Yeah," Kevin answers. "Today is more of a fan favorite. The purse is nothing compared to the big event Saturday. Two thousand versus one hundred thousand."

"Makes sense," Aubree says.

"Yeah, Blaine decided the risk of tearing up the car wasn't worth it."

"Because of the championship?"

"No. This race isn't a points race, which means it doesn't count toward the championship. However, it gets your name out there, and the purse is nothing to shake a fist at," Rick chimes in.

"So, it's for the money?"

"No, Aubree. It's not for the money. It's for the love of racing. For the notoriety that comes with saying you won the Dirt Late Model Dream at Eldora Speedway. It's for hundreds of reasons."

"Blaine!" my mother scolds me.

"I'm out. Thanks for breakfast." Tossing my plate in the trash, I put Camber on her leash and take off to walk the pits. Distance, I need distance. I stop at a fellow driver's trailer, John Frankie, and offer my help. I set Camber up in the shade, and get to work. It's a nice change of pace to not worry about the race and just enjoy working with my hands. This is exactly what I needed today.

CHAPTER Eleven

Aubree

AFTER BLAINE STALKED OFF, ROBIN, Ashley, and I opened up the T-shirt trailer for a few hours. We were swarmed with business, and it didn't take long for me to realize that Blaine "Checkmate" Bishop is a definite fan favorite.

"Now what?" I ask. We've just finished restocking the shelves from boxes and closed up shop.

"Now it's time to watch a race. You ready for this?" Ashley asks.

"Yeah, I'm kind of excited about it, really," I confess. "This is a new experience for me."

"Here's the thing about racing," Robin chimes in. "You either love it or you hate it. I, for one, am a fan," she adds with a laugh, pointing to the Bishop Racing T-shirt she's wearing.

"I admit, I looked it up online. I'm excited to see what it's like in person."

"I have a good feeling that you're going to love it." Robin winks, causing us all to laugh.

I follow them to the pits where the hauler is parked. I don't ask where Blaine is, no matter how curious I am. I feel kind of bad that he stalked off. I'm sure if I weren't here, it would have been a different day for them all together.

"Coming?" Ashley asks, walking toward the back right side of the hauler.

"Yes." I stand and follow her. She stops at a small ladder and begins to climb. "Uh, Ashley, what exactly are you doing?" I ask her.

She looks down at me, her grin wide and infectious. "We're watching the race, silly. There is no better view that on top of the hauler."

"Can we, I mean, is that safe?" I can't help but worry. That's me, that's who I am. Growing up without affection and in constant worry you are going to do something wrong or say something that might set your father off in a fit of rage does that to a person.

"Yes, we can. We are, and it's perfectly safe. Are you afraid of heights?" she asks.

"I don't know," I confess. I've never really been in a situation where I needed to find out.

"How is that even possible?" Blaine's deep voice asks from behind me.

Slowly, I turn to face him. "Didn't have a lot of... experiences growing up."

"Come on now, you've never been to an amusement park? Ridden a roller coaster? What about the county fair?"

"No, no, and yes, but I wasn't allowed to go off on my own and ride rides. When I was old enough to go alone, I was working or spending time with my Uncle Bobby. He wasn't in the best of health." I don't know why I spill all that to him, but the words are out before I can stop them.

"Bree," he says softly.

"Hey, what's the holdup down there? You're going to miss the race," Ashley calls out.

With more courage than I actually feel, I grab ahold of the ladder and slowly begin to climb. As my foot hits a new rung taking me higher, I find I'm not really of fan of being in the air. Then again, maybe it's this tiny ladder and the fact that I'm climbing on top of a trailer. What if I fall? My hands begin to shake and my knees begin to quiver.

"Hey," his deep, husky voice greets me. Not just that, but I can feel the heat of his body pressed against mine. "I've got you. I won't let you fall."

"I-I should just go back down," I manage to croak.

"Bree." His lips are next to my ear, his hot breath sending shivers down my spine. "I've got you. I promise you, I won't let you fall."

"Y-you don't even 1-like me," I remind him.

He chuckles. "Trust me, liking you is not the issue."

I want to ask him what he means, but now is not the time for deep, meaningful conversations. My palms are sweating, and I feel as though my hands are going to slip and I'll be the cause of both of us falling to our death.

"Death? We're maybe four feet off the ground."

"S-shit," I mutter. "I didn't mean to say that out loud."

"Come on, you. We're going to miss the race. I'm going to keep one hand on you at all times. I will not let you fall," he says with conviction.

"Okay," I agree meekly. "My hands are sweaty."

I feel his large hand grip my hip. "I've got you. Wipe one then the other on your shorts, then slowly make your way up. I'm right here. Right behind you."

I do as he says, slowly wiping my hands. Then, without further instruction, I grip the ladder and move up a step. Blaine is right there behind me, his body heat soothing me, his words encouraging as I continue to the top. When I reach the final step, Rick is there with his hand out, I take it and let him help me up onto the top of the hauler.

"You good?" he asks, squeezing my shoulder, bending to look me in the eye.

"Yeah, I'm okay." I can feel my face heat with embarrassment. I'm an adult and acted as though I was a three-year-old. I'm humiliated, but at the time, there was nothing I could do to stop it.

"Come on over." Ashley gives my arm a gentle tug and pulls me to a row of lawn chairs looking out over the track.

"Wow," I say, taking in the sight before me. You can see everything from this angle.

"Pretty cool, huh?" she asks.

"You sure you're okay?" Rick asks.

"She's fine." Blaine joins us and hands me a bottle of water.

"Thank you." I don't get a reply as he turns to Kevin and they begin to talk racing. Something about the track being hooked up… whatever that means.

"Look at you," Ashley whispers.

"Huh?" I turn to look at her, I'm sure wearing a look of confusion from her laugh.

"You have them falling at your feet." She nudges me with her shoulder.

"What? Who?"

"Blaine and Rick, and I'm sure Jacob would be too if he were up here. He met up with a few friends of his to watch the race."

My mouth falls open in shock. "What are you talking about?"

She links her arm through mine and lowers her voice, so only she and I can hear. "Both of those guys are ready to offer you the universe," she teases.

"First of all, Rick is just grateful that I helped him. He's being nice. And, Blaine, well he hates me, but felt sorry for me I'm sure." Even as I say the words, I can't help but wonder. He's hot and cold with me. One minute he's all sexy and tempting and the next he's back to being an asshole.

"You know, it's funny, what sometimes is right in front of us is invisible."

"Are you talking in riddles?" I laugh.

"Nope, think about it. Often we don't see what's right in front of us."

"I see it, Ashley. I see a race track, lots of fans, some dirt," I tease. I also see him. Just like I can also feel his body pressed next to mine. The attraction that seems to ignite between us. I keep telling myself to ignore it, that it will go away.

"I'm telling you, sparks are flying. Maybe not with Rick, but with Blaine." She wags her eyebrows.

"He hates me."

"There is a thin line between love and hate."

"Not that thin." I smile, shaking my head at her theory.

"I know him. He's different around you. Although I don't know you well, I can see it. The hopeful way that you look at him." I thought I was doing a good job of hiding my body's reaction to him.

Guess not.

I close my eyes and cover them with my hands, which causes her to laugh out loud.

"What did we miss?" Kevin calls out.

"Nothing, dear, just girl talk," Ashley calls back. He smiles at her as if she's the answer to every unanswered question he's ever had. "Blaine's a good guy," she assures me.

"Yeah, I'm sure he is, but he's mean and short one minute and then nice and sweet the next. He gives me whiplash. Not to mention, he's a fling type of guy. He told me that himself. I'm not sure I'm made for that."

"He's focused. He really wants to win the championship this year. He wants to make history. He loves the sport, hell, they all do. He wants this for them, his team, his parents, and himself. That's a lot of pressure."

"I get pressure, but he's… an asshole."

"You talking about me again, Bree?" Blaine chuckles from beside me.

"If the shoe fits," I banter back, proud of myself for not jumping at his interruption.

Before we can take it any further, the announcer starts the race. He introduces the drivers while they drive slowly around the track. When the green flag drops, dust flies, the wind whips, and the crowd is on their feet cheering. It's exciting and unlike anything I've ever been to. I don't know who I'm supposed to be cheering for, but the car leading is number eighteen with the name Babb written in the bottom of the number. He's leading, and that's good enough for me. I cheer him on when the car behind him gets close.

"Go, Babb!" I hear myself cheering for him. I turn in circles watching the race, not wanting to miss a minute of it. It's a lot to keep up with. There are cars on all areas of the track, so much so that I can't watch them all, so I keep my eyes on the leader as he flies across the finish line and takes the checkered flag. I'm covered in dirt, my hair is a mess from the wind from the cars, and I'm surprised to find I don't care. I loved every minute of it. This is nothing like the races my father used to watch on TV on Sunday afternoons.

"Thought you'd never been to a race," Blaine says from over my shoulder.

Turning to look at him, he's closer than I thought. He leans down and our noses touch. He grins and backs away. "I haven't but he was winning." I shrug.

"What if he was my biggest competitor?"

"Am I supposed to cheer for you?"

"You're a part of the Bishop Racing team, you cheer for me," he says, stone-cold serious.

"Oh, am I a part of the team?"

"Come on now," he says, placing his hand over his heart as if he's been wounded.

"Could have fooled me. I thought I wasn't welcome."

"It's the distraction that you bring," he explains quietly.

"I told you I would stay out of the way," I counter.

"Bree." He shakes his head, resting his hands on his hips. "Are you breathing?"

"What?" Is he losing his mind?

"You heard me, are you breathing?"

"Obviously," I sass.

"Exactly." He throws his hands in the air.

"How is that a distraction?"

He steps closer. "It's you, Aubree. All you. Your green eyes, the red hair, those long tan legs. You are one gorgeous distraction. So, yeah, if you're here and breathing, living in my hauler, you're a distraction."

I open my mouth to reply, but no words come out. Nothing. He's rendered me speechless.

"You guys coming?" Ashley calls out as she stands on the top rung of the ladder. She's wearing an "I told you so" grin, and suddenly I'm worried if anyone heard him. He's messing with me, and I don't want her to take his comment for more than what it is. She already has crazy ideas in her head.

"I wish," he murmurs just for me, before turning to face her. "Yeah, we're right behind you." When he turns back to me, he holds out his hand. "Ready to do this?"

Just like that, he turns off the attraction, or the flirting, or whatever it is he does like a light switch. I don't know how he does it. "Yeah, I can't stay up here forever," I say, taking his strong, slightly roughened offered hand, and let him guide me to the steps.

"I'll go first, then I want you to follow right after me. I'll tell you when to step. I'll be right behind you the entire time."

I can already feel my knees start to shake. "I'm not so sure this was the best idea." There's an obvious quiver in my voice.

"Hey." His voice is soft and soothing. "I've got you, Bree. I won't let you fall. Just take it slow and I'll help guide you."

I nod. "The sooner we do this, the sooner my feet are back on the ground."

"Is it the height or the ladder that scares you?"

"Both, but I admit once I was up here I settled down, especially with the excitement of the race."

"Yeah? You a dirt track fan, Bree?"

"I can see the appeal. I mean, tonight was my first race. I wouldn't go as far as saying I'm a fan."

"You're right. We'll save that moment of clarity for when you see me out on the track." He grins and turns, stepping on the first rung of the ladder. "Come here." He holds his hand out for me.

With wobbly knees, I turn my back to him and bend to hold the ladder, taking my first step on the top rung. "O-okay?" I ask as I white knuckle the bars.

"Relax." His hot breath touches my neck. "I'm right here. I'm going to keep one hand on your back and leave the other on the ladder. I'm going to take another step down. When I tap you like this—" He taps my back to show me "—I want you to take another step down."

"Got it," I say with more confidence than I feel. I actually feel pretty ridiculous; I'm a grown woman freaking out about a ladder. However, on the flip side of that, I do have the sexy Checkmate at my service. It's kind of a win situation for me. Step by step, we make our way down the ladder. When my feet hit the ground, my legs wobble just a little, but strong arms wrap around me.

"You good?" His voice is husky.

"Yeah." I step away from him. "I'm actually pretty thirsty.

I'm going to go grab a drink." I turn to walk away toward the concession stand when he reaches out and stops me.

"There are plenty of options in the hauler."

"I know that, but I'm not freeloading. I need to take a walk on my shaky legs anyway. Thanks for your help." I turn and walk as fast as I can to get some distance between us. I should have shut him down, told him that I didn't need his help, I could have managed on my own. I could have, but having his attention on me when he's being nice is something that's hard for me to say no to.

This is going to be a long racing season.

CHAPTER *Twelve*

BLAINE

"HELL YES!" I SHOUT, POUNDING my fist on the steering wheel. I just took the checkered flag for the main event. I'm the new Dream winner, and a hundred grand richer. Of course, I'll be passing along some of that to my crew. They are with me day in and day out. I couldn't do this without them. That includes my parents.

Slowly, I make my way to the scales. When I drive on the platform, I keep my eyes on the light, and when it turns green, the crowd roars. I didn't expect to not make weight, but I've seen it happen plenty of times to my competitors. Driving away from the scales, I head to victory lane. My team is there and waiting as well as the track officials and the trophy girls. I kill the engine once I'm up on the platform and pull off my helmet, setting it to the side. Kevin is there and hands me a bottle of the same nasty-ass energy drink that sponsors me. As always, I play the game. This is my life. I get paid to do what I love, and I'm damn good at it. This win solidifies that I need no distractions. We are on our way to making Dirt Late Model Racing history. I will make that happen. There is no other alternative. I have my crew, my family, and my sponsors. The car is on point, nothing is going to stop us from our third consecutive championship.

We've got this.

I've got this.

With my helmet off, I take a minute to catch my breath, both from the intense racing and the exhilaration of winning. Climbing out of the car, Kevin is the first one to greet me with a slap on the back. Followed is a hug from Ashley, and my parents, and pats on the back from Jacob and Rick. Then, she's there. Aubree's smile is wide, her eyes shining as she launches herself at me. I catch her easily and wrap my arms around her.

"That was so amazing. You killed it," she says, backing away.

Her cheeks are flushed, and her lips have never looked more kissable than they do right now. Reaching out, I place my hand on her hip, intending to pull her to me and do just that, consequences be damned, when an interviewer shoves a microphone in my face. I know I should let her go, but I don't. Instead, I throw my arm over her shoulders to make the moment seem less intimate, when all I want to do is make it intimate, and maybe even a little inappropriate.

"I'm here with Blaine 'Checkmate' Bishop. Checkmate, you dominated the track tonight. How's it feel to take home the win?" the interviewer asks.

"Anytime I can bring home a win is a good night," I reply just as Mom comes up and tucks herself under my other arm. The rest of the crew gathers around as well.

"You dominated the track tonight. This is your second career win here at Eldora Speedway, and although it's not a points race, it looks good on the resume." He laughs.

This guy is a real tool. I hate this part. The interviews, the questions, the jokes that they think are funny that are really anything but. "I couldn't do it without my team and of course my sponsors. Knoxville Health Partners has a full-time person with us keeping the crew healthy as we travel." I go on to list my various other sponsors, all not nearly as big of a contributor to the team as KHP.

"Great job out there tonight, Checkmate." He shakes my hand and walks away to interview one of the other drivers. I'm not sure who finished where, but I do know I'm taking home the one hundred grand win.

"Fuck yeah!" Jacob screams, pumping his fists in the air. "You killed it, man."

"*We* killed it," I tell him. I can be an asshole a lot of the time, but I do give credit where credit is due.

"Let's get this car loaded, and we can celebrate," Kevin says, wrapping his arms around Ashley. Mom steps away and even though I don't want to, I know that means I need to drop my arm from Aubree's shoulders. I still want that kiss, and I have every intention of getting it.

Rick climbs in the car and drives it back to the trailer, while the rest of us follow along behind him. When he climbs out of the car, he yells in pain, bending over holding his back. Aubree rushes to his side.

"Tell me what you're feeling. Where does it hurt?" she asks him.

"My back. The same pain as before. I must have tweaked it climbing out of the car."

She looks up at me. "Can you help me help him inside the hauler?"

"We got it." Kevin jumps in and gets on one side of Rick, while I get on the other. Slowly, we make our way inside and help him to the couch.

"Rick." Aubree's voice is calm and soothing. "I need you on your stomach. Are you okay to lie like that?" He grumbles a reply and winces as he stretches out like she asked. "Let me grab my bag." She scurries off the hauler, to I assume the under-belly storage. She had a black bag with her with the KHP logo on it when we loaded her bags.

She comes back and gets right to work. Kevin leaves to help Jacob and Dad load the car, exactly what I should be doing, but I can't take my eyes off her. With practiced ease, she slides his shirt up, explaining every step of the way what she's doing. She pulls a couple of lotions, and a few other massage tools out of her bag and gets to work. She talks softly to Rick, asking about the race, and how long he's been on the Bishop Racing Team. She has laser focus for him, and even though I know she's just doing her job, it irritates me.

Rick moans and she chuckles softly.

"Really, man?" I ask, my irritation showing through.

"You have no idea," he says, his face buried in the couch. "Her hands are magic."

That too pisses me off. I want to be the one with her magic hands all over me. I want her lips fused with mine, her body pressed tightly against me. And, I'm going to get that kiss. This is just a delay in the inevitable. I saw it in her eyes. When she met me in victory lane, she was feeling it too. We're going to explore this. I'll convince her to my way of thinking. I have to. Otherwise, I feel as though I might lose my mind not knowing the taste of her lips, or the feel of her soft skin. If we can keep it about sex and not let our feelings get involved it would be the perfect situation. We can both relieve some tension, and I don't have to worry about all the other priorities that come with a relationship. I don't have to worry about her feelings, if she's feeling left out while we're working on the car. Just sex and limit the distraction. That I could handle.

We could make that work.

"We're good here," Aubree tells me, never removing her hands from his back.

"I need a shower," I say, stalking off toward my room to grab some clothes. I take the fastest shower known to man and rush through getting dressed, at least enough to be decent. Dressed in jeans and no shirt, I exit the tiny, hot-as-hell bathroom and slide into the booth that is our kitchen table.

"All right," Aubree says, finally lifting her hands from his back. "Slowly, I want you to sit up for me."

Rick does as she says and this time there are no yells of pain. "Damn," he says, standing, "it still hurts, but it's so much better."

"I'm not a doctor, so if this keeps happening, you might want to go get checked out just to be certain it's just a strained muscle," Aubree tells him.

"What? I've got you." He winks at her.

"Dad's grilling," I say to change the subject and hopefully chill myself out a little.

"Thanks again, Aubs, I'm glad you're here." Rick squeezes her arm then slowly, although not as slow as he was when we brought him in here, makes his way to the door and out of the hauler. I follow behind him and turn the lock.

"Congratulations," she says, tucking a loose strand of hair behind her ear. "You mind if I grab a bottle of water? I'm parched after all of that cheering."

"You're welcome to whatever you want," I tell her. I watch as she makes her way to the small fridge and pulls out a bottle of water. Twisting off the cap, she brings the bottle to her lips and tilts her head back. I can't help but watch the column of her neck as she sucks the bottle dry. I'm a man, and that thought alone is putting all kinds of ideas in my head. She doesn't stop until the bottle is empty. I keep my eyes trained on her as she replaces the cap and places the now empty bottle in the trash can.

"Better?" I ask her.

"Much. I don't know why I've been so thirsty lately. I guess change of environment. I'm outside a lot more than normal."

"Yeah?" I ask, taking a step toward her. She's nervous, causing her to take a step backward. When her ass hits the counter, she braces her hands on either side as if she has to in order to keep herself standing upright. I don't stop until I'm standing right in front of her, toe to toe, just like we were in the love tunnel. "So, you did a lot of cheering, did you?"

She blushes, a slight reddened tint to her cheeks that has my cock stirring in my jeans. I'm glad I still have my racing suit on to hide the evidence. "I mean, I am here for Bishop Racing, am I not?"

Not able to take it, I reach out and run my index finger over her cheek. "You mean you're here for me." My voice is husky with desire. Desire for her.

"Well," she licks her lips, "you are Bishop Racing, right?"

Lightly, I brush my thumb over her plump bottom lip. "That I am," I say, leaning in toward her. Again, her tongue darts out and passes over her bottom lip, just where my thumb was seconds ago. With ease, my hand slides behind her neck, and I pull her into me. "What do you think, Bree, does a win deserve a kiss?" I don't give her time to answer before closing the remaining distance and pressing my lips to hers. Her lips are just as soft against mine as I imagined them to be. I'm just about to go deeper, kiss her harder when someone tries to open the door. Bree goes stiff in my arms as they knock on the door.

"Blaine, we're ready to eat," Mom says through the door.

"Be right there!" I yell back.

Exhaling, I rest my forehead against Aubree's and close my eyes. Her hands are gripping my shirt. I have one hand on her hip, holding her to me, and the other is still on her neck. I trace her soft skin with my thumb. "I want to do that again," I whisper huskily. She doesn't reply, but then again, she doesn't have to. Her grip, the one that she's not releasing tells me all I need to know. I'm not in this alone. She can say she's not interested, but right now, right here tells me otherwise.

"We better get out there."

"Yeah." I place a tender kiss to her forehead, lace her fingers with mine, and step toward the door.

"Wait." She pulls back. "What are you doing?" She holds up our joined hands.

"It's time to eat."

"This…." She holds our hands up again.

"This is me not ready to let you go yet."

"You have to," she replies softly. "Look, I wanted you to kiss me. Being honest, I want you to do more than that to me." Her cheeks are a deep red, matching her auburn hair. "I want that, I do, but I don't play games. I want structure and dependability. You said that's not what you're looking for. I have no doubt that we would be… great together. I just can't risk it. I know me, Blaine. I know that I can't separate sex from feelings. I also know that I'll fall for you. I've had enough heartbreak in one lifetime."

"No one knows," I tell her. "No one has any idea how relationships are going to work out. You have to risk getting your heart broken to see the end result. It could be a good thing."

"Is that what this is? Are we in a relationship?"

"No."

"Exactly. You don't want that, and I do. We can't do this. I'm sorry." She removes her hand from mine, and I let her. I stand here and watch her unlock the door and step out of the toter home.

I know what she's saying is right, she warned me, but I want her. Telling myself that I can't have her isn't working. I need to find a way to chase away this craving, this appetite I have for her. Either way, this is going to be a long fucking season.

Stepping out of the toter home, no one even gives me a second glance. I hear Aubree talking to Ashley about being in the restroom and feeling a bit overheated. She's covered for us, and even though I should be thankful, as we don't need interference, I'm not. I'm irritated that I can't tell them that those soft lips of hers were pressed against mine. That her hands, they're soft and smooth next to mine that are rough and calloused. I grab a plate and take a seat across the fire from her. Rick and Jacob are talking her ear off, and I want to punch them both. I want to tell them that she's mine, but I can't do that. I don't do that.

I'm fucked.

CHAPTER Thirteen

Aubree

IT'S MONDAY MORNING AND I would normally be at work. Instead, I'm sitting alone in my apartment. When we got home yesterday, I sped away from Blaine's like my ass was on fire. I needed to put some distance between us. He's too sexy, too tempting, too… everything. I needed some time and space to get myself in check. When he kissed me, I wanted to drag him back to the bedroom and let him have his way with me, or you know, I could have had my way with him. Either scenario would have worked for me. Instead, I did the right thing, the responsible thing and turned him down. It's times like these when I wished that I could be carefree, live on the edge every once in a while. I've worked my ass off to be independent. I promised myself that I would only engage in true relationships, those that I know will stand the test of time. Maria, I knew the day I met her that she would be that friend for me. Blaine, I can't tell. I want to think that maybe he would change his mind, but I know from experience a tiger doesn't change his stripes. I refuse to set myself up for heartache.

The laundry is done, and there is really no point in going grocery shopping since we leave to go out of town again on Thursday morning. Our next track is in Kentucky, only a few hours away. I have three days to fill, and I have no idea how I'm going to do it. I'm contemplating a nap even though I'm not tired when there is a knock at the door. Taking a look through the peephole, I see Maria standing on the other side.

"Hey, you," I greet, opening the door wide for her to come in.

"Tell me everything." She glides into my apartment and sets the large pizza on the coffee table.

"Tell you everything about what?" I ask, not really sure what she's talking about. I just talked to her last night and filled her in on my weekend. Well, I left out the kiss. I was still, *am* still processing the kiss.

"About whatever it is you didn't already tell me." She grins then turns toward the kitchen. Shutting the door, I watch her grab a couple of plates and a roll of paper towels, before snagging two bottles of water from the fridge. "I know you, Aubs," she says, plopping down on the couch.

Defeated, I take my seat next to her. "He kissed me."

"And?"

"And, he almost did it the day before, and then he kissed me, and I wanted him to never stop." The words tumble out of my mouth.

"Now we're getting somewhere." She laughs, handing me a plate with two slices of pepperoni. "Keep going," she urges.

"He's so damn frustrating. One minute he's a total jerk to me, and the next he's got me backed against the wall in the Love Tunnel and all I can think about is how badly I want his lips fused with mine."

"Oh, the Love Tunnel." She wags her eyebrows. "Do tell."

I spend the next few minutes explaining the Love Tunnel and how I ended up seeing it with Blaine. "He's all dark hair and sexy hazel eyes. He's built, but not bodybuilder built. His arms are huge, but he works out, holding on to the steering wheel at high rates of speed, he has to stay in shape."

"Uh-huh, keep going." She grins before taking a huge bite of pizza.

"When he's being nice, I can see myself falling for him."

"You know the theory of the little boy who pulls the girl's pigtails because he likes her. I think this is the adult version."

"What?" I laugh. "You've never even met him."

She nods. "I know, but I know you, Aubs. I know that in order for this guy to affect you the way he has, that he has to have some good inside of him somewhere. I think he wants you, but he just doesn't want to, or maybe he doesn't know how to deal with it."

"No, he's made it clear he doesn't want anything serious. All he wants is to win this championship. He'll be the youngest driver to win three in a row."

"He's got goals. I like that in a man."

"Maria," I whine. "You're not helping me here. I have to spend the next several months with him. How am I going to do this?"

"Take a risk, Aubree. For once in your life, don't worry about where each decision is going to take you. Don't worry about if he wants to be serious, have fun. A summer fling."

"I can't do that. I know me, I'll fall for him." I'm not sure I haven't already started falling.

"Then you fall for him." She shrugs. "Sure, you may get your heart broken, but what if you don't? Tell me, what if you have a fling and he falls for you too? What happens then?"

"Come on, Maria, this is not a fairy tale. We're not going to ride off in his late model into the sunset."

"You could. It's a definite possibility, but you'll never know because you're too afraid to try."

"I've had enough heartache to last a lifetime." My throat

grows thick as I fight off the emotions that thinking about my past brings.

"I know." Her face softens. "But life is full of heartache and happiness. It's how you choose to handle both that defines you. So, you do this thing and it ends. Your heart is broken, but you pick up the pieces. I'll help you and you move on. Or it's wonderful and amazing and you live happily ever after."

"Do you hear yourself right now? You want me to go into this… whatever-it-would-be fling, I guess knowing I'm going to get hurt in the end. Why would I do that?"

"Because, my dear friend, you don't know. You don't know if you will be hurt or if your heart will be so full that it's bursting with love from him to you and you to him." She reaches over and places her hand over mine. "Do me a favor, Aubs. Live. If only for this summer, I want to see you living life and enjoying yourself. You're twenty-three years old and have less of a social life than my grandmother. I get it. I know why you have your walls up, I do. However, I want you to let them down. Let go of the fear, and see what happens. Just know that no matter the outcome, I'll be here. Whether it's to bring over ice cream and wine or if it's planning your bridal shower, I'm here."

"It's hard for me to trust."

"I know that. You don't have to tell him all your secrets, just take advantage of the fun the two of you could have together, in and out of the bedroom." She winks.

My pulse quickens at the thought of letting Blaine take advantage of me. "I'll think about it." I want to, more than anything I want to. I've never had this kind of connection, if that's even what you call it, to a man before. I've never had this constant ache to be more with anyone else. Just Blaine, and of course he has to be the most emotionally unavailable man on the planet. "Wait, what about work? Technically, I'm there working."

"Sure, but you don't work for Blaine. He has nothing to do with your paycheck."

"I know that, but if KHP… if Jonah finds out, I'm sure he wouldn't hesitate to fire me."

"That's not going to happen. They sent you because they know how good you are. Besides, there are other jobs out there. If you could choose riding off in the sunset with Blaine or your job at KHP, which would you choose?"

"Love," I say without having to think about it. My eyes widen with shock.

She gives me a satisfied grin. "There you go. You don't work for him, you're not breaking any rules. Take it day by day and see what happens."

"Eat your pizza," I tell her, ending the conversation. Although I hate to admit it, she has a point. I've been guarded in life, and I do keep people out. Maybe she's right. Maybe I can just throw caution to the wind and see what happens. I can live through a broken heart, hell, that was my life growing up. Having Blaine break my heart would be minor compared to my father not loving me, and telling me that on a daily basis, and losing my Uncle Bobby, the one person in life who was on my team.

We spend the next hour catching up. They're going to start trying for a baby and my heart swells for her. I want that for them. After she leaves, I take the nap I had been contemplating earlier. I'm emotionally exhausted from our conversation. I lie here for what feels like hours before falling asleep, but as I drift off, I've decided. I'm not going to fight it. I'm just going to go with it, and see where it takes me. If anything, at least my battery-operated boyfriend will get a break. It's been too long for me, and the idea that Blaine could be the one to break my dry streak has me drifting off with a smile on my face.

It's been three weeks since my talk with Maria. Three weeks of watching him, and to be honest, wanting him. That first week we went to a track in Kentucky, two and a half hours from home, so the travel time was cut short, which I was thankful for. Ashley also stayed home, so I spent most of my time with Robin and Brian in the T-shirt trailer. When Blaine won, we all met him for pictures on the front stretch, but I made sure to keep a body in between us. It's safer that way.

The next week, we were at a track here in Tennessee; it was only a twenty-minute drive, so we didn't leave until Friday morning. I've learned that Blaine likes to be one of the first to arrive. He claims it's to get a good pit spot, but Robin tells me that he's always been that way when it comes to racing. He truly loves the sport and wants to be relaxed when it's time to hit the track. You can't do that if you're late getting there from traffic or any other reason that might cause a delay. Again, we had limited interactions. A few looks across the fire, a brush of his arm against mine as we were moving in the hauler, but nothing more. Nothing like the kiss that first weekend. I'm both disappointed and relieved. So basically, I'm a mess over him, over the possibility of us.

Every time I talk to Maria, she asks how things are going, and I'm honest when I say I have nothing to report. She went as far as calling last night and telling me to make my move this trip. This weekend we're going to Pennsylvania. The track is nine hours away. That doesn't include stopping for gas and food or traffic. It's going to be a long one.

That brings me to now, bright and early Wednesday morning, five in the morning to be exact. I park my Impala in the same spot, and grab my bags out of the trunk. One for me, and one for work, that I've only needed once. That's a good thing of course, but it would give me something else to focus on.

"You got what you need?" he asks from behind me. I would recognize his voice anywhere. Blaine Bishop is in no way forgettable.

"Yeah, just my usual," I say, holding a bag up in each hand.

"I'll take them." He reaches for the bags.

"I can get it."

"My momma raised me better than that. Hand 'em over,

Bree." He reaches for them again, and I let him take them. There is no use in arguing anyway, he'll win, and besides, if he insists on the heavy lifting, he can have it.

"This is a long one," I say, trying to make small talk that's safe.

"Yeah, nine hours straight through. We will have to stop a couple of times for fuel and food. Dad and I are tossing around driving halfway today and the other half tomorrow. The race isn't until Saturday night, so we have plenty of time."

"I'm just along for the ride," I say like an idiot.

He mumbles something about you and ride, and I ignore it. I can feel the blush coating my cheeks. Instead of sticking around so he can see, I open the door to the toter home and find, Rick, Kevin, and Jacob already there. Kevin is behind the wheel, while Rick is occupying the passenger seat. "Am I late?" I ask, worried I've put us behind schedule.

"Nah, we're just all early. We are still waiting for Robin and Brian to get here," Kevin explains. Just as the words leave his mouth, headlights pull in. I watch as Brian backs up to the T-shirt trailer. He gets out and says a few words to Blaine, before climbing back in his truck and pulling out of the drive, trailer in tow.

"Ready?" Blaine asks, climbing on board.

"I'm going back to sleep." Jacob stands and moves to his bunk, climbs in, and pulls the curtain.

"He can sleep in any situation." Rick laughs.

"Let's get this train moving," Kevin says, putting the vehicle in drive and following Brian.

I'm sitting at the table, and to my surprise, Blaine slides in across from me. "What are you looking at?" he asks, pointing to my laptop.

"I thought I'd try to find a movie to watch."

He raises his eyebrows and I point to the mobile hot spot that I purchased after our first weekend. "Ah, you know we have one here." He points to a small square box mounted to the wall.

"No, I mean, I know you do in the T-shirt trailer for credit card transactions, but I didn't know there was one here too."

"Yeah, password is Checkmate." He chuckles. "You can thank Ashley for that one. She set it up. You should use ours, save your data."

"I bought the unlimited plan." I shrug.

"What are you watching?"

"Not sure yet. Any ideas?"

"Don't really watch much TV."

"I'm more of a reader," I confess.

"Yeah? What do you read?"

Again, I blush. I'm not embarrassed but confessing my love for my books to Blaine, is… a little intimidating. "Romance," I finally say.

He nods. "I can see that about you."

"What does that mean? You can see that about me?"

"Chill, Bree, it's not a bad thing. You're not like anyone I've ever met. The women I meet throw themselves at me for my name, my status. None of that even seems to register with you."

"Not really. I mean, you're just a man. A man who has made a successful career out of doing what he loves. I might not have the status, but I've done the same."

He nods. "So, what are we watching?"

I have to bite my lip to hide my smile as I click through the options, knowing I need to choose something that will hold both of our attention. Finally I click on the first *The Fast and the Furious* movie. "You coming over here?" I ask, unsure.

"Why don't we move to the couch?"

I nod. Sliding out of the booth, laptop in hand, I move to the couch. Reaching up, he grabs a couple of pillows and a blanket out of the overhead storage and settles in beside me. He motions for me to lift the laptop so he can throw the cover over me.

"What are you doing?" I ask softly.

"You always seem to be cold when we're on here. Thought you might want this," he replies just as soft.

Looks like the sweetheart in him is out today. Not that I'm complaining. I hit Play and he chuckles. "I didn't peg you for a F&F kind of girl."

"Paul Walker," I say, deadpan. He turns to look at me, a confused expression on his face. "Vin Diesel," I add. "There's not a woman alive who will turn down watching those two men in action," I confess.

I expect him to give me a hard time, but he surprises me when he leans in, his lips next to my ear. "You got a thing for guys who drive fast cars, Bree?"

My immediate thought is to deny, deny, deny, but then I think about Maria and our conversation, and I make a decision to take a chance. "Just one guy really," I say, turning to face him. He's close, so close that if either of us leans in just a little, we'd be kissing.

"Yeah?" His voice is gravelly.

"Uh-huh, now let's watch the movie." I turn to face the screen. I've put it out there. Now we just have to wait and see.

CHAPTER Fourteen

BLAINE

IF SOMEONE WOULD HAVE TOLD me that this season I would have a sexy redhead tagging along, I would have laughed at them. If they would have told me that that same sexy redhead would have me by the balls, I would have told them to get fucked. However, here I am sitting beside her, her head on my shoulder as she's curled up under one of my blankets watching *The Fast and the Furious.* Jacob is still sleeping, and I've seen the glances that Kevin and Rick have been giving me, but I can't find it in me to care.

It's been a struggle these past few weeks to stay away from her, to limit my exposure to her, but today, this trip, I knew that wasn't possible. I decided I would try and play it cool, be the nice guy. Forget that I remember the feel of her lips or the way her body felt pressed against mine. That lasted all of fifteen minutes. When she settled on the couch beside me, I knew that any plans I had for pretending were shot.

She's addictive.

Now here we are, the last few minutes of the movie, and she's sleeping peacefully on my shoulder. Normally, this kind of thing—cuddling—gets to me. In fact, it's not something I've done since high school. I never let myself have time. I had, no, scratch that, I *have* goals, and this is my year to make history for the second time. That's my plan, I have a mission, and a means to make it happen. I just didn't expect her. Now that she's here, my plans are still the same, but I'm hoping that the beautiful Aubree can be the perfect amount of distraction that we both need. From her comment earlier, I'm optimistic that she's coming around to my way of thinking. We can keep this fun, and just between us. No pressure, just the way I like it.

When the movie ends, I close the laptop and then my eyes. I'm not ready to move. I like being close to her. I can't explain it, and at this point, I don't even care to try to. It is what it is, and we will be what we will be. I just hope that includes her underneath me. Hell, who am I kidding? This is Aubree, and even though I can't believe I'm saying this, I'll take her any way I can get her.

When the toter stops moving I know we've made our first stop. I assume Mom or Dad need a bathroom break. I keep my eyes closed, not wanting to hear the questioning that I'm sure will come from Kevin, or the pissed-off look I know will come from Rick. He's got a thing for her, but I've got news for him. So, do I, apparently. And it's not going away. I hear Jacob snoring and I know he's not waking up anytime soon. I swear he can sleep through anything. I guess that's a good thing with this kind of job.

I wait until I think the coast is clear to open my eyes. Sure enough, we're all alone, well, unless you count the snoring Jacob. I don't know if she needs anything, and I hate to wake her, but I do it anyway. Turning my head to the left, I place a featherlight kiss on top of her head. Then, reaching over with my right hand, I ever so gently run my index finger down her jaw. "Hey, Sleeping Beauty," I say softly.

She stirs, and with another soft caress of her cheek, her eyes flutter open and then immediately close. "Please tell me I didn't fall asleep."

"I can't do that." I chuckle softly.

"I'm sorry." She scrambles to move away from me, but I'm faster. I place my arm over her shoulders and pull her into my chest. "I don't mind," I tell her.

"You do make a good pillow," she finally says. "I didn't mean to fall asleep."

"You were tired. There are no rules against taking naps."

"I blame you. You got me this blanket and then let me snuggle up next to you. How am I supposed to resist that?" she asks, this time her voice is a little lighter, a little more awake.

"You're not. I don't want you to resist me."

"Funny, I'm not sure I can even if I wanted to."

Am I hearing this right? Is my mind playing tricks on me, because I've thought about nothing but her for weeks? "What does that mean, Bree?"

"It means that I know that I could be putting not only my heart but my job on the line. It means that even though I know that I'm going to fall hard for you, I'm okay with it not being more. It means that having a little piece of you is better than none at all. I've tried to ignore this, but it's not going away."

I tighten my grip, holding her just a little tighter than before. "I don't want to hurt you."

"I know, but that doesn't change the fact that you will."

I hate the thought of hurting her. "You don't know that. You called me an asshole, remember? Maybe we'll find out that this attraction was simply wanting what he can't have."

"Maybe," she says, not really meaning it. "Or maybe I'll know what it's like to take a risk on something I want. Maybe I'll learn that not all men are like my father. And maybe I'll learn that no matter what the outcome, I'm strong and independent and I will survive the heartache."

"Fuck, Bree. That's not what I want, not at all." She's crushing me here.

"I know that." She sits up to look at me. "I know that's not your intention, but I also know me. I know that if I let this go one step further, one minute longer, that I'm going to be falling harder and deeper. I know that you don't want that, and I'm okay with it." She pauses as if she needs to collect her thoughts. "Can we, maybe just keep whatever this is between us? We can be friends, and that's all anyone needs to know. It will be easier for me when it's all over."

"Jesus, Aubree." I want her. I want her more than I've ever wanted another, but that's selfish because I can't give her what she wants. "This is a bad idea," I tell her, running my hands through my hair.

"No." She surprises me by climbing onto my lap and straddling my hips. "I live on the safe side, always. Growing up, life was hard, and there wasn't a lot of love or security. I've made that for myself, and I'm… complacent. No one has ever sparked this… need inside of me, not until you. I don't want to play it safe with you, Blaine. I want everything you're willing to give me. And when you walk away with my heart, I'll have the memories and the knowledge that I was brave enough to go after what I want."

"What do you want?" My hands grip her thighs. Internally, I'm pleading for her to say me; it's all kinds of wrong and selfish, but with her, I can't help it.

"You, Blaine, I want you." She leans in and kisses the corner of my mouth. "The one rule is that this stays between us. I don't want any of the crew or your family to know."

"Anything you want," I tell her. She sways her hips, rubbing herself over my cock and with that one move, I would promise her the world.

We hear voices and she hops off my lap, and stands. "I'm going to go get some snacks. Want anything?" she asks, as if she didn't just light a fire inside of me with that sexy little move of hers.

Before I can respond, the door opens and Kevin walks in. He eyes me suspiciously, until Aubree distracts him. I know the feeling.

"Is that a homemade donut?" she asks, leaning into him to get a better look at what he's holding in his hands.

"Yes, and this is my third one." He moans as he takes another bite. "I might have to stop here on the way home and pick one up for Ash."

"I'll be quick, but I have to get me one of those." She grabs her purse and dashes off the toter in search of a donut.

"What are you doing, Blaine?" Kevin asks immediately.

"What?" I'm able to pull off confused because I'm still processing what just happened. What we just agreed to.

"With Aubree, what are you doing?"

"We watched a movie."

"Uh-huh," he says, not believing a single word that comes out of my mouth. He shouldn't, not when it comes to her.

"She's different." This is from Rick. I didn't even hear him come back in.

"You think I don't know that?" Fuck me, do I know that. I can feel it too, and to be honest, it's scaring the hell out of me.

"Just be good to her."

I stand so that we are eye to eye. "Have you ever seen me treat a woman with anything but respect?" I ask, fists clenching at my sides.

"No." He doesn't say another word, just climbs behind the wheel to take his leg of the driving.

"Let's have it, before she gets back," I tell Kevin.

He holds his hands up in the air. "Nothing." He grins. "Nothing at all." He too takes his spot, which is now in the passenger seat. I'll be taking the final leg of driving, that is if we decide to do it all in one day.

Aubree, true to her word, was quick as she climbs aboard.

"Oh my word, Blaine, I got one for you and Jacob, if he ever wakes up." Smiling, she hands me a box of donuts.

"This is a dozen," I say, shaking my head, taking one out of the box.

"You can't have just one." She offers another to Kevin and Rick, and they take her up on it.

"Knock, knock," Dad says, climbing aboard, Mom right behind him. "We wanted to touch base. You all thinking we drive the entire way today?"

"I don't know," Kevin chimes in. "Might be too early to tell. I say we play it by ear and see how we're all feeling when we stop for lunch."

"Where's Jacob?" Mom asks.

"Sleeping," I tell her.

"You guys have to try these." Aubree holds the donut box open for them.

"Oh, Kevin already filled us in. We have our own box in the truck," Dad tells her.

"All right, well, we'll see you all at the next stop." They head back to their truck and then we're off.

"He does all the driving?" Aubree asks.

"Yeah."

"We should probably stop then, I mean, unless Jacob or someone wants to give him a break. You all take shifts."

"Yeah, more than likely we'll stop and all get a room for the night."

"I like that plan. I've never really been able to travel, so it sounds fun. I've only ever stayed in a motel, you know the kind where the door opens to the outside. Never stayed in a hotel before."

"Really?"

"Nope. I stayed in a motel when I first left home. It was cheap, and I needed cheap until I found a place to stay." She must see the question in my eyes. "My dad was a jerk. Hated me, blamed me for my mother leaving. My childhood was… well, not really one to talk about. My Uncle Bobby, he's really the only person I had growing up who cared about me. I was going to move in with him as soon as I turned eighteen. He passed a few weeks before that. He didn't have much, but what he did have he left to me. It was enough for me to get out of town, find a shitty studio apartment, and enroll in school. I worked two jobs all the way through to support myself."

"I'm not sure I know what to say to that," I admit.

She shrugs. "Nothing. That's my life, my story if you will. I don't want or expect your pity. I'm who I am because of it."

Shit, and here I am telling her we will never be anything. How am I any different than her father?

"No." She settles in the booth, and I take the seat across from her just as we start to move. She glances over her shoulder — my guess is to gauge if the others are paying attention to us. Reaching across the table, she laces her fingers with mine. "I want this with you. I want the excitement, and I need to see what this is. This… overpowering draw that I have toward you. I know what the consequences are. I have my eyes wide open, trust me on this one, Blaine. I didn't come to this decision lightly."

"Okay." What else is there for me to say? I'm a selfish bastard, and I want her.

She gives me a soft smile, just the corner of her lips tilting upward. "Okay."

We spend the next couple of hours talking about movies and playing cards. She even convinces me to watch *Cars* with her. Little did I know it was an animated film about racing. I have to admit it kept my attention, although I would never say so out loud. Surprisingly, it's the most fun I've had outside of the race car in too damn long.

CHAPTER *Fifteen*

Aubree

IT'S JUST AFTER FIVE AND we've decided to stop for the day. We hit traffic, and have about another five hours of driving, at least that's what Kevin says. So, we're at the hotel, spending the night and even though I know it sounds childish, I'm excited. Blaine insisted on paying for my room, even though I protested. He wouldn't hear of it. When Brian chimed in to let his son pay, I gave up the fight. I wasn't going to win anyway.

"How about everyone gets settled in their rooms and then we head to dinner? The hotel has a restaurant. Is that good with everyone?" Robin asks. She's not only Blaine's mother, but she seems to take care of all of them when they're traveling.

"That's a good plan," Jacob says. He's the least tired of all of us, never ending up taking a turn driving. He slept several hours.

"Here are the keys to your rooms. We're not all on the same floors. I tried, but no such luck. Kevin, Rick, and Jacob, you guys are on the second floor. Mom and Dad, you're on the third." Blaine turns to me. "You're on four and I'm on five." He hands me a room key.

I smile, not because he's paying for my room, but because of where we are. I'm staying in a hotel, with a card key. It's the little things in life, but I keep my excitement to myself. "Thank you." I smile up at him. He nods.

"Right. So that gives us about thirty-five minutes to get settled. Meet here in the lobby at six," Robin says, pushing the button for the elevator. All of us, with bags in tow, follow her on board. The guys are dropped off first, then Robin and Brian. When the doors open for my floor, I step out, as does Blaine.

"What are you doing?" I ask him.

"Just making sure you get into your room okay."

"I'm a big girl, Blaine Bishop," I remind him.

"I know you are, Aubree Chase," he says huskily, causing warmth to radiate through my body.

I follow the signs and keep my eyes glued to the room numbers until I find mine. With reined in excitement, I slide the card into the door and hear the lock click open. Pushing into the room, I can no longer hide my smile. There is a decent-size bathroom, a king-size bed, a table, dresser, TV, chair, and a mini-fridge. "Blaine, this is too much." I turn to face him. He's dropped his bags and is standing right behind me.

"Let me have that." He takes my bag and tosses it gently to the floor. "This room is a standard room, Bree. We all got the same one."

I look around again, before turning back to face him. "This is the nicest place I've ever stayed," I confess.

"Yeah?" He steps closer. Reaching out, he snakes his arms around my waist. "I'm glad," he whispers, his lips just a breath from mine.

My chest rises and falls as my breathing grows faster, louder. "Do it." I exhale the words. I want him to kiss me. I can see it in his eyes, that's his intention, but he's hesitant. I don't want him hesitant. I want him to kiss me.

Not needing further invitation, he presses his lips to mine. With the gentle stroke of his tongue against my lips, I'm opening for him. He's tentative as his tongue brushes against mine. My hands grip the back of his T-shirt, holding him to me. I want him closer, and I can't seem to get him there. Releasing my grip, I slide my hands under his shirt and dig my nails into the defined muscles of his back.

"Fuck, Bree," he murmurs before kissing me harder. There is no hesitation in the way his tongue invades my mouth and battles for space, or the way he tastes me. His hands grip the back of my thighs and suddenly, I'm airborne as he tosses me on the bed. He crawls on the bed after me, holding his weight with his arms on either side of my head. "You sure this is what you want? You know I can't give you more," he reminds me. My heart pounds like a bass drum in my chest.

"I want this, Blaine. I want you." I keep my eyes locked on his, willing him to believe me. There is no backing out, not on my end. I've fought this long enough, and the idea alone of the excitement of being with him fuels my desire even more so. I want to live a little. I want to experience this deep-rooted passion that we seem to share. Heartbreak be damned.

"I need more time," he whispers against my lips.

"What?" I ask, confused. I thought we were both on board with this.

"I need to trace every inch of your skin with my tongue. I need to worship these." He lightly brushes his index finger on my breast. "I need more time," he says again. I must still have a confused look on my face. "We have to be downstairs in twenty-five minutes, but I can give you this." He settles beside me, propping his head up on one hand while the other travels down my body, only stopping when he reaches the button of my blue jean shorts. The button pops and I suck in a deep breath.

"You okay?" His hand is still, waiting for me to give him

permission.

"Yeah." I look over at him. His eyes are filled with heat, his lips red from our kiss. I run my fingers through his hair. "I'm more than okay." I'm no virgin, but this is all new to me. This overbearing need to have his hands on me and mine on him. This want for him to devour me is all new.

He proceeds to slide the zipper down, making room for his hand. Immediately, I feel the warmth of his skin even through my panties. Gently, he strokes a finger over my clit. "Bree," he breathes. I want to feel ashamed that I'm soaked, and I know he can feel it, but I can't seem to find it in me to care. Cautiously, he runs his fingers over me, and even with the barrier of my silk panties in the way, his touch lights me on fire.

"More," I say, my lips next to his ear. My hands are buried in his hair, pulling him toward me. My mouth latches onto his and he doesn't disappoint. He kisses me as if I'm the air he needs to breathe. I take in a deep breath when his hand slides under my panties.

"Talk to me," he demands.

"Don't stop," I pant, closing my eyes and letting my head fall back onto the pillow. He kisses my neck, his stubble scratching me, but it's a sensation I crave. His tongue is crazy talented as he licks and sucks on my neck. His fingers equally so as he slides them through my folds. I try to open my legs wider for him, but my shorts are restricting.

"I've got you," he murmurs, nipping at my ear.

His thumb circles my clit just as his fingers press inside. He works me over, slow at first, letting my body get time to adjust to him. That doesn't take long, I don't think I've ever been this turned on, this ready in my entire life. When he adds another digit, I lift my hips, needing something, but not knowing what it is. I can feel my orgasm building. It's a slow, torturous climb, equal parts maddening and bliss. Sensing I need more, he moves his thumb faster while thrusting in and out of me with his fingers.

"Blaine," I moan from the intense satisfaction it brings me.

"Bree," he answers. He doesn't slow his pace. "Open your eyes." I do as he says and find his intense stare focused on me. "I want to see you when you fall apart."

As if his words are what I needed to do so, my orgasm comes thrashing through me. One hand is buried in his hair, while the other digs into his arm, the one that is currently bringing me to the abyss of pleasure.

"Fuck, you're squeezing my fingers. That's so hot," he says, not stopping his ministrations. As my body comes down from its high, only then does he slow. He removes his thumb, but lazily strokes his fingers inside of me. "So wet," he says with awe in his voice.

"So worth it," I finally say, making him chuckle.

"We have about five minutes before we have to be downstairs. Let me help you clean up." He kisses my lips quickly and climbs off the bed. I know I need to get up, but I can't seem to find the will or the want. If I could stay in this room just the two of us forever, repeating that, I would. No questions, no hesitation.

"Stand up for me." Opening my eyes, I see him standing by the bed, offering me his hand. Reluctantly, I place my hand in his and let him pull me to my feet. Dropping to his knees, he slides my shorts and my panties down my legs. It's not until I feel the warm damp cloth do I realize he's cleaning me up. Taking care of me. My heart squeezes in my chest. It's been a long time since I've allowed anyone to do so. It's not lost on me that it's Blaine. I knew I was falling for him. I know that it's going to end in heartache, but the certainty of that doesn't keep me from wanting to do this.

"I'll grab some clean panties," I say, my face heating. I close my eyes, not wanting to see his face. I feel his lips press just below my belly button before he stands and kisses my lips one more time.

"Good idea," he says. "These"—I open my eyes and see him

holding my black silk panties—"are soaked." He then proceeds to shove them into his pants pocket.

"What are you doing?"

"These are mine, Bree. I need something of you for when I can't have you. You wanted this to be just between us and I agreed to your terms. However, after that—" He points to the bed. "—it's going to be hard as fuck to stay away from you, regardless of who's around. So these"—he taps his jeans pocket—"will be what gets me through."

I open my mouth to argue, but quickly shut it. It's hot, and I like the thought of affecting him this way. So instead, I reach into my bag and pull out another pair of panties. I take my time stepping into them and sliding them up my legs and over my hips. I reach for my shorts and do the same.

"Ready?"

He reaches into the front of his pants and adjusts his hard length.

"I can... I mean, won't that be painful?" I ask, again feeling my cheeks flood with embarrassment.

"I'm good," he assures me. "Besides, that was just an appetizer." He steps closer. "After dinner, I plan to have dessert."

"Crap!" I look at the clock and see it's two minutes past six. "We're late."

He laces his fingers through mine and leads us to the door. "I've got the key." He holds up the card and shows me before shoving it into his back pocket. He doesn't let go of my hand until the elevator stops at the lobby level and the doors slide open. We walk side by side, closer than necessary but unable to fight the pull. We find everyone waiting for us just outside the restaurant.

"Sorry we're late. We had to stop at every floor on the way down," Blaine excuses.

"We're waiting on a table anyway. How's your room, dear?"

she asks me.

"It's very nice." I turn to look at Blaine. "Thank you." It's more than just a thank you for the room, and by the heated look he gives me, he knows it too.

"Bishop party of seven," the hostess calls out.

We fall in line to head to our table when I feel his hand on the small of my back and his hot breath against my ear. "Never thank me for giving you pleasure, Bree. It's equally as much for me as it is for you."

And just like that, another pair of ruined panties.

CHAPTER Sixteen

BLAINE

PARTY OF SEVEN, TABLE FOR eight. Somehow, I managed to get seated on the opposite side of the table than Aubree. Mom is sitting on her right, and Rick to her left. The seat next to him is open, so he had a choice of where he sat. Of course, he chose right next to her. Dad distracted me when we got to the table, talking about the weather that's headed toward Pennsylvania. They are supposed to have storms, which could mean potential rain, possibly delaying or canceling the race altogether.

So, now here I am, wondering if this long-ass drive is for nothing, watching one of my closest friends flirt with my girl. Okay, technically she's not mine, but while this thing—whatever it is between us—is happening she is. While she spends her nights in my bed, she's mine. I not only don't do serious relationships, but I don't share. I never have. I'm an only child and a selfish bastard. Apparently, especially when it comes to Aubree. I've imagined throat punching Rick a thousand times in the last hour. He's sitting closer than he needs to, and he's monopolizing all of her attention.

I guess I should be glad it takes the heat off of us, but I find that when it comes to her, I don't give a fuck who knows. I agreed to her terms because I want her. I'm not usually one for displays of affection. I keep my conquests to myself. However, it's been a long damn time since there has even been a hookup in my life. My singular focus has been my career, until the gorgeous redhead sitting across from me came crashing into my world.

"Blaine," my dad says, pulling me out of my thoughts.

"Yeah?" I turn to look at him. He's grinning.

"I said your name three times."

"Sorry, just thinking about the race." Not a complete lie.

"That's what I was trying to talk to you about. Maybe we should stay here tomorrow, and see how this plays out. Save us ten hours of drive time there and back to this point if it looks like it's going to be a wash."

Immediately, my mind goes to Aubree and me in her room, or hell, in mine the one I've yet to see because all I can see is her. "Yeah, not a bad idea. I guess leaving home this early wasn't the best move."

"I think it was. We're five hours away from the track, and just about the same from home. This could go either way. If they run, we don't show up at the last minute. If they don't, we don't have to drive ten hours to get home."

"Good point."

"What's going on?" Mom asks.

"We were just talking about the race. The weather is coming in. Says severe storms Friday through Sunday. There's a chance they're going to cancel."

"We should stay here another night then," Mom says.

Dad smiles at her. That loving "you could be cussing my ass out" look, and I'd still worship you. It's the way he's always looked at her. "That's what we were thinking," he finally says.

"Damn, I wish Ash could have made this trip," Kevin

comments.

I don't know how he does it. He looks at Ash like Dad looks at Mom. I couldn't imagine spending so much time away from someone I loved so much. Kev makes a good living as my crew chief, but it's not about the money, rather it's Ashley's decision to have her independence. I can see her giving that up when, and if, they have a baby. Which to hear Kev talk could be soon.

"She's welcome anytime. I've told her that over and over again," Mom says.

"Yeah, she knows. My wife is stubborn to a fault. She enjoys working."

"Nothing wrong with that," Dad chimes in.

"I get it," Aubree adds. "I worked hard in college and to be where I am in life. To give that up, to trust someone else to take care of me, I'm not sure I could do it."

Rick places his arm on the back of her chair. "You just need to find the right guy." He wags his eyebrows at her. Rage bubbles over, and if it were not for the chance I might hit Aubree, I'd kick him under the table.

"Even then," Aubree says. "I've been dependent on a man who hated me. It's not anything I would ever wish on anyone. My job ensures I'll never have to again."

"Oh, honey, don't let one bad relationship turn you off love," Mom tells her.

"It's hard to do when that relationship is your father." She slaps her hand over her mouth as soon as the words are out. Mom convinced her to have a glass of wine with dinner, and she's a little freer with her words than normal. The table is eerily silent, and I find myself wanting to hold her, capture her in my embrace and protect her, tell her everything is going to be okay. I've never felt the need to comfort anyone, but I've already established Aubree is not just anyone.

"Aubree girl," Dad speaks up. His voice is calm and clear. "Please forgive me for talking ill of your father, but no man deserves the title of father who makes his child feel that way.

I'm sorry for what you've been through, and I can promise you that the men sitting at this table, none of them are like that. You can trust us, sweetheart," he adds.

Mom places her hand over Aubree's that's resting on the table. "We're all here for you," she says, keeping her voice low, her words meant only for Aubree.

When a tear trails down her cheek, I've had enough. Dinner is done, and we've all just been sitting around chatting. I stand and hand Dad my business credit card. "Take care of this, will you?" I don't wait for his reply, I know he will. Instead, I walk around the table, and place my hands on the back of her chair. I bend down and whisper just for her, "Let's get you settled." Her reply is to scoot back in her chair and stand.

"I'm sorry," she says, head hanging, eyes glued to her feet.

"Aubree." Dad says her name with authority, which causes her head to snap up and look at him.

"You have nothing to apologize for. You get some rest. We'll see you in the morning."

With that, I place my hand on the small of her back and lead her to the elevators. As soon as the doors slide and close us in, I wrap my arms around her and hold her tight. She holds onto me as if I'm her lifeline. When the elevator stops on the fourth floor, I let go of her and she whimpers. "Hey," I say soothingly. "Put your arms around my neck." She does as I ask, allowing me to pick her up and carry her to her room. Carefully, I set her on her feet and unlock the door, pushing it open for her and following in behind her.

I don't really have a plan, not anymore. All thoughts of ravishing her are gone but not forgotten when I saw her tears.

"Blaine." Her soft voice pulls my attention.

"Yeah?" I step toward her and cup her face in my hands.

"Make me forget."

"Bree, I'm not sure that's the best idea. You've been drinking and obviously you're upset."

"I'm not drunk, Blaine. I let the truth slip free, and you're still here."

"Of course, I am. Where else would I be?"

"You have your pick of… companions," she says.

"I pick you," I tell her, tracing her cheek with my thumb.

"Then make me forget."

"Aubree." Her name is a plea on my lips. Although I'm not sure what for. For her to not ask this of me, or because she is? She trusts me to make her forget.

"Do you want me?" she asks.

"You know I do."

"Then show me. I want to know what that feels like. My uncle was family and obligated to want me around. He was nothing like my father, but family all the same. I've never known what it feels like to truly be wanted. By a man," she adds.

There is protest on my tongue, but she drops to her knees, has my pants unzipped and my cock in her hand before I can voice it. "Aubree," I say again. I'm not sure if it's a plea or a warning this time.

She looks up at me under her lashes. Green eyes shining bright like emeralds, full of heat and desire that are directed toward me. "Blaine," she says huskily, just as she wraps her mouth around my cock.

"Son of a bitch," I rasp, reaching out for something to hold onto. Luckily, the wall is there to save me. I want to bury my hands in that red hair of hers, but I stop myself. She needs this. To feel as though she's the one in control. She needs to be able to see what she does to me. That saying that I want her is a mild interpretation of the way my heart is thumping against my chest as I watch her slide her soft lips around my shaft and pull me into her mouth.

Her hands grip my thighs, her nails biting the skin, but I relish the pain. I focus on that and not coming down her throat. She wants me to show her I want her, and that's what she's going to get. I've never wanted anyone the way I do her.

Never.

Just Bree.

"Aubree," I pant, feeling myself closing in on my orgasm. "Not before you," I tell her.

She sits back on her knees and a soft popping sound echoes through the room as my cock falls from her lips. "I want to," she counters.

"Not tonight. I need to show you." I know that will sway her to my way of thinking. She nods. "Come here." I reach out a hand and pull her to her feet. Her mouth is plump and wet, and I have to kiss her. Tasting the precum on her lips, my cock twitches. "I need you naked," I murmur against her lips.

Stepping back, she strips out of her T-shirt and shorts. She stands before me in a black silk bra that matches the panties in my pocket and a tiny light pink lace thong. "You're behind," she tells me with a soft smile as she reaches behind her and unhooks her bra.

Not needing further encouragement, I slide my jeans over my hips and kick them to the side. My underwear is next before I reach behind my neck, grab my shirt, and tug it over my head. It too is tossed to the side.

"Better." She smiles shyly.

I watch her as she slips her thumbs beneath the waistband of her thong and slides it down her legs. "You're gorgeous," I tell her honestly. I take a minute to take her in. To memorize every inch of her in this moment. Her eyes are blazing with desire, while her lips are red and plump, still wet from when she had my cock in her mouth. Her auburn hair is falling down over her shoulders, begging for my hands to be buried in her locks. Long slender neck, pert round breasts with cherry-red nipples begging for my mouth to feast on them. My trail leads along her stomach and to her pretty pink pussy, followed by her toned long legs. Her toes are painted the lightest shade of pink, and although I've never had a thing for feet, I want to suck each one of them into my mouth and drive her wild. The beautiful Aubree has definitely got me by the balls. In this moment, I'm good with it.

Dragging the covers back from the bed, I motion for her to climb in. She doesn't hesitate and I follow in after her, pulling the cover up over us.

"It's cold in here." She shivers.

"I can fix that," I say, drawing her naked body into mine. She places her hand on my cheek and presses her lips to mine. My hands roam over her body, tracing every curve, memorizing every dip and valley I can possibly get my hands on. My cock is hard as steel pressed against her belly. With her nipples hardened peaks against my chest, I want to suck on them, show them the attention they deserve, but not yet. Instead, I remain calm, my hands skimming her soft skin, and I kiss her. She wants to know what it's like to be wanted. I'm damn well going to show her. After tonight, she'll never have to wonder.

"Blaine." She breathes my name.

"Hmm?" I ask, my mouth trailing from her lips across her cheek and to her neck.

She throws her leg over mine and I can feel her wet heat. My control is slipping, but I'm determined to give her this. I might not be able to give her the happily ever after she yearns for, but I can give her this.

This night.

My lips move down her neck over her collarbone and to her breasts. "Lie back," I whisper. With one hand, I flick her nipple, causing her to arch off the bed, while my mouth latches on to the other. In tandem, my hands and my mouth lavish her with the attention she deserves. Nipping and sucking her nipple, soothing her with my tongue, I roll the bud of the other between my thumb and index finger.

It's not until I climb on top of her and settle between her thighs that I realize I don't have a condom. With a heavy exhale, I rest my forehead against hers, trying to get myself under control with the realization that tonight isn't happening. At least not how I planned it.

"What's wrong?"

"Condom. I don't have one."

"I bought some," she says. I pull back to find her smiling up at me. "At the gas station with the donuts. I wasn't sure we would need them, but you know." She lifts a shoulder into a small shrug.

I kiss her hard on the lips, just a quick meeting but enough that she gets the point. "Where are they?"

"In my purse." She points to the table where her purse is lying.

"Don't move a muscle." Throwing off the covers, I hop out of bed and dump her purse on the table. I find the box of condoms, and notice there are three as I tear open the package and bring all three of them back to the bed with me. I place two on the nightstand while ripping the package of the other with my teeth, and rolling it on my length. Quickly, I take my spot between her thighs and pull the covers back over us.

"I missed you," she says softly.

Something flips over in my chest at her words, but I ignore it. I have something far more important to focus on at the moment. With my hands flat on the bed on either side of her head, I rest my weight to keep from crushing her. Leaning down, I capture her lips with mine.

"Blaine," she says against my lips. Taking matters into her own hands, she reaches between us and fists my cock, positioning me at her entrance. She looks up at me, and I'm glad the light is on. We must have forgotten to turn it off when we left, but I've never been more thankful. Her green eyes are filled with desire. All for me. Not able to wait a minute longer, I push my way inside of her.

"Bree," I murmur, closing my eyes. She fits me like a glove. Her wet heat surrounds my cock like it was made just for her. When her hands trace up and down my back, I open my eyes to make sure she's okay.

"Hey." She smiles.

The corner of my mouth lifts. "I need a minute," I confess. "You feel too good."

"This isn't a one-time thing, you know." She lifts her hips, taking me deeper, something I didn't think was possible. "I'm yours for as long as you want me."

Forever.

That one word echoes in the back of my mind, but I push it away. Instead, I drop my elbows to the bed, encasing her, and slowly begin to rock into her. I kiss her lips, her chin, her neck, her ears… my mouth doesn't leave a single piece of skin that it can reach uncovered. I flick her nipple with one hand, while my mouth makes love to the other. I alternate back and forth taking my time, showing her with my body how wanted she is. How much *I* want her.

"More," she pants, hiking her legs up around my waist and locking them around me with her feet entwined.

No matter how much she begs, I'm not going to race to the finish. I'm taking this slowly, a first for me. Usually I chase my release, and I'm good to go for a few weeks, hell, months, but tonight, with Aubree, I don't want to chase mine. No, in fact, I want her to chase hers. I want to build the desire that's been burning between us for weeks, then together, explode into pure bliss. She deserves to be treasured.

Seconds, minutes, hell, hours tick by, but I don't notice. All I know is that I'm here with this beautiful creature — inside of her — with her warmth wrapped around me, and this is the closest thing to heaven that I can imagine. I'm close, but I hold back, refusing to go without her. I keep my rhythm steady, and even at our slow pace, I begin to break out in a sweat from the need to come… from the need to release this… passion I have for her.

"Oh, Bl-Blaine," she moans, and her pussy pulses around me.

She's close.

Placing my lips next to her ear, I talk her through it. "You feel so good, Bree. I can feel you squeezing me." I roll my hips and her nails dig into my back. "Let go for me, beautiful." And as if my encouragement was all she needed, she screams as her orgasm thrashes through her. With one more pump, I still and let mine do the same. I rest my weight on my elbows, careful not to crush her as we catch our breath.

"That was…." She doesn't finish her sentence as she sucks a deep breath into her lungs.

"How much I want you," I finish for her. It was more than that, so much more that. I'm not ready to dissect it just yet. Instead, I want to just lie here beside her and bask in the glow of our orgasms.

"Can you stay?" she asks.

"No place I'd rather be." After sliding out of her, I climb out of bed to get rid of the condom. I bring her back a warm cloth to clean up. I've never done this before. I've never taken the time to take care of a woman after sex. With Bree, I have this desire to care for her, to make her believe that she's someone special. Not just to me, but in everything she does. Once that's taken care of, I toss it back into the bathroom and climb in beside her. She snuggles up next to me and within minutes we're both sound asleep.

CHAPTER Seventeen

Aubree

I WAKE TO THE RINGING of my cell phone. Slowly, I open my eyes and take in my surroundings. I see our clothes lying on the floor and feel his warm embrace surrounding me as the memories of last night come flooding back. "Go back to sleep," Blaine mumbles.

"It might be important." I try to wiggle free of his hold, although a part of me just wants to stay in his warm embrace a little longer.

"What's important is you kissing me good morning."

"Uh." I cover my mouth with my hand. "I need to brush my teeth."

"You need to kiss me," he says, kissing my bare shoulder.

"How about I check my phone, brush my teeth, and then give you a proper good morning kiss?" Compromise is important in relationships, right? Even those with an end date?

"How about you brush your teeth, come back to bed, kiss me, and then check your phone?"

"Deal." I climb out of bed, and to my surprise, he follows me. "What are you doing?"

"Brushing my teeth," he says, following me into the bathroom. I really need to pee, but I'll wait until he's done. Instead of stopping at the sink, he goes to the toilet and lifts the lid.

"Blaine! Are you really doing that right now?" I've never been in this situation before. My high school hook-ups were in the back of a car, and the few I did let myself indulge in when in college were more of a "wham, bam, thank you ma'am" kind of situation. No morning afters.

He looks over his shoulder at me. "It's human nature, Bree."

"Yeah, I mean, I know but in front of me?"

"You've seen all of me." His eyes rake over my body. "I've not left an inch of you untouched, and this is too intimate?"

"No, I just… didn't expect it, is all." With the running water, and him doing his business, I've really got to go. He flushes and drops the lid, joining me at the counter. "Can you step out for a minute?" I ask him.

"Why?"

"I need to use the restroom."

"Go ahead, I don't mind." He grabs the toothpaste and places some on his finger before brushing his teeth.

"Gah!" Not able to hold it any longer, I take a seat on the toilet and relieve my bladder. This is all new for me. It's oddly embarrassing and comforting at the same time — to have this level of intimacy with him.

"Meet you back in bed." He leans down and kisses me. While I'm using the bathroom!

My mouth hangs open as I watch his bare ass, a mighty fine sight I might add, walk out of the bathroom and back to bed. Is this what normal couples do? I'll have to ask Maria or Ashley. I finish my business, and brush my teeth, then head back to bed. Grabbing my phone from the dresser, I see I missed a call from Robin.

"Hey." He grabs my phone and rolls on top of me. "Aren't you forgetting something?"

I want to smart off something cute and flirty, but really, I just want to kiss him. So that's what I do. Burying my fingers in his hair, I pull him into a kiss, one lacking morning breath I might add.

"Morning, Bree," he says before giving me another chaste kiss and rolling off me. He hands me my phone with an ornery grin.

"I missed a call from your mom," I tell him.

"Really?" He looks at his phone. "She didn't try to call me."

When I hit her number, it rings twice before she answers. "Hello, Aubree. I hope I didn't wake you?" she says politely.

"No, I was in the restroom when you called."

"Looks like we're going to be hanging out until we see what this weather does. I thought you and I could do some shopping. Are you up for it?"

Immediately, tears prick my eyes. I never knew my mother. I always dreamed of having her in my life, and in my dream, she is everything like Robin Bishop. "Yeah." I clear my throat. "I'd love to. What time do you want to leave? I just need about thirty minutes to shower."

"That will be perfect. Let's make it forty-five. We'll grab lunch here at the hotel and go out and see what we can get into."

"Perfect. Thank you, Robin."

"You're doing me a favor. I need some girl time." She laughs, and hangs up the phone.

"You okay?" Blaine tucks my crazy hair behind my ears. I know I look like a hot mess from my short trip in the bathroom. If I wasn't so emotional from the invite from his mother, I would probably be embarrassed.

"Yeah, she uh, she invited me to go shopping."

"I heard." He smiles. "Why did that upset you?"

I debate on whether or not to tell him and then decide to just go for it. He knows most of it anyway. "You know my mom left when I was a baby. Uncle Bobby never married, so I've never really had a mother figure in my life. When I was younger, I always dreamed of the day she would come back for me and in my dreams, fantasies really, she was a lot like your mom. Kind, understanding, unconditional love...."

"I'll share her with you," he says softly. "She has such a big heart, and I know without a doubt she would have loved to have a daughter."

I chuckle. "Yeah, and when this is over, how does that work?" His offer makes my heart happy, feel something I've not felt a lot of in my lifetime. If I'm honest, it's never felt like this. Nothing has ever made me feel the way Blaine does.

"We're adults, Bree."

"Yeah. And I'm an adult who's going to be late if I don't get moving." I jump out of bed ending the conversation. I was making things heavy when they're supposed to be nothing but fun between us. I need to remember that. No matter how much my heart screams otherwise. It pleads for me to let it love him, to not worry about the what-ifs, and embrace this—whatever is happening—with open arms. I went into this with my eyes wide open. I know the stakes and was willing to bet them.

I just lathered my hair with shampoo when Blaine walks into the bathroom. "Dad called. He wants to know if me and the guys want to shoot a few games of pool while you and Mom go shopping. Something to kill some time."

"Have fun," I say, rinsing the shampoo.

"I'm not leaving until you kiss me goodbye."

I peer through the glass shower door and he's leaning against the counter, legs crossed and arms crossed over his chest.

"So, what? You're just going to stand there and watch me until I'm done?"

"Yep. Trust me, if you could see what I see, you would do the same damn thing."

"Don't you need to shower?" I ask him.

"Yep."

"Will you not be late?"

"Nope."

"You could join me, if you want," I offer, already knowing it will make me late, but the temptation is too great.

"Nope. You and I both know that if I climb into that shower with you, neither one of us is leaving this room anytime soon."

He's right, so I keep my mouth shut and let him watch me shower. The act is just as intimate as if he were actually in here with me. My heart races and there's tingling between my thighs. When I'm done, he's there with two towels. I take one for my hair and the other he keeps. He takes his time drying me, slowly raking the towel over my wet body. He's taking care of me, which is also altogether new and exciting and a turn on. I know I can't be late to meet Robin. I don't want to be, so I keep my need for him to myself. For now. When he's satisfied, he throws the towel over the shower door. I watch him as he adjusts his hard length.

"Bree," he rumbles. "You can't look at me like that."

"Like what?" I ask innocently. I know exactly how I was looking at him.

"Come here," he growls, pulling my naked body into his fully clothed one. "Kiss me, so I can go. You're too damn tempting." Doing as he asks, I kiss him, teasing his lips with my tongue. "You're going to be the death of me." He laughs. "Get ready, and have fun. I'll see you later?"

"Yeah, I'll see you later." One more quick kiss and he walks out my door. The act reminds me that one day soon, when he turns and walks away, he won't be coming back. When we started this, I knew I would fall for him, I know myself. I just had no idea that the fall would be this fast and this hard. How am I going to move on without him?

I rush through getting ready, and manage to make it downstairs five minutes ahead of schedule.

"I hope you weren't waiting long," Robin says. "I lost track of time."

I want to tell her that her son almost made me late, but I keep that titbit of intel to myself. "Not at all," I say instead. "I just got here."

"I'm starving." She links her arm through mine and leads me to the bar. "We'll get served faster here than waiting for a table."

"Fine with me. I'm more thirsty than hungry." We take our seats at the bar, and talk about the weather and what that means for Blaine and the race.

"I'm sure he's been on pins and needles all night," she says, referring to Blaine.

"Yeah," I agree, trying not to blush.

"He hates it when the weather delays or cancels a race. I swear that boy lives and breathes this sport."

Our food arrives before I can comment, and I ask the bartender for a refill on my water. We scarf down our BLTs, and head out. "Are you looking for something particular?" I ask as we exit the hotel.

"Not at all, just a day out getting some girl time. I gotta tell you, it's nice that you're here. I used to be the only female except on days when Ashley could tag along. If you weren't here, I would either have dragged Brian with me or just did whatever they wanted, so thank you." She offers me a warm smile.

"Hey, glad I could help." We walk across the street to a small strip mall.

"Oh, I'm going to go look at these scarfs," Robin says, walking toward the back of the very first store we enter.

I browse around, nothing really reaching out and saying buy me until I come across a burgundy shirt made to look like lace. It has pieces of thinner sheer material that makes it see-through in places, but not enough to really stand out.

"I bought that exact one for myself the other day," a girl about my age tells me. "I'm Sara. Would you like to try that on?" she asks.

"No, it's uh, not really me?" It's more of a question than a statement. I usually stick to boring-casual or scrubs. This is out of my comfort zone, and I need some advice. Advice I'm hoping she offers.

"Of course, it is. It would be perfect with your hair color. Try it on."

My mind wanders to what Blaine would think, seeing me in this.

"Oh, what did you find?" Robin asks, scarf in hand.

"I'm trying to convince her this shirt would look amazing on her with her hair color," Sara explains.

Robin pulls the shirt off the rack holding it up to me. "Ooh, you're right," she tells her. "Aubree, you have to try this on."

"It's not really me, I mean, you can see through it."

"Just wear a nice black or even burgundy bra or cami underneath," Sara tells me.

"Go." Robin hands me the shirt and gives me a little nudge toward the dressing room.

I smile all the way to the dressing room. My back is to them so they can't see my goofy grin. Today is great. Shopping with Robin is another new experience, one I wish I could repeat often. After pulling my Bishop Racing T-shirt over my head, I take the shirt off the hanger, and try it on. Unhurriedly, I fasten the buttons and take a look. It's V-neck, showing just a hint of cleavage without being obscene. The sheerness is not as bad as it appears once you have it on. Luckily, today I have on another black bra, and it looks good.

"I wanna see!" Robin yells into the dressing room.

Slowly, I open the door and walk out.

"Wow, Aubree, that looks great on you."

"Yes, and we have a new line of lipstick, one this exact color that would set this off. Leave the shorts and the flip-flops, this is a cute outfit. I'm going to have to wear mine like this," Sara says, dashing off to, I assume, grab the lipstick.

"It's not too much?" I ask Robin.

"You're young, and it looks great on you. I say go for it."

"Where would I wear it?" I ask her. "I wear scrubs to work, and I have a uniform for the track."

"Wear it out."

"I don't go out. Not really."

"Huh, well, we're going out tonight. We're going to spend the night again, since the storm is slow-moving and see what happens. I'll gather the troops. It'll be fun," she says.

Just the thought of wearing this for Blaine, and the heat in his hazel eyes is enough for me to buy it. "Okay," I agree. Robin claps her hands and cheers.

"Here you go." Sara hands me the lipstick. "We're having a sale right now too so I can give you both twenty percent off." She winks. "It's friends and family only, but we're friends, right?"

"Yes," Robin and I say at the same time, and the three of us laugh. After we make our purchases, we hit a few more stores. I buy some lotion, a bottle of water because I'm still thirsty, and I find a cute black and white cell phone case. It's plaid, but it makes me think of Blaine and racing, so I buy that too.

"I guess that's all she wrote," Robin says when we exit the final store.

"Yeah, but we got some good buys," I say, holding up my bags.

"We did."

"Thank you for today," I tell her, fighting back the emotion that's clogging my throat. "This is a first for me. I've never really been shopping with a mom, or a mom figure, so today was... nice. Thank you." My voice cracks.

"Anytime, Aubs." She reaches out and hugs me, well, tries to with her bags in her hands. "You need a shopping buddy, even when the season is over, you call me. The men in my life live in that garage. I'm always up for some girl time."

We make plans to do it again soon on our walk back to the hotel. I meant what I said. Today was a great day. One that I've dreamed about having. I hope Blaine realizes how truly blessed he is to have his parents in his life.

BLAINE

MOM AND AUBREE STOPPED BY the hotel bar where we're still playing pool and sipping on beer. I have to make an effort to not drink her in. It's only been a few hours since I've had my hands and lips on her, but it seems as if it's been years.

"Who's winning?" Mom asks, taking a stool. Aubree follows her lead and takes the one next to her.

"We're playing pea pool," Dad tells her. "So far, Rick is out and the rest of us are still in."

"I think they were gunning for me," Rick grumbles.

He's not wrong, but this game makes it impossible to do so. I have no idea which numbers he drew, but that's not to say that if I did, I wouldn't have tried to knock him out.

"So, Aubree and I decided we all need to go out tonight, blow off a little steam. This girl Sara, at one of the boutiques we went to, said there is a place just a block from here called Stagger. Says that's the place to be," Mom says.

Dad laughs. "Sounds like a plan, babe," he tells her.

I watch as Mom bumps her shoulder into Aubree's with a wink. "What do you say? Seven? We can eat there. Sara says they have great food."

"You've been busy today," I tell them.

"Girl time," Mom replies. "We had a good day, huh, Aubs?"

"Yeah." Aubree holds up her bags. "We found some deals."

Why do I, all of a sudden, want to pull her into my arms and kiss her? I want to hear all about her day shopping, and I even want to see what's inside those bags. I can almost guarantee knowing Bree, and the fact that she was with my mom, it's nothing at all scandalous, but it caught her attention long enough to buy it, and I want to hear all about it.

"I think I'm going to go up to my room and freshen up a little," Aubree says, standing from her stool.

"Oh, don't forget to wear that cute shirt you bought," Mom tells her.

"You sure?" she asks.

I'm fascinated by how well the two of them get along.

"Definitely. You might find a nice young man to spin you around the dance floor." Mom winks.

I want to tell her that Aubree has a nice young man, one that she in fact raised, but I bite down on my lip to keep the words from spilling out. The thought of some other guy hitting on her pisses me off. Maybe going out tonight isn't the best plan, but I don't see a way out of it.

"Okay. I'll see you all in the lobby at seven." She doesn't even look at me as she turns and walks out of the bar.

I want to follow her, but that would be obvious, and she would hate that. I agreed to the terms and now I have to live up to them. I watch her until I can no longer see her before turning my attention back to the game. That's when I find all eyes on me. "What?" I ask as if I'm innocent.

"Nothing." Kevin grins before lining up and taking his next shot.

Mom excuses herself to take her bags up to their room, and we stay downstairs to finish our game. This one takes the longest and if I didn't know any better, I'd say Dad, Jacob, and Kevin are missing their shots on purpose. It's as if they know I want to go to her.

"What? You guys suddenly forget how to play pool?" I ask them.

All four of them, even Rick who's been out of the game since the beginning, cracks up laughing.

"You got somewhere to be, son?" Dad smirks.

"Nope."

"Uh-huh." He laughs, taking his shot and finally, he makes it.

The game goes on with the guys missing as many as they hit, which is not like them. When we finally finish, it's just a few minutes before seven. I'm convinced now more than ever that they were doing this on purpose. Delaying the game.

"Your mom just texted me and said they're on their way down."

The five of us wander out of the bar and into the hotel lobby to wait for them. Kevin calls Ashley to check in, while Dad, Jacob, and Rick look at the weather. I should be doing the same thing, in fact, any other time it would be me who is pulling up the weather keeping an eye on things, but right now, all I can focus on is the gorgeous redhead who is striding toward me with my mother. As they draw closer, I take in what she's wearing, and with just one glance, I'm ready to lose my mind.

"Ready?" Mom asks.

"Lead the way," Dad says, holding his arm out for her.

I let them walk a few steps ahead before I lean in close to her ear. "Are you trying to out us?" I ask Aubree.

She stops walking. "What are you talking about?" she whispers. Her eyes dart around to make sure no one can hear us.

"That outfit."

"You don't like it?" I can hear the hurt in her voice.

Knowing the risks, I grab her arm and pull her behind a tall column in the lobby. "Fuck, Bree, I more than like it. It's going to be damn hard to keep my hands off you." Her warm body pressed against mine is so damn tempting. All I want to do is drag her back to the room.

"Yeah?" she asks, hopeful, shuffling her feet.

"Don't do that," I warn her. "Don't look at me with those big green eyes. I can't seem to resist you." I lean in and kiss the corner of her mouth.

"We better go." She turns to walk away, and I stop her, pulling her into my chest.

This time, I kiss her on the lips, just a soft peck, but it's her lips against mine so I'll take it.

"Checkmate, you act like you missed me," she teases.

Her teasing makes me smile. She's really started to open up and come out of her shell. It's as if she's gaining confidence every day. I like to think I have something to do with that. The thought of being that person for her, it does things to me. Makes me want more than an end date. I realize that I did miss her, more than I thought possible. "I missed these lips," I say, instead of telling her the truth.

"Come on." She pulls out of my hold and steps out from behind the pillar. We're able to slip up behind the others, and it seems like they didn't even miss us. That gives me hope for sneaking some time with her tonight. I can only hope this place has dark corners to hide in.

Stagger is packed. It seems as though this Sara girl gave Mom and Bree the right information. Dad leads us to the back corner to an empty table, which is surprising considering the amount of people that are covering the dance floor.

"What can I get you ladies to drink?" Dad asks.

"Just a water, dear, oh and one of those pineapple upside-down cake shots." She smiles. "Get Aubree one too."

"No, just a bottle of water for me." She reaches into her pocket to pull out money and Dad waves her off.

"I've got this." He walks off toward the bar.

I'm sitting next to her this time, and no way in hell am I going to lose my seat to Rick or even Jacob, so I stay put. I'll grab something later.

"You not want anything?" Mom asks.

Just Aubree. "Nah, I'm good for now. I had a couple earlier." It's not a complete lie.

"You okay?" Aubree asks once Mom and Kevin are in a conversation. Jacob and Rick followed after Dad for drinks.

"Yeah." I place my hand on her leg under the table. I can't seem to keep my hands off her. I've never had that issue before. I'm a grown man who can control his urges.

Until Aubree.

Now I'm doing and saying things I don't usually say, thinking things I've never thought, and I'm not exactly sure how to handle it all.

"Here you go, ladies." Dad hands Aubree and Mom each a bottle of water and a small plastic cup half full of something that I'm sure is fruity and sweet knowing Mom.

"Aubree, these are so good. You can't even taste the alcohol." Mom holds up her plastic cup.

"I really shouldn't." Aubree tries to get out of taking the shot.

"I'm right here," I whisper in her ear. "I'll get you where you need to be safe and sound. Trust me. Just have a good time."

"I'm not much of a drinker," she tells us.

"Just one," Mom says. "I really want you to taste it."

My mother is one of those people who is really hard to say no to. She's genuine, a "what you see is what you get" kind of person, and you can tell that within seconds of meeting her.

"Just this one," Aubree concedes.

"You don't have to," I say for the table to hear.

"No, one won't hurt, but I'm not really a fan of not being in control. Of not having the assurance that I'll get home safely."

"You're safe with us," Rick chimes in.

I keep my eyes trained on her instead of turning to glare at him. It's a struggle to do so. "I've got you," I say, not caring if any of them hear me. "Have fun. I promise you I'll get you back to your room."

"Thanks, but this is plenty." She grabs the cup and taps it against Mom's.

I watch her as she tilts it back and takes a small sip. "Wow, this is really good." She smiles at my mother and tilts her cup back, finishing off the shot.

"Told you." Mom gives her a satisfied grin; she downed hers in one go. "I'm not really much of a drinker myself. Hate the taste of beer, and why anyone would drink whiskey to burn your throat is beyond me, but the fruity stuff I can handle."

"That tasted like an actual pineapple upside-down cake." Aubree laughs.

"Oh, honey, stick with me. I got the sweet and fruity covered." Mom laughs, holding up her hand for a high-five, which Aubree returns immediately.

The night flows on with good food, laughter, and talking. It's nice to unwind a little. I don't move from my seat beside Aubree. When she yawns for the third time in a row, I'm ready to drag her cute ass back to the hotel.

"You wanna go?" I ask her.

"You look exhausted," Mom tells her.

"I don't know why I'm so tired," she says over a yawn. "I think I'll head back to the hotel."

"I'll walk you." Rick stands, but so do I.

"I'll go. I want to check on the hauler anyway. You all be safe." I point to my parents. Mom is smiling wide while Dad nods, letting me know they will indeed be safe. I wave to the others, and they all return the gesture, even Rick. He's smirking, and that tells me all I need to know. He knows I'm invested and he's pushing me toward her. Good to know I don't have to punch one of my closest friends over her. I never thought I would be that guy, but with Aubree, everything is new.

As soon as we're out of the bar, I place my arm over her shoulders and pull her into me. "That was torture," I admit.

"Torture?" she asks, confused.

"Yes, Bree, torture. Sitting next to you in those shorts that are illegally short and this shirt, showing off your bra." I moan deep in my throat at the thought of peeling it off her.

"I'm sorry?" She says it like she's asking a question, making me laugh.

"You're sorry, huh?" I ask, pulling her a little closer.

"Sounded like the right thing to say."

"Well, never be sorry for being sexy as hell. You just can't help it." I kiss the top of her head.

She runs her hand underneath my T-shirt and hooks her fingers into my jeans. It's a simple act, intimate more than sexual, but the feel of her soft hands against my skin light a fire inside of me.

Back at the hotel, as soon as the elevator doors close, I push her against the wall and mold my mouth to hers. Again, her hands snake up under my T-shirt, and her nails grip my back. When the doors open, I have to force myself to pull away from her. We're both breathing heavily, and she has a beautiful smile on her face.

"We're going to get caught." She laughs as I lead her off the elevator.

"Would that be so bad?" I ask, because to me, that's not a bad thing. I want the world and every motherfucker that eyes her to know she's spoken for, even for just until whatever this is fizzles out. Yet another new discovery from me—that surprisingly I'm okay with her being mine. Not just for tonight, but for a hell of a lot longer. Even the word forever pops in my mind, and it doesn't bother me. Not when it comes to Bree.

"Yeah, Blaine, I really think it would. I like your parents, and when this is over, it would make things awkward. I have very few people in my life who I feel as though I can truly trust, and I trust them. I would hate to lose that."

What can I say to that? Nothing, so I don't even try. I simply place the key in her door, unlocking it. As soon as it shuts behind us, I push her up against the wall. "This," I say, kissing her neck, "was supposed to cool off a little once I got a taste of you." I continue nipping her neck gently and soothing it with my tongue.

"Yeah," she agrees with a breathy sigh.

"And this…" I pull back and turn us so it's my back that's against the wall. "…it's sexy as fuck, Bree." I trace my index finger from her collarbone to the bottom of the V-neck opening on her shirt. The one that shows me just a hint of cleavage that's hiding behind that black lace bra. "This shirt should be illegal, at least for you."

"Why me?" Her eyes are closed as she enjoys the feel of my finger tracing against her skin.

"Because I can't control myself around you. This sexiness only makes it worse."

"Yeah? Maybe I should take it off, you know to help you balance your control." Her voice is throaty and alluring as fuck.

Slowly she opens her eyes, and the heat I see there would bring me to my knees if I were not leaning against the wall. I watch her as she starts at the top button and unfastens it. I rest my hands on her hips, needing that connection to her, but letting her have her fun. She's teasing me, and we both know it.

As soon as the final button is free, I grip either side of her shirt and pull it away from her breasts. I keep an iron grip on her shirt, even though all I really want to do is strip her bare and show her yet again how much I want her.

"Aubree," I say huskily.

She slides one hand behind my neck and the other grips the neck of my shirt, fisting it, fighting her own battles with the inferno of desire that's blazing between us.

"Blaine," she says, leaning in close.

I pull on her shirt, needing her closer. Her earlier exhaustion seems to fade as the heat between us roars. When my phone vibrates in my pocket, she buries her head in my neck and begins to laugh.

"That might be important." She tries to pull away.

I stop her by keeping my grip firm on her shirt. "I'm not letting you go before I get a kiss."

She gives me a short peck on the lips, but that's not good enough. "Come on now, we can do better than that." Her emerald eyes tell me everything she's not. She agrees. Leaning in, I capture her lips with mine. My tongue traces her lips, prompting her to open for me. She does so without hesitation. That is until my phone vibrates again.

"You should get that," she says against my lips.

With a heavy sigh, I dig my phone out of my pocket and see two missed calls from Dad. Keeping one arm around her waist, I hit his name to call him back. Aubree rests her head on my chest at the same time he answers.

"Hey, what's up?" I ask before placing a kiss on top of her head.

"They just called the race. Wanted to see what the plan was for tomorrow. I'm on the fifth floor, which room are you in?" he asks.

"Uh, I ran downstairs to grab a bottle of water. I must have just missed you," I tell him.

"Why did you go all the way downstairs? There's a vending machine on your floor. I just passed it."

"Didn't bother to look," I tell him. The truth is, I have spent very little time in my room. Just long enough to shower and get dressed today. The rest of my time I've been with Aubree.

"Okay, well, I'll wait on you. Your mother wants to know if Aubree got to her room all right?"

"Yeah, she's in her room. Resting," I tell him. She is resting, I just leave out the fact that I just kissed her senseless and she's resting against my chest. This is my moment, just for me. "I'll be right there," I tell him before ending the call.

"Everything okay?" she asks.

"Yeah, Dad's on my floor looking for my room. They called the race so he wants to get a game plan for when we want to leave tomorrow."

"Okay." She lifts her head and steps away from me.

"Let's get you tucked in." I lead her to the bed, and help her undress, leaving her in nothing but her panties. I grab a Bishop Racing T-shirt, the one she was wearing earlier, and help her put it on.

"Night, Checkmate," she says, her eyes already closed.

"Night, Bree." I bend down and kiss her forehead before slipping out the door.

Luckily there is a vending machine on her floor as well, so I buy a bottle of water and head upstairs to my room. Dad is waiting just outside the elevators when I get there.

"Bree okay?" he asks.

"Yeah, I mean, she was when I left her."

"I'm not blind, son. I see the way you watch her. The way you refused to leave her side tonight."

Not wanting to have this conversation in the hall, I start walking toward my room. Once we're inside, I place my water bottle on the table and sit down on the bed. Resting my elbows on my knees, I bury my face in my hands. I can hear the chair move and I know from experience my father can wait me out. Finally, I look up at him. "It's nothing. We're just having fun."

He nods. "Yeah, but it's more than that, even if you don't want to admit it."

"She's fun to be around."

"She is. Your mother is already in love with her." He laughs.

"I'm glad. She's never had that."

"Blaine, I won't lecture you. You're an adult. What I will tell you is that girl has been through a life we've never imagined. Not knowing the love of her own father." He shakes his head in disgust. "If you're not in this, I mean, not *really* in this, you need to let her go."

"I can't do that, not yet."

"You're playing with fire, son."

"What happened to not lecturing me?"

"Fine, I've said my peace. Now what time do you want to leave tomorrow?"

Normally, I would want to leave early so we can get home, but I think about Aubree just one floor below all snug in her bed and waking up with her this morning. I want to do that again. I don't know when we will have this opportunity being in a hotel room, and our rooms spread out enough that no one will notice. "What time is checkout?" I ask him.

"Ten."

I nod. "Yeah, around ten works fine."

He raises his eyebrows; that was an answer he obviously was not expecting from me. "All right. Your mother and I will be ready."

"Thanks, Dad." He nods and walks out of my room. Quickly, I send a text to the guys, letting them know we're going to meet in the lobby at ten. Then I pack my bag. Making sure nothing is left behind, I head back to the fourth floor. Back to Aubree.

Reaching her room, I slide the keycard in and wince when it beeps, hoping that the sound doesn't wake her. I enter as quietly as I can and find her sound asleep. Once my bags are on the floor by the dresser, I strip down to my boxer briefs, and climb into bed beside her.

"Blaine?" she asks groggily.

I'm not going to think about what the fact that she calls out for me does to me. I'm not going to ponder why my heart seems to expand in my chest anytime she's near. "Shh, go back to sleep." She snuggles closer, and I wrap my arms around her. Having her in my arms makes me feel… content. It doesn't matter what else is going on, as long as she's right here, everything is right in my world. That's a feeling that's all too new but welcome all the same. I lie here, softly running my fingers through her hair. I'm tired as hell, but I don't want to go to sleep, not knowing when I'll have a moment like this again, if ever. This is only a temporary situation, or is it? That's my final thought before drifting off to sleep.

CHAPTER Nineteen

Aubree

IT'S BEEN FOUR WEEKS THIS week since my relationship with Blaine changed. I spent the Fourth of July weekend at his place. We hid my car behind the old barn, and as far as we know, no one has figured it out. I know they suspect, but I'm going to continue to pretend that we're living in our own little bubble. One that I know when it pops is also going to shatter my heart. The time I've spent with him, it's worth it. Any amount of heartache is worth the time we have together. What is it they say... *It's better to have lived and loved than to never have loved at all?* Something to that effect. Maria spouted if off to me the other day on the phone when I told her I was in love with him. Not just I *might* be, I'm in love with him. It's fast, I know. I've only known him for a couple of months, but we spend a lot of time together and we just... click.

We've yet to talk about how long we're going to let this go on, and I'm good with that. Ignorance is bliss. Today we're headed to Tampa, Florida. It's an eleven-and-a-half hour drive, so leaving today, Wednesday, gives us plenty of time. Blaine surprised everyone when he said he wanted to stop somewhere tonight and spend the night, finishing the drive tomorrow. Racing starts Friday at six in the evening, so pulling in Thursday night gives us ample amount of time, or so he says.

The mass text message he sent last night, the one I got when I was lying on the couch beside him says that we are leaving at eight this morning. It's a little after six, and I need to get moving, and pull my car around to the shop so no one knows I spent the night. That's something I've been doing a lot lately. So much in fact that Maria is complaining that she never sees me anymore. I can tell she's teasing, but I still feel bad. I promised her that we would have dinner next week before we head out again.

"Morning." Blaine kisses my bare shoulder. It's a wake-up that's become routine for us, and I'm already dreading the mornings when I will no longer have his lips against my skin, and his husky voice in my ear.

"Morning, we need to get moving."

"Just… a little longer." He yawns.

"Nope. I have to move my car and get my stuff packed and out to my car so it's not so obvious that I stayed," I remind him.

"Is it really that bad if they find out?" he asks.

"It has to be this way. It will be easier when you decide to end this." I focus on keeping my breathing deep and even, despite the twisting in my gut.

"When I decide?" he asks. "What makes you think it's going to be me who ends this?"

"I've known that from the very beginning, Blaine. I told you I won't be able to walk away. My heart can't separate sex from love." I shrug. "That's not who I am."

"Maybe that's not who I am either," he counters. His tone is even, not giving me any insight to how he's feeling. He ignores the fact, or maybe he just doesn't pick up on, that I basically told him I'm in love with him.

"Come on, Checkmate." I use his racing nickname. "Everyone knows including me that serious is not your thing. I knew that going into this. I'm okay with it." That's what I need to say, because that was our deal. What I want to say is we can make this work. That I love him enough for the both of us, but I can't.

"Why?" he asks, sitting up and letting the sheet pool around his waist. "Why are you okay with it, Aubree?" His voice is gruff, and I can't tell if he's pissed off or getting upset at the thought of what we have ending.

Climbing out of bed, I grab his T-shirt from the floor, and pull it on before turning to face him. My emotions are already bare to him. I need clothing as a barrier, as if it can hide my true emotions, can hide my heart. "Because that's who you are, Blaine Bishop. And I happen to be pretty damn fond of you."

"Bullshit. Tell me the real reason," he pries.

"I just told you." Kind of. I left off the part about being in love with him. He doesn't want to hear it anymore than I want to say it. Saying it makes it real. Makes the fact that my heart is surely going to be broken one day in the near future a certainty. One I'm not ready to deal with.

"Bree," he says softly.

"I'll take a shower first." I grab some clothes and rush off to the bathroom. Although, I know it's immature, I shut and lock the door behind me. I need a little distance if we're going to get moving and get me out of this house before anyone else gets here. Under the hot spray, I let the tears that have been threatening to fall have their freedom. Silently, I cry for what I know I'm about to lose. The pain in my chest is so much worse than I could ever have anticipated.

Twenty minutes later, I'm opening the bathroom door to find his room empty. Packing my bag for the trip, I hide the rest of my stuff in the closet, just in case, and head downstairs. "Blaine," I call out. Nothing, no response. Grabbing a bottle of water from the fridge, I down half of it before heading outside.

I see my car is moved, so I go ahead and walk to the toter home and toss my bag into the underbelly storage. I've started keeping my massage bag there instead of packing it back and forth each week. I've only needed it the one time, and although I'm grateful that no one has been injured, I'm wondering if KHP is going to call and pull the plug on this little adventure they sent me on. I hated the idea at first, and now, thinking about not being there when he races, it causes an ache in my chest. One I know that I will one day have to get used to.

Just as I'm shutting the underbelly storage door, Kevin and Ashley pull in. She's going with us this time, and I'm excited. She's not tagged along since my first weekend. She and I text often. I keep her in the loop of how things are going since Kevin is always busy working on the car. We even met up a few weeks ago for drinks. I met her friends, Susanne, Beth and Lisa. She was right, they're a lot of fun to be around and when they invited me to do it again sometime, I found myself saying yes. I'm even looking forward to it.

"Hey, you," she says as soon as she climbs out of their SUV. "You ready for this one?"

"You bet. Two new states. I just wish we had time to see the ocean while we're there."

"You've never seen the ocean?" she asks.

"Nope. Never traveled out of Tennessee until I took this assignment."

"I'm seeing a girls' trip in our future," she says.

"I'm in."

"In for what?" Blaine asks, joining us.

"My wife is planning a trip for your… for Aubree and her to go to the beach. A girls' trip," Kevin says. I can't help but wonder what he was going to call me. It's obvious he's also onto us. Maybe Ashley told him. I know from the looks and the hints that she's been dropping that she knows. Or at least suspects. I just ignore it, what else can I do? I don't blame her for not wanting to keep secrets from her husband.

"Girls' trip, huh?" he asks.

"Yeah. Aubs has never seen the ocean. If that's not excuse enough for a girls' trip, I don't know what is," Ashley tells him.

The rest of the crew pulls in, followed by Robin and Brian who back up to the T-shirt trailer and hook to it without even getting out of the truck. The rest of us pile in the toter home.

"I got first leg today," Blaine says, climbing into the driver's seat.

"Aubs, why don't you take shotgun?" Ashley suggests. "This is a new state for you. You should take in the sights."

I can tell that's not the only reason she suggested that I sit up front with Blaine, but I take the seat anyway.

Blaine looks over and winks. "You ready for this?"

"Let's do this!" Jacob chants, way too chipper for this early in the morning, causing us all to laugh.

Blaine is quiet and so am I as I take in the scenery. It's beautiful, and it's pretty cool to be sitting up this high on the highway. It's not something I'm used to. I snap a picture of the welcome sign when we cross over into Georgia. I'm excited to pick up a new state, but not even the excitement can hold its own with the lull of the wheels on the road as I drift off to sleep.

"Hey, beautiful." I hear his deep voice and feel his lips against my cheek. As I start to wake up, I remember where we are. My eyes pop open and I sit up quickly in my seat, looking around. "Hey," he soothes. "It's just us. We're stopping to stretch our legs and fill up. I thought you might want something."

"Thanks," I say, my heart rate slowly returning to its normal rhythm. "I am thirsty," I say, realizing how dry my mouth is.

"What do you want?" He moves to climb out of his seat.

"I'll come with you."

"Okay, but first..." He helps me up and pulls me into his arms. "It's been hours since I've kissed you," he says, softly pressing his lips to mine.

"Blaine, someone might walk in," I scold him but not

bothering to pull away.

"Let them." He gives me another quick kiss before releasing his hold on me. "After you." He holds his hand out toward the door and I can't hold back my smile.

"Thank you, kind sir," I say dramatically.

"It's purely selfish on my part. Have you seen your ass in those shorts?" he whispers next to my ear.

I'm blushing. I can feel it. And I have a feeling that as soon as I open that door, there will be someone there to witness it. So, instead of replying, I take in a deep breath and try to cool my hormones down. When I open the door, sure enough, Ashley is there, and she jumps back. "Sorry, I didn't mean to scare you."

She laughs. "No worries." She steps out of the way to let us pass.

Her smile was knowing, and it's only a matter of time before she corners me to ask what's going on. Maria knows, but it would be nice to talk about this, whatever it is that's going on with us with someone who knows him.

Rick takes the next leg of driving with Jacob as his copilot, his words not mine. Kevin and Ashley give Brian and Robin a break even though Brian insisted he was fine, which leaves Blaine and me and his parents. We're all four sitting at the table when Robin suggests we play a game of cards.

"Do you know how to play Euchre or maybe Rummy?" she asks me.

"No, but I'm sure I could learn."

"Let's go with Rummy. I can see her cards that way and help her," Blaine suggests.

So, that's what we do. We spend the next four hours playing Rummy, laughing and joking, and it's a really good time. Brian and Robin are great people, and well, Blaine is Blaine. He keeps leaning into me to look at my cards, and I can't say I'm upset about the gentle touches and the closeness. I can't help but think about the fact that if we were... more than what we are, this could be our life. Hanging out with his parents on the holidays and during the season. I push that thought to the back of my mind. Those kinds of wishes bring nothing but more heartache, and I know for certain, I'm up for a healthy dose of that soon enough. The day isn't even here, the one where he tells me he's done, yet already I'm starting to feel broken on the inside. My heart aches, and I know that I have to create some distance.

CHAPTER Twenty

BLAINE

IT'S GO TIME. THE STANDS are packed and the fans are cheering ready to see a race. The track was hooked up in the heat races, just the way I like it. Dad and the guys are checking over the car one last time, making sure we're good to go. Mom, Ash, and Bree are standing here with me while I suit up. They've been in the T-shirt trailer all day, and I've missed her. I want to haul her to me and kiss the hell out of her, but I refrain.

"You're good, man," Kevin says, walking up behind Ash and wrapping his arms around her. Dad places his arm over Mom's shoulders and my eyes immediately dart to Bree. She's watching me, a small smile tilting her lips. Rick walks up and hip checks her, and I can't prevent my glare even if I wanted to.

He smirks.

Bastard.

They know. They all fucking know, but none of them other than Dad and Kevin have hinted at it. Rick likes fucking with me, and I'll admit it's working. I've never been the jealous type, but then there has never been anyone like Aubree. She's special, something I've known from the beginning, but it's more than that. I've fallen for her. I swore I wouldn't, that racing was my top focus, but somehow over the last couple of months, she wormed her way into my heart. All this time she's been certain that this… situation of ours would end with her having a broken heart.

Not on my watch. At least I hope not.

I never want to hurt her. I know she loves me. I can see it in her eyes. I care about her, more than I've ever cared for another woman, but is it love? I'm not sure, and until I am, I'm keeping this to myself. I need to be certain that this is true, and not just the rush of all the time we've been spending together. The sneaking around.

"Good luck out there." Kevin shakes my hand while Ashley gives me a hug. Rick and Jacob follow suit with a handshake and a slap on the shoulder.

Then there's Bree. She steps forward and wraps her arms around me in a hug. "Be safe, Blaine," she whispers.

I inhale, pulling her scent, and a hint of peaches surrounds me. A smell I know is her shampoo, because I've used it a time or two when she left a bottle at my place. All too quickly she's pulling away and stepping back. I want to pull her back and kiss the hell out of her, but I don't. Instead, my eyes follow her until Mom steps into my line of vision.

Mom steps into my embrace. "Have fun, and be safe. That's what's important," she tells me. It's the same line before every race, has been since I was a kid. I squeeze her tightly before letting her go.

"Son," Dad says. Instead of the handshake I normally get, he pulls me into a hug. "Trust the push," he says, just low enough that I can hear. He pulls back and offers me his hand.

"Dad, I'm pretty sure I've got this." I laugh.

He nods. "You're a damn fine driver," he agrees. He steps in close. "But I'm not talking about the car, Blaine. I'm talking about Aubree."

I nod. No use in denying that I care about her. Apparently, I'm not hiding it as well as I thought I was. "Yeah, I'm getting there."

With a grin, he says, "Good. We'll see you after, in victory lane."

"Don't jinx me, old man," I call after him as he's already walking away.

"Never," he says with a laugh over his shoulder.

Aubree lifts her hand to wave before turning and following my parents and Ashley. I watch her go, until I can no longer see her. Shaking out of my thoughts, I get my head in the game.

"You ready for this, Checkmate?" Kevin asks. Apparently, he too can see that she's occupying my mind.

"Yeah, let's bring home a win." I climb into the car and prepare to start the race.

When the green flag drops, I hammer down and make my way to the front. The track is fast as hell and smooth as I fly around the corners. Lap after lap, I hold strong in first position. The flagman gives us the sign that we're halfway there.

Twelve laps to go.

As I slide around turn three, on the inside, I see the lap car in front of me spin out. I don't have time to adjust and nowhere to go when I slam into him. My HANS device, and five-point harness seat belt do their jobs to keep me in place, but when my car flies through the air, end over end, I still feel the impact of the fall when I finally land. My hands shake as I take a minute to gather my bearings. I'm safe, not hurt from what I can tell, just shaken the fuck up. Literally and figuratively. I've flipped before, but this time, I was end over end more times than I could count before my car finally landed. I don't move just in case something is broken or hurt, not that I could if I wanted to. My hands are trembling so bad, I can't even grip the wheel.

Emergency personnel appear at my window asking me

questions about if I'm hurt, what I feel, if my legs are trapped. I answer them to the best of my knowledge. Reaching in they, unhook my HANS device, and help me take off my helmet.

"You good?" one of them asks me.

"Yeah, just get me out," I say, my voice shaky. I'm not sure if it's the adrenaline or the fear. This is a dangerous sport, I know that. We all do. It's a risk climbing into this car week after week. It's not that a driver has a death wish, but we love the sport. I'm trembling and I admit it was scary as fuck, but it won't keep me from getting back in my car and racing.

It's in my blood.

For safety purposes, they cut the door of the car to get me out. Once I'm out, the crowd goes crazy, cheering and clapping. With an emergency worker at my side, I make my way to the ambulance to get checked out. I go through the motions, answering questions. I'm not hurt, just startled from the adrenaline of the crash. They release me with a list of things to watch for, a list I have memorized. I've been lucky during my career. I've not had many accidents like this one, but it only takes one for you to know the drill.

When I exit the ambulance, we're in the infield. My car is on the back of a wrecker as they pull it to the pits. A track official waits for me on a Gator to take me to my hauler. When I get there, Mom rushes me and hugs me tight.

"Oh, thank God," she says, fighting back tears.

"You good, son?" Dad asks, pulling Mom out of my arms.

"Yeah, just a little shaken up."

"You're going to be sore tomorrow," Kevin says. Ashley steps forward and gives me a hug, not nearly as tight as Mom's.

"We've got the car," Rick chimes in. "You go in and get a shower, or whatever," he tells me.

"We'll take care of it," Jacob adds.

"Thanks."

My eyes dart around looking for Aubree. I find her standing

off to the side, her arms crossed over her chest, and although she might not realize it, her heart on her sleeve. I can see the worry from the way she's biting on her bottom lip. I can see the fear from the wetness of her eyes. I don't care who sees me. I stalk toward her with my arms open. She stands still, not moving, watching me.

"Come here, Bree," I say when I stop just inches away from her.

"Are you okay?" she asks, her voice cracking. Her eyes roam over my body looking for injuries.

"I will be once you come here," I say again.

"What if —" I don't wait to hear what she has to say. I close the remaining distance and wrap my arms around her.

"I don't give a fuck who sees," I say, keeping my voice low and even. "I care about showing you I'm okay."

A sob breaks free from her chest as she grips the front of my fire suit and holds on, as if she were to let me go, I might disappear. "I didn't know what to do." She sniffles. "I wanted to go to you, but...."

"Hey." Pulling back, I place my index finger under her chin and lift her gaze to mine. "I'm okay. A little shaken, and I'm sure I'll be sore for a few days, but I'm good."

She steps out of my hold and wipes her eyes. Standing to her full height, she says, "I can help you, I mean, the soreness, that's why I'm here, right?" She turns and opens the underbelly of the toter home and starts pulling out her bag.

"Bree." I grab her arm to get her attention. "Let me shower and let us all calm down a little. We'll get to that."

"But I can help you." She wipes another tear from her cheek.

"I know you can, but let's take a breath, okay?"

She nods. "Yeah."

"Son." Dad places his hand on my shoulder. "We're thinking a hotel for the night. Will do you some good to soak in a tub, and we could all use a good night's sleep."

"I like that idea," I tell him.

He turns to Aubree. "You okay, sweetheart?" he asks softly.

"Yeah." She stands up taller. "Just hard to watch when it's someone you know."

He nods. "That it is. Go ahead and load up. We're packing up out here, and the T-shirt trailer is already closed down. Ashley is booking us rooms now."

"I can help," Aubree offers.

"Actually, can you stay with him? Not that we expect anything, but for a few hours, we need to keep a close eye on him. That's probably just the dad in me coming out, but I'd feel better."

"Sure." She nods and her shoulders seem to relax a little. "Let's get you settled." She moves to stand beside me and takes my arm, guiding me to the door of the toter.

"I can walk, Bree."

"I know, but I just… let me help you."

I don't need her help. The adrenaline rush is starting to come down, and I'm no longer shaking. I think she needs this more than me, so I'll give it to her. Whatever she needs to believe that I'm okay, that's what I'll do.

"I'm sorry," she says once we are inside and I'm sitting on the couch.

"What for?" I reach over and tuck a loose strand of hair behind her ear.

"The way I acted. I know this is supposed to be fun, and we agreed to not tell anyone. I just couldn't control it, Blaine. When I saw you flip—" She bites down on her lip again as her voice cracks.

"Don't ever be sorry for feeling how you feel. I don't care if they know. That's the least of my worries."

"Can I get you anything?" She offers me a small smile before turning and walking to the fridge. "You should take some ibuprofen. You're going to be sore." Reaching inside, she grabs a bottle of water and a bottle of headache medicine from the cabinet above the sink. "Here." She opens the bottle of water and hands it to me, followed by a couple of tablets.

"Thanks." I swallow the tablets and down the entire bottle of water. "Come sit with me."

"I can't," she says, leaning back against the sink. "I'm barely keeping myself together. I just need a minute to get it under control before everyone joins us."

"Aubree," I say tenderly.

"I was so scared, Blaine. I mean, I know you were in the car, and I can't imagine what you were thinking and feeling, but seeing that." Her voice cracks again and her eyes well with tears. I swallow back my own emotions remembering the crash and seeing her reaction. Her pain, her worry, it's all for me. It's real and true and another piece of the wall that's been surrounding my heart crumbles.

Before I can counter, the door opens and everyone piles in.

"To the hotel we go," Rick says, taking a seat behind the wheel. They all know that I need normalcy. For a driver after that kind of accident, I need normal. The worry and the fear leads to second-guessing. I need to be 100 percent the next time I climb into that car. My crew, my parents, they know that. My Bree, she doesn't, but to see her hurt for me, that does something to me. Instead of fear, it's longing. For her. I motion for Bree to come to me, and I'm surprised when she does. She sits next to me on the couch, pulls a pillow into her lap, and holds onto it as if it's her lifeline. She remains that way the entire drive to the hotel.

CHAPTER Twenty One

Aubree

WHEN WE STOP, I STAND, tossing the pillow onto the couch, and climb out of the toter home. As soon as I'm outside, I take in a deep breath. Mentally I have to remind myself that he's okay. He's not hurt. It was my idea to hide us from everyone, thinking it would be easier, but in all my life, I've never regretted that decision more than I do tonight. I had to make myself stand back and watch as everyone greeted him. I couldn't get too close; I was barely holding onto my composure as it was. Then when he came for me, the tears that were threatening to break free finally fell.

I'm sure my reaction is confusing to them, but I couldn't hold it in. Now here I am trying like hell to act as collected as possible, to be the professional I was trained to be. It's time for me to do the job I was assigned to do. The real reason that I'm here, with him. The reason that brought us together in the first place.

Opening up the underbelly compartment, I grab both of my bags and sling them over my shoulders.

"Let me help you with that," Jacob offers.

"No, thank you." I try to be polite and keep my voice calm. Nothing at all like the shaking emotional mess I am on the inside.

"Let's get checked in." Ashley links her arm with mine and we head inside the hotel.

I want to argue that I need to be with Blaine, that he might need my help, but he's okay. Not to mention, there are four men who are more than capable of helping him.

"Here, this is y'all's room." She hands me a key. I stare up at her in confusion. "Aubs, I see it. There are separate bedrooms in case I'm wrong, but I'm pretty sure I'm not."

"I can't stay with him. What will everyone think?" It's a halfhearted plea and we both know it. I don't even bother to ask her how she knew. I know that my actions in the last couple of hours speak volumes.

"They won't know. Blaine gave me the credit card. I booked the rooms. We're all on opposite floors. Your secret is safe with me."

I nod as the tears build behind my eyes. "I thought he was hurt or worse," I croak.

"Come here." She pulls me into a hug, and I don't hesitate to hug her back, holding on tightly, soaking up all the comfort she's willing to give. I know it should be Blaine who's being comforted, but my heart... I don't think it beat until I saw him climb out of that car. "Here they come," she says softly.

Pulling away, I wipe my eyes and stand tall. Blaine catches my attention as soon as he sees me, raising his eyebrows in silent question, asking if I'm okay. I give him a subtle nod.

"Right, so Bree has her key," Ashley says. "Here is one for everyone else. Check out is at eleven." She passes each person a key including Blaine.

"I'm in for the night," Blaine says. "I see a hot bath and room service in my future."

"Honey, you should let Aubree work on you. That might help with the soreness tomorrow," Robin suggests.

"What do you think? Will it help?" he asks me.

"Yeah, I mean, you're going to be sore regardless, but your muscles won't be as tight."

"All right. Let me get a shower, and I'll call you."

"You need help?" Kevin asks him.

"Nah, I'm good. You all go enjoy your night. Nothing a hot shower and a good night's sleep won't cure."

We all pile onto the elevator, and each of us pushes a button or calls out our floor number. Blaine and I are on the sixth, everyone else is on three and four. I don't call out a number, not wanting to lie to them more than we already have. Sounds crazy considering.

"Oh, good," Robin says when we stop on the fourth floor and I make no move to exit the elevator. "I'm glad you're on the same floor in case he needs anything." She turns to Blaine and gives him another hug, while Brian holds the elevator doors open. "You call us if you need something. You too, Aubs, we know he can be a pain in the ass." She smiles, trying to make light of the situation. I can see the worry in her eyes, but they're all putting on a brave face for him. Then again, maybe it's for me. I've done a shit job at hiding my emotions.

When the doors close, Blaine reaches out and laces his fingers through mine. Neither one of us says a word. When the doors open for the sixth floor, I lead us down the hall and to our room. "Ashley, she, uh, got us a two bedroom," I say as we enter.

"Remind me to thank her," he says, pulling me into him.

Carefully, not wanting to hurt him, I wrap my arms around his waist and bury my face in his neck. We don't speak. We just hold one another letting time pass us by. Finally, I pull away. "You should shower," I tell him.

"Yeah," he agrees.

"I'll get a few things set up out here for when you're done."

He leans in and presses his lips to my forehead. "Thanks, Bree."

Once he disappears into the bedroom, I set up the other one with my lotions, and a few massage tools I keep with me. He's going to be sore all over, both from the massage and the accident. My hope is that I can make it a little less painful, helping his muscles relax.

When he exits the bathroom, he's wearing a towel around his waist and his hair is still damp. I run my eyes over every inch of exposed skin looking for injury.

"Hey." He slides his hand underneath my hair around my neck. "I'm okay, Bree. I have a bruise on my right arm. Other than that, I'm okay," he says, reassuring me.

I nod. "I have everything set up in the other bedroom." I turn, causing him to drop his hand from my neck and head to the other bedroom. This is set up like a small apartment. I hate to think of what Ashley had to pay for it. Well, technically it's Bishop Racing that's paying so that defaults to Blaine. "Lie face down," I tell him. I go to my supply of lotions I have set up on the dresser and choose the BioFreeze. It will heat and soothe the muscles as much as the massage will. My clients seem to like it best.

Without a word, I begin to work his muscles. Starting at the middle of his back, I work my way to his waist, then back up to his shoulders. We're both quiet except for a small moan or sigh when I touch a tender spot or relieve one. I spend extra time on his shoulders and arms before I move to his legs.

"Turn over." When he does, his eyes are closed and his hands are fisted at his sides. "You okay?"

His eyes flutter open. "Do you know how hard this is for me? Literally?" My eyes immediately dart to his hard length. "Your soft hands…" He reaches out and laces his fingers through mine. "…it's torture, Bree."

"You should relax."

"Touch me."

"Blaine." My tone is a warning.

"I'm fine. I know it's scary, but I'm right here, and I want you. You are the only person who can make this better."

"I don't want to hurt you."

"You won't."

"We don't know that. You were just in a horrible accident. Your car flipped through the air. Sex is the last thing you should be thinking about."

"I'm not thinking about sex, at least I wasn't. I was thinking about you," he says, his voice low. "Then these soft hands touched every inch of me, and now I'm thinking about sex. Sex with you." He takes my hand and tries to place it over his length. "This is all you."

Pulling my hand back, I grab a towel. "Don't move," I warn him before going to the bathroom and washing my hands. The last thing he wants to deal with is having BioFreeze on his dick.

"What are you doing in there?" he calls out just as I'm walking back into the bedroom.

I hold up my hands. "Had to wash off the lotion. You don't want that… there. Trust me."

"It would have been worth it to have your hands on me." He reaches down and strokes himself, never taking his eyes off me.

"Blaine," I choke out. I fight against the onslaught of emotions the day has brought seeing him flying through the air like that. I have to remind myself that he's here and he's safe.

"Aubree," he counters, his voice husky with desire. "I'm okay," he assures me. "I need you."

My feet carry me back to the bed, and I replace his hand with mine. He places his on the back of my thigh, gripping tighter with each stroke.

"So much better when you do it."

Slowly, I stroke him root to tip over and over again. His grip on the back of my thigh grows stronger with each pass. I try not to squirm, but it's a challenge when I'm this turned on. Watching what my touch does to him… I mean, I'm sure if any female were here, he would have the same reaction, but it's not just anyone. It's me.

Removing my hand, I step back, causing him to drop his hand, and I kick off my shoes. Next, my KHP Bishop Racing polo falls to the floor, before I pop the button on my blue jean shorts and wiggle my hips, letting them fall as well. I'm standing before him in my dark-red lace bra and panties.

"Keep going," he instructs huskily.

Reaching behind my back, I unfasten my bra and slowly slide the straps down each arm before letting it fall to the floor. My eyes are locked on his, and I can see when desire pools in their hazel depths.

"Come here, Bree," he rasps.

As I step toward the bed, he reaches out and grabs ahold of the waist of my panties and tugs, causing them to rip. He lets go and they fall to the floor. I should yell at him, those were one of my favorite pair, but I can't seem to find the fight in me. Not after today. Material things are not what's important in life. Not to mention, that the act alone has my legs quivering with desire.

Life.

The people you love.

That's what's most important.

Blaine.

He's here and he's safe, so he can rip all of my panties. I'll buy more. It's moments like these with him that I'll cherish the most. Placing one knee on the bed, then the other, I straddle his lap. There is nothing between us, we're skin to skin. He runs his calloused hands up and down my bare thighs, causing goose bumps to break out across my skin.

"You cold?"

"No. It's just you," I tell him honestly. I'm too raw after today to hide my emotions. "You're hell on wheels, Blaine Bishop."

"Yeah? Does that mean you're going to drive me like you stole me?" He gives me a lopsided grin.

"Yeah, that actually sounds like exactly what I want to do."

"Your skin is so soft." His fingers caress my thighs.

Placing my hands over his, I bring them to my breasts. Tenderly, he traces his thumbs over my nipples. Every time he touches me, it's as if he sets my soul on fire. His touch causes me to squirm, which in turns has me rubbing my wetness all over his length.

"Jesus," he murmurs. I do it again, and then again, driving us both crazy with need. "Aubree." His tone is half warning, half plea.

Rising up on my knees, I fist his cock in my hand. "I'm clean," I blurt out, realizing we don't have a condom. I have some in my bag, but it's out in the other room, and to be honest, nothing, not even that could pull me away from him right now.

"Me too. You're the only person I've been with since I was last checked," he says, his grip firm on my hips. It's as if he wants to pull me down on him, yet his hold helps keep me suspended in air.

"Do you want this?" I ask him. "I can go dig through my bag —"

"I want this. I want you. Just like this. Only you." He's talking in short sentences, his hazel eyes burning with need.

"I've never... I mean, you know." Heat floods my cheeks.

"Neither have I. But I want to. With you," he says again in short sentences.

As if he can read my mind, he takes his cock in one hand and the other that's on my hip pushes down. He watches me closely, gauging my reaction to him. To us joining together as one. He's biting down on his bottom lip as he feels me bare for the first time. Once he's fully sheathed, both hands grip my waist as he closes his eyes tightly. "Fuck, Bree," he murmurs. Slowly, I begin to rock, but he stops me, holding me still. "I just… need a minute. I can't… so warm, so…." His jaw is locked tight, and his grip is firm.

I remain still until he slowly opens his eyes. They're filled with… something I can't name. Tenderness maybe? He begins to guide me as I slowly move my hips back and forth. Back and forth. He never takes his eyes off me. I can feel his gaze deep in my soul.

"Blaine." His name is more of a moan as tingles race up my spine. His hands find their way back to my breasts, and although I want to go faster, I want to chase the release that I feel building inside of me, I don't. It's not far from my mind that he was in a bad accident today, and to be honest, we probably should not be doing this; he should be taking it easy. However, I think we both need it. This connection that tells us both that he's here and he's okay.

Slowly, we make love like we never have before. Our bodies merged as one, and in sync, we chase our release. Blaine lifts his hips, and I cry out from the sensation. Resting the palms of my hands on his chest, I begin to rock faster.

"Take what you need," he says gruffly. I swirl my hips, and a murmured, "Fuck," falls from his lips. "Bree, you're going to have to stop that. I'm not coming without you."

"I-I'm close." My nails dig into his skin as my orgasm takes hold and has me screaming out his name.

"Fuck, Bree," he pants, stilling my movements as he releases inside of me.

I collapse on his chest, and he wraps his arms around me. "That was—" He stops to catch his breath.

"Incredible," I finish for him.

"Best sex of my life," he adds.

I take in a deep breath, savoring the moment, glad that he feels the same. It too was the best sex of my life. I'm both euphoric and sad at the same time. How many more moments like this will we have? Although I don't want to, I sit up and move to his side. "I'm, uh, just going to go clean up," I say, moving to climb out of bed.

"Hey." He places his hand on my arm. "You okay?"

"Yeah." I smile big, even though my heart is crying. I know I said I was good with the heartbreak that was inevitable at the end of this… agreement we have, but now, after tonight, I'm not sure I'll ever recover. Racing to the bathroom, I shut the door and take my time cleaning up, giving myself a few minutes to collect my thoughts and get my emotions in check. I made the rules; it's too late to back out on them now.

A few minutes later, I climb in bed beside him. He doesn't hesitate to pull me into his chest, keeping his arm held tightly around me. "Night, Bree," he whispers.

"Goodnight, Checkmate." The use of his nickname is a reminder to both of us, that this, the way we've spent the last few months is not what he wants and will soon come to a grinding halt. I need to make an effort to keep reminding myself of that. Maybe it will lessen the pain.

Not likely.

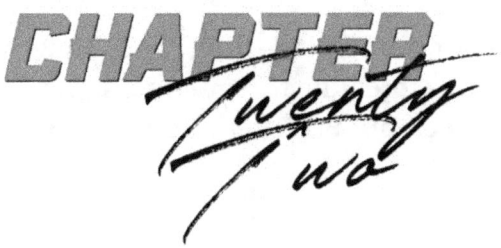

CHAPTER Twenty Two

BLAINE

I WAKE UP HUGGING MY PILLOW, and I immediately roll over and reach for Bree, only to find the bed beside me cold. Forcing my eyes open, I see where the bed is rumpled, so I know I didn't imagine last night. Fuck, even my imagination isn't that good. Last night was... life changing. I know now that it's not just lust I'm feeling. I'm in love with her. It's not something that I meant to let happen, but then again, it's not like you can plan it. Falling in love just happens, and I'm a lucky son of a bitch for it to be Aubree.

Sitting up in bed, I hear the shower running. That's unlike her to be up and going when we have the morning to lie in bed together. Glancing at the nightstand, I see it's just after nine. I've got time to join her. Climbing out of bed, my sore muscles protest, but it's not as bad as I was anticipating it would be. Thanks to Bree, I'm sure.

As soon as I push open the bathroom door, she shuts off the

water and steps out of the shower. "Damn, I was hoping to join you," I say, taking in her glistening wet naked body.

"You snooze, you lose." She grins, flipping her head over and wrapping her hair up in a towel.

"We have time, get back in," I say, reaching for her second towel.

"Nope. Your mom texted you, and they want to meet downstairs to have breakfast. I got the same message. We're meeting at ten, check out is eleven. Your dad is hoping to be on the road by then."

"What's the rush?" I ask.

"What? Mister, I Have Every Minute Planned isn't ready to get home?"

"No. What I'm ready for is to spend the morning in bed with you." I reach out and snake an arm around her waist, pulling her into me. "Morning," I say, kissing the corner of her mouth.

"I'd love that. However, I told your mom I would be there, and I'm sure if you don't reply to her message, she's going to be knocking on that door wanting to check on you. She thinks you're in this room all alone."

"Fine," I grumble. She's right. Mom is more than likely pacing the floor waiting to hear back from me. "I don't like waking up without you," I admit.

She kisses my chin. "Go, I need to get ready and get my things packed up."

"Bree."

She stops to look at me. "Blaine." She smiles. "Go. We're going to get busted."

"I don't care."

"I do, now go."

I try not to let her words sting. She doesn't know that in my eyes, our arrangement has changed. She still thinks she's headed for heartbreak when we end this. She doesn't know that I don't want this to end.

Grabbing my phone, I type out a message to Mom letting her know that I just woke up, that I'm doing fine, and I'll meet everyone downstairs at ten. Tossing my phone on the bed, I head to the bathroom to take a shower.

Aubree is already dressed and is blow-drying her hair. I stop behind her, placing my hands on her hips. She smiles at me in the mirror tilting her head to the side. I take advantage of what's in front of me and kiss her neck.

"We have twenty minutes," she reminds me.

"I can be quick." I rub my hard cock against her back.

"Nope. Not happening. I am not meeting all of them after being ravished. I've already made a show with my emotions yesterday, no way am I giving them more ammunition to figure us out."

"Is it really that big of a deal if they do?"

"Yeah, Blaine, it is. I don't want their look of pity when this — " She swallows. " — when this is over."

"Aubree, what if — " Her phone rings on the counter and she races to pick it up.

"Hey, Ash," she says in greeting. "No, I'm good. Thank you for everything. I'll see you in a few." She hangs up and meets my eyes in the mirror. "She wanted to know if we needed help with our bags. We now have fifteen minutes. I need to finish getting ready so I can pack up both of my bags."

Dismissed, now is not the right time. We're on the brink of running late, and she's right, we are meeting my friends and family, and we can't continue this conversation with them. When we get home, I'll sit her down as we need to talk about this. She has to know that my feelings for her run deep. That my outlook on us has changed. I'm not going to end this. I never want it to end.

She leaves a few minutes before me, leaving me to pace the suite on my own. Now that I've admitted it to myself, I want to scream it from the rooftops, but I can't do that. We need to talk without an audience. I've been an ass, just like she said I was all those months ago when we first met. I've made her my dirty little secret, when she's anything but. She's by far the best part of my day, and I crave the time I get to spend with her. Suddenly, I'm worried she's not going to believe me.

It's been five minutes, which is more than enough time, so I grab my bag, do one final sweep of the room, and something catches my eye under the bed. Reaching under, I find her ripped panties. The ones that I tore off her last night in my need to have her skin pressed against mine. Slipping them into my bag, I make a note to buy her a new pair.

"There he is," Mom says, walking toward me and giving me a hug. "How you feeling?"

It doesn't seem to matter how old I am, she still inquires as if I'm a minor in her care. "I'm good, Mom." I kiss her cheek. "A little sore, but Aubree's massage helped with that." I don't look at her for fear of giving us away. I've never had a massage, they're relaxing and something I'd definitely do again. However, Bree's massage was altogether different. I get the saying "happy ending," and my mind instantly wanders to all the others guys she's given a massage to. Her hands all over their bodies. My fists tighten at my sides.

"You okay, son?" Dad asks.

Forcing my hands to unwind, I give him a nod. "Yeah, fine. Let's eat." Everyone follows along behind me as I ask for a table large enough to accommodate us. Lucky for me, Aubree chooses the chair next to mine, which has the tension in my shoulders releasing.

"You in pain?" she asks me.

"No. Just a little sore. Nothing I can't handle."

She eyes me suspiciously but takes my answer as the truth and begins looking over the menu. I watch as Kevin whispers in Ashley's ear and she leans in close to him. I'm pissed off at myself for letting this charade go on as long as I have. I've known for a while that she was special, that I cared deeply for her. I should have told her then. Instead, I get to sit here and wish that I could hold her close and whisper in her ear. Yeah, we are definitely going to have a long talk when we get home.

After breakfast, we load up. I send a text to Dad and Kevin, who is driving the first leg home. I have a surprise for my girl, and they're all on board. It's just about a twenty-minute drive so I keep her occupied along with Rick and Jacob, who I also texted so they know what's going on. Aubree and Jacob are playing war when we stop.

"Stopping already?" she asks, craning her head to try and look out the window.

She's not having any luck. I closed the blind as soon as we came on board, not wanting to spoil the surprise.

"Aubs, I need to stretch my legs. Take a walk with me?" Ashley asks.

"Sure," she agrees, however hesitantly. She knows this isn't our norm, but she's rolling with it. Just something else for me to love about her. She's the farthest thing from high maintenance that I could get, and I wouldn't have her any other way. She's not afraid to get dirty at the track, never complains if I'm working on the car. She's perfect. In more ways than one.

She scoots out of the booth and meets Ashley at the door. I'm right behind her. "Care for some company?" I ask them.

Bree opens her mouth to stop me, but Ash beats her to it. "Sure, Kev, you coming?"

Kevin too joins us, and the three of us follow Ashley off the toter home. Kevin parked so that we're looking at the street. Jacob, Rick, and my parents are now with us as well.

I place my hands over her eyes. "So, we have a surprise for you." I'm sure she can hear the waves by this point.

"What's going on?" she asks, smiling.

"Just trust us," Ashley says, linking her arm through hers, while my mom takes the other.

I remain behind her with my hands over her eyes. "Slow steps," I instruct.

"Come on, guys, what's going on?"

We stop just short of the sand that would be a sure giveaway. "Open your eyes, Bree," I say, my lips close to her ear. Slowly, I remove my hands and she gasps, whipping around to face me.

"What?" She turns back to face the ocean. Then again, back to me. "You—" She turns back to the ocean. "I can't...." She takes a step forward, placing her feet on the sand. I watch as she kicks off her flip-flips and buries her toes in the sand. "It's soft." She laughs. It's a musical sound.

"Go on," Mom urges. "Go check it out."

Bree turns back to face me. "I can't believe you did this."

"It was a group effort."

The look she gives me tells me that she knows otherwise. The shimmer of tears in her beautiful green eyes sparkle from the sunlight. "Blaine." Her voice cracks.

"Hey." I step next to her and pull her into my arms. I couldn't give a fuck less who sees me. She's upset and I have to fix this. "I thought you would want to see the ocean," I say softly as she buries her face in my chest. "No way we could leave Florida without that."

"I do. I just… no one has ever done something like this for me. I mean, I've never had anyone who—" She stops.

"Now you do," Dad says firmly. "Go on and check it out." He pats her shoulder. The old man is a big softie when it comes to family, and it seems as though that includes Aubree as well.

Stepping back, I hold my hand out for her. "Come on, I'll go with you." Her smile is blinding and full of love when she takes my offered hand, and I lead us to the water. A wave comes rolling in, splashing us, causing her to laugh. I would not have believed it had I not seen it with my own eyes, but her smile grows even wider. We spend about fifteen minutes just the two of us. We're no longer holding hands, but our backs are to everyone and I don't have to hide how I feel about her. I don't have to worry about schooling my expression. Not that it matters. They're on to us. I know they are.

"Got ya!" Ashley chants as she kicks her legs through the water and splashes Bree. They take off running and splash in the water.

I watch them smiling at her laughter. We should have brought Camber this trip. She would have loved running up and down the beach. These long trips are hard on her so she goes to doggy daycare. They spoil her rotten there.

"You plan on telling her?" Dad asks, joining me. Mom is at his side.

"Yeah," I confess.

"Oh, honey," Mom gushes.

"Mom," I groan.

"What? She's wonderful. I already feel like she's a part of our family."

"Well. Hold off, all right. I don't need her scared off before I can convince her I'm a safe bet."

"Are you?" Dad asks.

"The safest," I assure him.

He places his hand on my shoulder. "Funny," he says with a grin, "what can happen when you trust the push." He chuckles.

"What on earth are you yacking about? This is not the time to talk racing." Mom shakes her head.

"You're right, dear." Dad kisses her temple and her scolding is long since forgotten.

We stay on the beach for a couple of hours before we finally need to hit the road and head home. I figured Aubree would be disappointed we have to leave, but she just smiles and gives every one of us a hug to say thank you.

"The best day," she says once we're back on the road. She and I are sitting on the couch with her head on my shoulder. Jacob and Rick are riding with my parents, giving Dad a break and them some company. Kevin insisted that he was good to drive the next leg as well. So, here we are. The two of us.

"Yeah? I'm glad. I promise I'll take you back to the ocean

when we can stay longer."

"Don't—" She places her hand over her mouth covering a yawn. "Make promises you can't keep."

Lifting my arm, I pull her in close. "I intend to keep it, Bree," I say softly. She doesn't reply, and by the way her breathing has evened out, I know she's fallen asleep. I settle back into the couch and close my eyes, and it's not long before sleep claims me as well.

CHAPTER Twenty Three

Aubree

IT WAS THE EARLY HOURS Monday morning when we finally got home. We drove all the way through from Florida. The same day, I had meetings at KHP, and by the time they were over, I was drained. It's a shame really. I've gone soft apparently. I used to pull ten- and twelve-hour days on my feet when needed and recently, I'm lucky to be up for eight and not need a nap. I guess that's what happens when you travel all the time.

Tuesday was declared a girls' day with Maria. We haven't spent much time together since I took my new assignment, and we were long overdue. Of course, I had to fill her in on everything that's been going on with me and Blaine. I've been texting her and we talk on the phone as much as we can, but it's just not the same as having her here. She thought the ocean stop was sweet and thinks that he's falling for me.

I know he cares about me. I can see it in the way he looks at me. I can feel it in the way he touches me. Something shifted between us that night he got hurt. I can't put my finger on it, and if I'm honest, I haven't really tried to decipher it. Anytime I think about it, I push it to the back of my mind. My heart hopes that it means we're more, but neither my head nor my heart are ready to deal with the pain and the loss if it's not. I've spent the last few days staying busy so I could avoid thinking about it.

I'm a coward.

Blaine wanted me to come over after Maria left, but I was emotionally drained and just wanted to go to bed. I'm not sure if he believed me, and I'm aware it sounds as though I'm making up excuses, but I'm not.

That brings us to today. It's Wednesday, and Blaine has already called twice asking when I'm going to be there. He's waiting for me at his place. He and the guys have a new body on the car, and we're ready to go for this weekend's race. It's another local track, just about an hour and ten minutes away in Tazwell, Tennessee. That means we don't leave until Friday around noon. Blaine still insists we get there early.

I miss him.

I miss him so much that my heart aches, but I know me and I'm too invested. I must start distancing myself for when the day comes that we are no longer. That doesn't stop me from coming to see him. Case in point, I'm pulling into his driveway, only it's already full. I notice Jonah's BMW and start to panic thinking that they somehow found out about us. Not only will I lose Blaine, but my job too.

"There she is," Jonah says as I climb out of my car.

"Hi." I wave awkwardly, grateful my sunglasses are hiding the scared-as-hell look I'm sure is showing in my eyes.

"Didn't know you would be here." He looks over at Blaine and grins.

"Yeah, I uh—" Camber comes rushing toward me and nudges my leg with her nose. "Hey, girl." I bend to pet her, grateful for the interruption. That's when it hits me. "Camber and I have a date," I say, looking up at my boss's boss.

"Camber, huh?" he asks suspiciously.

"Yeah. I can't have animals in my apartment, and this one and I have become close. Blaine said I could take her to the park today."

He looks over at Blaine and he nods, although reluctantly. "Yeah, the traitor seems to prefer her over me anyway," he says good-naturedly.

"It's a girl thing, huh, Camber?" I ask, snuggling in close to her neck. "What's going on?" I ask, trying to play it cool.

"Just stopped by to see my cousin." Jonah grins.

"Cousin?" I ask, confused.

"Yeah, did I forget to mention that? Blaine's mom and mine are sisters," Jonah explains.

I look to Blaine for help and he shrugs. "No, no one bothered to mention that," I say calmly when my insides feel anything but. "So, this, me being here, that's what? A favor to your cousin?"

"You could say that. It truly is marketing genius. Our visit rates are up, and we've hired two new massage therapists."

"Really? Does that mean I don't have a job when this is over?" I ask, and even I can hear the concern in my voice.

"Of course not. Your job will be there when the season is over."

"Why me?" I finally say. "I mean, I know what you told me, but this is a new development, so why me?"

Jonah laughs. "Kevin talked highly of you. He called me after and said you were great with Rick. You didn't go all fangirl over this one." He points to Blaine. "That's a rarity. You were perfect for that reason alone. Not to mention, your skill and work ethic. That was all true, Aubree."

I let his words roll around, and I'm not sure if I'm just shocked or angry. I mean, Blaine knew Jonah was my boss, his cousin, and he didn't mention it. He knew that this was way riskier than what we first thought, especially with his family and friends with us, watching us. I know they know. I just pretend otherwise. I need some time. "Ready, girl?" I ask Camber.

"You're leaving?" Blaine blurts.

"Yeah. I'll have her back in a couple of hours."

"No need to rush off," Jonah tells me.

"That was the plan, taking this pretty girl," I pet Camber on the head, "for a walk. See you." I call for Camber and turn to my car.

"You need her leash," Blaine calls out.

"We'll be fine. She minds well." With that, I open my door and point. Camber doesn't hesitate to jump in and settle into the passenger seat. I can feel his stare, but I don't look at him. Instead, I drive away, never looking back. As soon as I'm out of the driveway, my phone is vibrating in the cupholder. Camber looks at it as if it's disturbing her trip. "I know, girl," I say, reaching over to pet her. "He's mad that we left, but what else was I supposed to do?" I ignore the constant reminder of my vibrating cell phone the entire ten-minute drive to the park. It's more of a school playground, but it's abandoned, and I know that as soon as he gets the chance, he'll come after me. He won't think to look here. I just need some time. Time to grieve, time to sort out my feelings. His cousin, my boss, is now involved and that takes this... secret to a whole other level. Is my job in jeopardy? How will I work with Jonah once this is all over? Will he pity me? Too many scenarios are bouncing around in my head. I just need some time to sort them all out.

Once we're parked, I grab my phone and keys and climb out, Camber hot on my heels. I spread the blanket I got from the trunk out under the large oak tree at the back of the playground. Camber curls up beside me and sighs as if she's been waiting for a day like this forever. Reaching for my phone, I see several messages, all from Blaine.

Blaine: You didn't have to leave.

Blaine: Come back.

Blaine: Are you mad?

Blaine: I should have told you.

Blaine: Bree...

And the last one, sent just two minutes ago.

Blaine: I'm sorry.

My fingers hesitate over the keys, but instead of texting him back, I close out of the screen and pull up my contacts, hitting Maria's name.

"Hey, you, I thought you had plans today."

"Well, I did, but they changed. I'm at the old elementary school underneath the old oak tree in the back." Camber barks, causing me to chuckle. "Correction, Camber and I are under the old oak tree."

"Camber?"

"Blaine's dog."

"Are you dog sitting or something?" she asks, confused.

"Not really. I kind of dognapped her, except Blaine was standing there, so it's more like I borrowed her for a couple of hours."

"Are you feeling all right?" she asks with a chuckle.

"Yeah." I go on to tell her about Jonah being there and the fact that he's Blaine's cousin.

"Wow."

"Yeah, wow."

"So, what are you thinking?"

"I have no clue. I don't know why he wouldn't tell me. I mean, we've been together for months as more, you know, and his family and friends, they all know, Maria. I know they do. I mean, I know Ashley knows, but they all must know. We're not that good at keeping it hidden."

"I know you're not. You wear your heart on your sleeve."

"Yeah, so they know and what if they tell Jonah, or maybe they already did, and he was there today to see for himself? I could lose my job. I could lose everything I've worked for."

"Did you get that vibe from him?"

"What?"

"From Jonah, did you get the 'I know you're sleeping with my cousin so I'm here to fire your ass' vibe from him?"

"No."

"Then maybe you're thinking too much about this."

"He should have told me," I counter with a huff.

"Yeah, he should have, but really he's not paying you, so it's not like you're sleeping with your boss."

"No, but Jonah, his cousin is paying me to sleep with him."

"Really, Aubs. That's a little dramatic. He's paying you to do a job, which you are doing perfectly. He even told you visits were up and that his marketing plan was working."

"Yeah, but he doesn't know that I'm sleeping with Blaine either. At least I don't think he knows, not yet anyway. It's only a matter of time before he finds out."

"You don't know that."

"You're right, I don't, but, Maria, this was only supposed to be temporary."

"Yeah, but plans change, Aubs."

"They can. They can also stay the same." The plan has always been to let this fling play out, and when my time was up, we would be done. That's still the plan. Blaine knows it, and so do I. What wasn't part of the plan is falling in love with him.

"Aubrey," Maria says softly, and I know it's coming. "You can't plan falling in love. The heart doesn't work that way."

"I know." I sniff, losing my battle as tears well up in my eyes. Camber rests her head on my lap, offering me comfort. I'll miss her too. "I didn't mean to, and yet I let it happen knowing I was going to be heartbroken in the end."

"Talk to him, see what he has to say."

"This was always going to end," I say again.

"I know you're scared of being hurt even more, but this could all turn out to be your happily ever after."

"My life is not a romance novel," I huff.

"It could be. Your life is what you make it, Aubs. You know that. You are a product of that. You had a shitty childhood. You grew up, worked hard, and now you have made a nice life for yourself. *You* did that. You chose to be where you are today. You could have very easily taken a different path."

"Right," I agree half-heartedly.

"Just take some time to gather your thoughts. Talk to him, listen to what he has to say."

"Yeah," I agree, but not really committing.

"You're already shutting down. I hate this for you, Aubree. These past few months you've been vibrant and happy. He brings that into your life. Don't be so quick to throw it away."

"I'm not throwing anything away, Maria. This has been and still is the plan. To part ways. I just need to… distance myself a little more. It will be easier in the long run." I was already on that line of thinking, and this just solidifies that I was right.

"Stubborn," she murmurs. "I'll be here for you no matter what, but please just think about this, and talk to him before you make any major decisions."

"I should go," I tell her. "Camber and I need to go get some water. It's hot as hell out here."

"All right. Be safe. Call me and let me know how you're doing."

We end the call and I lie back on the blanket. Camber moves to rest her head on my belly as I run my fingers over her soft fur. I always wanted a dog growing up but was never allowed. One day, I hope to have one just like Camber. My heart cracks at the thought of everything I'm going to lose. I've built relationships not just with Blaine and his dog, but his friends and family. I'm going to miss them all. There's going to be a huge void in my life, and I have a feeling I'm never going to be able to fill it. Not this time.

I wake to the sound of laughter. Opening my eyes, it takes me a minute to realize where I am. Camber slumbers at my side as the sun begins to set. Reaching for my phone, I see eighteen missed calls and several text messages from Blaine.

> **Blaine:**   He's gone.
>
> **Blaine:**   Please come back.
>
> **Blaine:**   We can talk about this.
>
> **Blaine:**   I'm sorry.

That was about three hours ago, the messages start to grow with concern as I read on.

> **Blaine:**   You've been gone for a long time. Please come back.
>
> **Blaine:**   Bree, please don't be mad.
>
> **Blaine:**   At least let me know you're okay.
>
> **Blaine:**   Aubree, where in the hell are you?
>
> **Blaine:**   Please, call me.
>
> **Blaine:**   Please.

It was never my intention to stay away this long, and I didn't mean to worry him. Hitting his contact, the phone barely rings before he's answering.

"Bree?"

"Hey, sorry. I fell asleep."

"Where are you? I'll come and get you."

"I'm fine. Camber and I took a nap under the old oak tree at the elementary school."

"I've been worried sick. I have the guys driving around looking for you."

"I parked my car behind the building. The tree is in the very back of the lot."

"Stay put. I'm on my way."

"Blaine. Stop. I'm fine. We're fine. I'm leaving now. I'm going to grab us a drink and then I'll drop Camber off safe and sound."

"It's not just my fucking dog I'm worried about, Aubree. You were missing," he says, raising his voice.

"I hardly call a few hours of missed messages and calls missing." I fight the lump in my throat. He was worried because he's a good guy. I wish it was more, but he warned me. He doesn't do serious. I knew the rules.

"What was I supposed to think? You left mad and upset and then I can't find you. You're not where you say you're going to be and hours pass with no word from you."

"I said I was sorry. I'll be there in fifteen minutes." I don't wait for a reply, ending the call. "We better go, girl. He's not happy." We load up in the car, and I drive us through the drive-thru and get a small cup and two bottles of water. Camber and I both finish ours off before I pull back out on the road and head toward Blaine's.

When I pull into his driveway, Camber is wiggling in the seat, happy to be home. Before I even have the car in park, Blaine is pulling open the door. I take my time shutting off the engine and unbuckling my seat belt. As soon as I do, he's offering me his hand and helping me out of the car. When my feet hit the ground, he engulfs me in a hug. It's so tight I can hardly breathe.

"Ease up there, man," I hear Kevin tell him.

He relaxes his hold but doesn't release me. "Don't." His voice wobbles. "Please don't ever do that again."

"It wasn't intentional," I pant, still trying to catch my breath from his crushing hug. You would think that I'd been gone for days the way he's acting.

"Give the girl some room." This from Ashley. I feel her hand on my arm as she tugs me out of his embrace. He doesn't look happy about it, but that doesn't stop her.

"Camber's fine," I say, pointing to the dog that's bouncing around her owner's feet, waiting for some attention.

Absently, he reaches down and pats her on the head, never taking his eyes off me.

"You had us all worried," Ashley says softly.

"Just went for a drive. We fell asleep under the old oak tree at the elementary school."

"We drove past there, didn't see your car," Kevin says.

"Yeah, I parked in the back. The tree is at the very back of the lot."

"Yeah," Blaine says, placing his phone next to his ear. "She's here," he tells whoever it is he's talking to. "Okay. Thanks for your help. No, we're good," he tells them before hanging up. "Mom and Dad say hello and they're glad you're safe," he tells me. I feel terrible that I had them all worried. I've never had this many people in my life who cared. My breath bottles up in my chest as I realize these people matter. Not just Blaine, but all of them matter to me, and me to them. For the first time in my life, I have people.

"Rick and Jacob went on home. I called them and told them you'd talked to her," Kevin tells Blaine, pointing at me.

"Thanks, man."

"Well, crisis averted," Ash smiles. "We're going to get out of your hair." She hugs me again.

"This is not that big of a deal," I tell her. "Just a couple of hours of sleep under a tree."

"Maybe not to you," she whispers just for me, tilting her head toward Blaine.

He doesn't take his eyes off me or even bother saying goodbye to his friends. He just stands there, his hands at his sides, and an unreadable expression on his face.

"I'm sorry I took her and stayed gone so long."

"Bree," he murmurs, stepping closer. He doesn't stop until he's close enough to cup my face in the palm of his hands. "I was worried about my dog, don't get me wrong, but you—" He shakes his head. "Just the thought of something happening to you."

"I was fine."

"I didn't know that. I knew that you were upset when you left and not responding to any of my messages. I knew that you were not where you said you would be. I knew that I hurt you, and I was afraid I would never get the chance to say I'm sorry."

"Why didn't you tell me?" I croak, already feeling my throat clogging from his heartfelt speech.

"Honestly, I don't know. I started to, but then this... attraction that I have for you won out. We said this was casual, and I didn't want you to worry about your job. You were worried enough as it was. I'm a selfish bastard that wanted you. So, I kept it to myself."

"I could get fired," I say, taking a step back, causing his hands to fall to his sides.

"You won't. Jonah's not like that."

"He's my boss, Blaine. My boss! He's your cousin, and you failed to mention this to me. What if they told him, huh?"

"Who?"

"Your family, your friends, that's who." He opens his mouth to protest and I cut him off. "Don't pretend like they don't see it. Not after the way I acted when you wrecked. They know, and they're just being nice and not saying anything."

"I never wanted to hide it in the first place."

"I told you, I came from nothing. No family support. Nothing." I emphasize the word. "I've busted my ass to get where I am. I love that job, Blaine. That's all I have. My job, and you risked that. You risked me losing the one thing in life I have to call my own."

"Bree—" He reaches out for me. "I'm sorry. I know I was wrong, I should have told you."

"I think we need to slow this down a little." The words are

out of my mouth before I even realize I'm saying them.

"What? Why would we do that? What we have, it's good, right?"

"Yeah." I smile softly. It is good. Being with him makes me feel alive and vibrant. Like I'm the twenty-three-year-old I am.

"Come in, let's get you some food, and we can talk some more."

"I'm really tired."

"You just slept," he says with a little bite in his tone.

"And I'm still tired."

"Okay," he concedes. "We can go to bed, just don't leave. Not yet."

"Blaine."

"Please, Bree. Just let me hold you, okay? Let me feel you next to me and know you're okay. I was scared as hell something had happened to you. I know I fucked up, I do, and I'm sorrier than you will ever know, but can you give me this? Please, just let me hold you."

I'm weak. I know I need to put distance between us. I know he should have told me about Jonah, but at the end of all of that, there is still me, just the girl who is madly in love with him. The thought of lying in his arms is something I know I'm not going to have much more of. So, instead of going home like I know I should, I nod and let him lead me into the house. Camber at our heels.

He guides me to his room, and strips me out of my clothes. When he pulls one of his T-shirts over my head, I'm grateful. I really just want him to hold me. Hold me so I can pretend that everything is fine, that we're fine, and that he's mine to keep. Hold me so that I can pretend, just a little while longer.

Pulling the covers back, he climbs into his bed, and holds them open for me. I slide in beside him and he wastes no time wrapping me up in his arms. The room is silent and I hear Camber sigh as she settles in on her bed on the floor.

"I was so worried," he says, his voice a quiet whisper into the dark room.

"I'm okay."

His reply is to tighten his hold on me. It doesn't take long before the warmth and security of being in his arms pulls me to sleep.

CHAPTER Twenty four

BLAINE

IT'S FRIDAY MORNING AND I woke up alone, much to my disappointment. I've gotten used to waking up to her red hair covering my pillow and the feel of her pressed up against me. Not today. Yesterday at breakfast she was quiet, and I know she's still upset with me. She claimed to have loads of laundry and emails from work to catch up on. I tried to get her to bring it here, even offered to come to her place, but she refused. In the end, after we cleaned up the kitchen, she left, and I haven't seen her since. I did talk to her last night before bed. She sounded tired, and I can't help but feel guilty. I know she's worried about us; she has no idea that I never intend to let her go. At least not without a fight. When she disappeared for those few hours, I was in full-on panic mode. If anything ever happened to her— No, I can't even think about it.

She thought I was upset that she had Camber that long. I wanted to scream at her and tell her how much I love her. That even though this started out as fun, it's way more than that. She's way more than that. She's the beat of my heart, and I know without a doubt, she's all I want. The words were on the tip of my tongue. I held back. I don't want to tell her while we're fighting. I don't want to tell her when either of us are upset. I know Aubree, and she would assume it's the heat of the moment. So, telling her during sex is not really an option either. No, my girl needs a spur-of-the-moment, casual I love you. Nothing elaborate. No fan fair, just the two of us doing something mundane. That's why I haven't told her. The time hasn't been right, and I want it to be perfect. One, because she deserves nothing less, and two, it must be right for her to believe me. I warned her I wasn't capable of love, that I didn't do long-term. Now, I've changed the rules, so it has to be the right moment when I tell her that I'm madly in love with her.

I have a feeling I'm going to need to convince her, once I do tell her. I'm okay with that. I'm okay with showing her she's everything. Somehow, she's managed to do what no other has done before her. I'd say she's a miracle worker, but it's just her.

Just Aubree.

The love of my life.

Climbing out of bed, my gaze lands on Camber, who lifts her head and lazily climbs to her feet, stretching. I grab a quick shower, and head out to the shop. Everyone should be here any minute, including Bree. It's been almost twenty-four hours since I laid my eyes on her, since my lips have been pressed to hers, and it's about to drive me insane with want. With need. She's my addiction, one that I never want to cure.

She's usually the first one here, but today it's Rick, followed by Jacob, Kevin, and Ashley. Still no Aubree. I look at my watch and will myself to keep cool. She's not late technically. Right at eleven, she pulls in behind my parents. It's as if she planned it so I can't ravish her. She's distancing herself from me, and I hate it. If I didn't know she would hate it, I would stalk to her car, pull her out, and kiss the living hell out of her. I don't give a damn who sees me. Then, I would tell her that I love her. That she is the keeper of my heart, one I never thought I would have. However, I won't. She's private, and I love that about her. I love that she's not like anyone I've ever met.

"You all loaded up?" Dad asks.

"Yeah, Aubree, you have anything you need to load?" I ask.

"Nope, all my work stuff is still on board, and we'll be home tonight so I don't need a bag." Her cheeks flush, and I want to press my lips against them to feel their heat.

"Okay then, let's head out."

"We stopping for lunch?" Mom asks.

"Yeah, we can do that. You all lead the way." I climb on board and take my seat behind the wheel.

"You sitting up front?" Rick asks her.

"You can if you want. Ash and I need to catch up."

Damn it. I want to scream and yell and stomp my foot like a toddler, but I know better. I know she would hate that, and it wouldn't solve anything. It would piss her off and put me further in the dog house. Further away from her. I hate it, but at least it's only a little over an hour's drive. I can do that without her by my side. I don't want to, but I will. I always want her as close as possible. A change for me, which I'm embracing all because it's her.

At the restaurant, Bree, Mom, and Ash sit at their own booth, leaving me, Dad, and the guys alone at a table. It was Mom's idea claiming she needed girl time and didn't want to talk racing. It's as if the universe has it out for me. To make things worse, Ash and Bree end up riding the rest of the way to the track with my parents. Something about a new book they're all reading or something. I want to feel bad for my dad, but I know him too well. He's all too happy to listen to Mom rave about her latest book. Of course, he is; she's there beside him.

I get it.

Now I finally get it.

I want that.

With Aubree.

As soon as we get to the track, the three of them rush off to set up the T-shirt trailer and again, I miss her. She's here, but I can feel this disconnect between us. It's been there since my accident, and I don't know what to do to bring her back. Telling her how I feel now will just make her think I'm playing games to get her attention. That couldn't be further from the truth.

Pushing through, I go over the car with the guys and my father. We check the lug nuts, make sure the tank is topped off, check the air in the tires, and Dad makes sure that I have fresh tear-offs on my helmet. We're race ready. I just need to see her before I go out on that track. There is this nagging feeling in my gut, and I need her here. It's as simple as that. The sport I love no longer holds the shine that it used to, not when placed next to Aubree.

"You ready?" Mom asks from behind me. My eyes meet hers before looking over her shoulder to see Ashley and behind her is Bree. My Bree, with Camber at her side.

"Yeah," I say, exhaling a breath. She's here.

"Bring it in." Mom laughs, pulling me into a hug. I can't help but smile at her. We go through our pre-race routine, she steps out of the way and Dad steps in with a handshake. The guys do the same before Ash steps forward. She hugs me and wishes me luck. Then there she is. She's in her issue KHP Bishop Racing polo, cut-off jean shorts, tennis shoes, and her hair is pulled back into a hat that reads *Race hair don't care.* She's perfect.

"Hey." She steps a little closer, but not close enough.

"Hey." I reach out and brush my thumb over her cheek. I don't care who sees. "You and me, we need to talk, tonight after the race." I can see her face change, and she thinks she knows what's coming. She has no clue. I step toward her. We're toe to toe. "It's a good talk, Bree. I feel you pulling away from me, and I… let's just say I don't want that. Not at all." I'm being vague, but fuck, we have an audience, and I have to climb into this race car and win this race. I need my head in the game.

"Okay," she replies softly.

"Look at me, Bree."

Her gorgeous green eyes capture mine. "It's all good, I promise you that. You're not getting rid of me that easy." I keep it light because I need to be in the right headspace in about twenty seconds. I need to know she's going to be ready to talk when I pull off that track. Regardless of why she thinks I'm telling her, I can't go another day without her knowing how much she means to me. Without telling her that I love her, more than anything.

"Be safe, Blaine."

"Always." I lean in and kiss her on the forehead. When I pull away, she's wearing a confused look, but the corner of her mouth slowly tilts, giving me a small smile. That's what I needed to see. Now, I can do my job, then take care of my girl.

Climbing into the car, I give her one last glance before pushing everything out of my mind except winning this race. At least that's the plan. I'm not, however, successful. As I'm taking the track, all I can think about is getting back to her. To telling her I love her. I'm ready for whatever she wants. House, kids, more dogs, whatever she wants.

I'm all in.

CHAPTER Twenty Five

Aubree

I STAND HERE UNTIL BLAINE pulls out on the track, and I can't help but wonder what he wants to talk about. Dread washes over me. Is he done? Was my little stunt not returning his calls too much for him, the worry and he's ready to cut me loose? My mind wanders with how this conversation is going to go. Will I be able to hold myself together? My gut tightens and that's when it hits me. I break out in a sweat, and my hands start to shake.

Fear.

What else could it be? This is the first time I've seen him race since the accident and honestly, the way my heart is racing and the way I feel right now, I can't do it. I can't watch him maybe wreck again. It's too soon, and I feel… not good. My head starts to pound and suddenly, I need to get out of here.

"I don't feel well," I tell Robin. "I think I'm going to go back to the hauler and lie down."

"Oh, you do look flushed." She reaches out and places the back of her hand against my forehead. "You're sweating. You want me to come with you?" She's looking at me with motherly concern, something I've never had in my life. My heart twinges even more for what I've lost and what I will lose in her when this ends.

"No, I think it's just nerves." I grimace and place my fingertips to my temples. This headache came out of nowhere. "I just need to drink some water and lie down."

"Okay, if you're sure." She still does not look convinced that I should be going anywhere on my own.

"I'm sure, it's not that far. I'll be fine," I assure her. Camber nudges my hand with her nose. "You can come too, girl," I tell her.

"You sure you're okay?" Robin asks.

"Yeah, just need to get past it." With a wave, I lead Camber back to the hauler. I can't watch him. By the way I'm feeling, I don't know if I'll ever be able to watch him again. I guess it's a good thing this is just a fling.

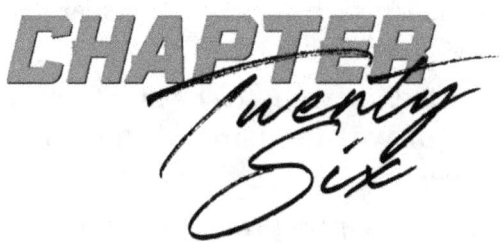

CHAPTER Twenty Six

BLAINE

ONLY THREE LAPS IN OF twenty-five and I feel cagey. Like something isn't right. I can't pinpoint what it is. The car is driving great, all the gauges are showing good, but something feels... off. Lap after lap passes by. I'm leading the race, and that's good, that's what I want, but I can't seem to shake this feeling. It must be Bree and everything I've left unsaid. As soon as I win this race, I'm telling her. What if there is another accident, and I don't get the chance? I grip the wheel tighter. That's not something I need to be thinking about right now, but damn, the thought guts me. No more waiting. I have to tell her.

When I take the checkered flag as the winner I don't celebrate; instead, I make my way to victory row, where I know she'll be. Instead of taking my time climbing out of my car, I rush to pull off my helmet and Kevin is there to greet me.

"Hell yeah!" he cheers, pulling me into a hug and smacking me on the back. Rick, Jacob, and Dad follow suit, then there's

Mom.

"You did good." She grins up at me before giving me a hug.

Looking over her shoulder, I try to see Bree, but it's just Ash. She steps forward. 'Good race, Checkmate." She smiles.

"Thanks." I drop my arm that is around Mom's shoulders and pull Ash into a quick hug, my eyes searching for Aubree. "Where's Aubree?" I ask them.

"Oh, she wasn't feeling well, so she and Camber went back to the hauler. I think it was too hard for her to watch you, you know after last weekend," Mom says.

I try not to let the disappointment wash over me. I want her here, with me. This is a big moment—another win for me and my team—and I want to share it with her. It just doesn't feel the same without her here. The win doesn't seem to have the same luster as it used to. Not without Aubree. If I didn't already know, I would for sure in this moment. I love her. I can't wait to finish this dog and pony show, the interviews, the pictures, all of it so I can go to her.

"Checkmate, congrats on another win. You've had a great season thus far. What do you think your chances are at winning your third championship in a row?"

Is this guy serious? I'm antsy as hell. I need to go to her. I feel… off somehow. I need to wrap my arms around her and tell her. "I have a good team," I say, shaking out of my thoughts. "They work hard, alongside myself and my sponsors. We're having a good year and looking forward to what's to come." I can tell by the expression on his face that's not the answer he was looking for. This interviewer likes to stir shit up. That's not happening, not with me. He goes on to talk about the race, and how the car performed. By the time I finish my sponsor spiel, I'm over it. Hell, I was over it before it started. As soon as he walks away, Jacob hops in the car and takes it back to the hauler, the rest of us walk along behind him. Fellow drivers, those who aren't jealous, call out congratulations, and I'm stopped by a few fans for autographs. That's all fine, but I really have somewhere to be.

As we grow closer to the hauler, I can hear the faint sound of barking. I'm not the only one to bring my dog to the track, but with each step we take, the barking is louder and my anxiety peaks.

Something's wrong.

I take off in a run to the hauler and throw open the door. "Bree!" I call out, racing to the bedroom to look for her. The bed is empty, the bunks are empty, she's not here. Still the barking.

"Blaine!" I hear Kevin scream my name.

Rushing back outside, I walk toward the barking, and as soon as I turn the corner, that's when I see her. Aubree is lying on the ground, between the hauler and the trailer. Jumping over the hitch, I drop to my knees.

"Don't," Mom warns. I didn't even realize she was there. I feel her place her hand on my shoulder. "Don't move her. We called the ambulance. We don't want to injure her. We don't know what happened," she says through choked tears.

Lying down on the ground, I brush her beautiful red hair out of her yes. "Bree, baby, open your eyes for me. Come on, beautiful, let me see them," I say, my lips next to her ear. Nothing happens. No reply, not even a flinch or a flutter of her eyes. "Baby, please," I beg her. Reaching out, I lace her fingers with mine, careful not to jostle her arm. "Bree, it's me, open your eyes, baby." Still nothing. I feel hands on my shoulders trying to pull me away from her, but I'm not budging. "No!" I shout. "Bree, please," I plead with her, having no idea if she can hear me.

"Sir," a deep voice says from behind me. "You have to move so we can take care of her."

"Come on, son." Dad pulls on my arm to get me to move out of the way.

I don't stand; instead, I move over a few feet, where I'm not crouching on my knees, her head in front of me. I watch them as they check her vitals. "Bree." My voice cracks with emotion I don't bother to hide. Not for her. Never again. "Please, God," I pray. "Please let her be okay."

I can hear the paramedics asking questions, but I can't answer them. I can't do anything but sit here and watch helplessly while I plead with God and anyone who's willing to listen to not take her from me. Not Aubree. I just found her and she doesn't even know that I love her.

I scramble to my feet when they load her onto the stretcher. She's lying there so lifeless. Reaching out, I take her hand again, holding it in mine. "Bree, please," I beg. I just need her to open her eyes. To show me she's going to be okay.

"Sir, we need to go."

"I'm going with you."

"Are you family?" he asks.

"Yes." It's not a lie. My heart belongs to her. That makes us more than family. That makes her my life.

"You can ride with us, but you need to let us do our jobs," he tells me.

"Where are you taking her?" Dad asks.

"General is the closest. The physicians there will assess and go from there."

"We're right behind you, Blaine," Dad assures me.

I don't acknowledge him, I can't. I keep my eyes trained on her as I walk with the EMTs to the back of the ambulance with her hand in mine.

"Sir, you have to let us load her," one of them says.

Reluctantly, I release her hand and allow them to load her in the back of the ambulance. As soon as they're settled, they give me the okay to climb on board. I'm pushed onto a metal box near her head and told not to move.

I don't.

I sit here, my eyes locked on her. In my mind, I'm begging her to come back to me. The trip is a blur, but when we stop moving and the back doors open, I know this could be it. She's still unresponsive, but I have to have faith she can hear me. Bending next to her ear, I whisper, "I love you, Aubree. Please come back to me, baby." The words are barely out of my mouth before they are lifting her out of the ambulance and rushing her through the emergency room doors.

"Come on, son." I hear my dad say.

My feet move on their own accord as we enter through the automatic double doors. The smell of hospital hits me instantly. It's unmistakably disinfectant that takes over your senses. It's a smell that coincides with loss and pain. Neither of which are comforting. Dad tries to lead me to the waiting room, but I turn to the receptionist's desk.

"Aubree Chase," I croak out her name. "Can I see her?"

She types on her keyboard. "Are you family?"

"Damnit!" I yell. "I have to go back there." I start for the door, but I feel strong arms grab ahold of each of mine.

"Calm down, man, you're not doing her a bit of good if you get your ass thrown out of here," Kevin says.

"I have to see her," I say with less fight but no less desperation.

"Ma'am, we're her family. Can you please let us know when we can see her?"

We don't stick around for her reply. Kevin guides me to a small corner of the waiting room where Mom, Ashley, Dad, and Jacob are waiting.

"You good?" Rick asks before releasing my arm and taking a seat.

"Sit down," Kevin says sternly.

"Fuck you," I say with zero heat.

"Blaine!" my mother scolds. I'm twenty-five years old and still getting scolded by my mother. Perfect.

I take a seat on the edge of the chair and rest my elbows on my knees. "What happened? Why was she there?"

"S-she said she wasn't feeling well. She was sweating and

blamed it on nerves. You two have been... quiet and I didn't want to make her feel uncomfortable. She seemed okay, just a little uneasy when she left. She took Camber with her," Mom explains.

"Camber, where is she?" I ask as an afterthought.

"She's in the hauler. The door is locked and the air is running. She'll be fine," Jacob tells me.

My mind races with what could have happened. There were no signs of injury. Did someone attack her? Was she really not feeling well or was it nerves? I can't get the image of her lifeless body lying in the dirt out of my head. "She has to be okay," I whisper, burying my face in my hands. That's when I feel the wetness in my eyes and on my cheeks.

I'm crying.

I don't remember the last time I shed a tear. Elementary school maybe when I fell off the monkey bars in first grade? I keep my face buried in my hands, not so much to hide my tears, but to give them the freedom to fall. *Please, God, if you're listening, let her be okay. Please bring her back to me.* I send up a silent plea.

"I love her," I say to whoever wants to listen. My voice is thick and grainy filled with emotion. "I love her and I've never told her, not until tonight. Right before they wheeled her in here, I told her, but who knows if she heard me. Fuck!" I scream. Lifting my head, I see my closest family and friends staring at me with sorrow in their eyes. Mom and Ash are wiping their tears, while the guys look on the brink of shedding their own. I don't bother to wipe mine away. "I'm an idiot," I add.

"Blaine," Ashley whispers. "She loves you too. She might not have told you, but we all see it."

I nod. I'm pretty sure I've known that for a while and just refused to see it. Refused to accept it and trust it. Trust in her. "Yeah," I agree. "Doesn't make it any easier though, you know? I've had all this time with her and never told her. Hell, on the track tonight, I had finally decided I was going to. I was going to tell her how I feel and that I want her. Forever."

"Son." Dad's voice is strained.

"I didn't do it, Dad. You told me to trust the push, to let her break down my walls and trust in that, in her, and I didn't do it. I fought it, told myself it was just for the season." I pause, taking a deep breath. "She deserves better."

"Oh, Blaine, don't you see?" Mom asks.

"You did trust it, trust her," Dad clarifies.

"Never seen you like you are when you're with her," Kevin adds.

"She brought down your walls, one brick at a time. We all watched it crumble to the ground." Ashley smiles. "You did the same for her." She glances around the room. "I got to know her pretty well and she's had a rough life. Never had much in the way of love and support, and she flourished with you. From the first day I met her until now, she's more confident and she smiles all the time. You did that, Blaine. You make her happy."

"You all knew?" I ask them.

"Yeah," they all say at the same time, causing each of them to chuckle.

"It's hard to miss the sparks flying between the two of you." Rick laughs.

"I should have told her."

"You'll get your chance. You just have to have faith."

"Aubree Chase, the family of Aubree Chase," a nurse calls out.

I jump to my feet, and in just a couple of long strides, I'm standing before her. "Can I see her?"

"Not yet. Are you family?"

"Yes."

She nods. "The doctor would like to speak with you." She looks over my shoulder. "Who are all of these people?"

"We're her family."

"Well—" She pauses. "Come on back. I'll put you in a conference room." We follow her down the long, cold, sterile hallway. There don't appear to be any patient rooms on this end of the building; trust me, I've looked at every door as we pass. "You can have a seat in here. I'll let the doctor know you're ready."

All seven of us pile into the tiny room and take a seat around the small conference table. No one says a word as we wait for the doctor. My hands are clasped tight together resting on the table and my leg is bouncing up and down.

"All of you are family?" the doctor asks when he walks into the room.

"Yes," is a chorus from each of us around the table.

"How is she?" I ask before he can say anything else.

"I'm Dr. Connor, I've been working on Aubree since she was brought in. She's stable," he finally says.

"Is she awake? Can I see her?" I ask in a rush.

"She's still unconscious. It appears as though her blood sugar dropped too low. Has she been taking her medication?"

"What? Medication?" I look across to the table to Mom and Ashley, and they are wearing the same confused expression. "She's not on any medication."

He nods. "Well then, it appears as though Aubree is a diabetic. Without her medical records, or her herself giving us her history, from what you've told me, I'm inclined to treat this as a new diagnosis."

"Diabetic?" I think back to the last couple of months and nothing stands out to me.

"She's a young healthy woman," Mom chimes in. "How is this possible? Would we not have seen the signs?"

"Not necessarily unless you know what you're looking for. Has she been tired a lot, thirsty?" he asks.

"Yes," I tell him. "She falls asleep easily claiming exhausting, and she's always thirsty. Damn it, I should have questioned it."

"No, it's possible that she's had this for some time. It's not something a non-medical professional would recognize unless maybe you are a diabetic yourself."

"So, when can I see her?"

"As I said, she's stable, but remains unconscious. There is a knot on her head, so I'm thinking maybe her sugar levels dropped and she fell to the ground, hitting her head. From the report I received from the paramedics that's how you found her?"

"Yeah, she was just… lying there," I choke out the words.

"We're doing everything we can. We're admitting her to ICU. Once she's in a room, I'll have a nurse come and inform you. Only two people are allowed in at a time, and visiting hours are eight in the morning until eight in the evening. You should go on home until then." He stands to leave.

"I'm not leaving her."

He looks over his shoulder at me and is quiet for more heartbeats than I can count. "Fair enough. You can stay. Cause any issues, and I'll have you removed. The rest of you go on home and get some rest." With that, he turns back around and exits the room.

"Go on back. Check on Camber. I'll call you if there are any updates," I tell them.

"We're good for a while and so is Camber," Dad speaks up. "Let's get our girl in a room and settled and then we can decide where to go from there."

The room is quiet for a long time, nothing but the sound of the ticking clock and my heartbeat that I know they must be able to hear, fill the room. "Guys, I'm not leaving her. Not until she's out of here. We might as well go ahead and get a plan together." None of them say anything, so I forge ahead. "Get some rest and head on home. We can rent a car when she's released."

"Nonsense," Mom speaks up. "We're only an hour from home. We'll figure it all out, right now, let's just get her into a room and settled."

I don't argue with her. I don't have the energy. Besides, she's right. There is time to figure it all out, and we are just a little over an hour from home. It's not like we're states away. That reminds me, I should call Maria, but I don't have her number. My mind races and then it hits me. Jonah. Surely she listed someone, namely Maria, as her emergency contact at work. Pulling out my phone, I send him a text.

Me: Hey, I need a favor. I need to get ahold of Maria. She's Aubree's friend.

Can you check her file and get her number for me?

Jonah: I can't just give her number to you, Blaine. Work out your lover's quarrel another way.

Me: She's in the hospital. Unconscious. I need that number.

Jonah: What? Why in the hell didn't you start with that, dick?

Jonah: Give me five to log into the database.

I stare at the screen waiting for his reply. Minutes pass by and I'm just about to text him again when the nurse knocks on the door. "We've got her in a room up in the fourth floor. Dr. Connor says that one of you is staying with her tonight."

"Me, and I'm not leaving until she does," I say, stepping forward.

"All right then, the rest of you," she looks around the room, "will have to wait until morning. Visiting hours start at eight." She reminds us. "You can follow me."

I don't have to be told twice. I'm on her heels as we make our way up to the fourth floor. Our family and friends are right behind me. When we all pile onto the elevator, the nurse just shakes her head, a smile tilting her lips.

"She's a lucky girl to be so loved."

It's an innocent statement, but I have to bite back another sob threatening to break free. She is lucky, but so are we. She would be even luckier if she knew how much I love her, how much we all do before this happened.

The nurse stops outside of her room and pushes open the

door. I follow in behind her. She steps back and lets me pass, and I stride straight to her side. "She looks like she's sleeping," I say aloud.

"Essentially, yes."

"Can she hear me?"

"Some patients say they could hear their loved ones while in this state, others not. It's hard to tell. I'd like to think she can. You should talk to her."

"Can I... can I touch her?" I ask, sitting in the chair next to her bed and moving it as close to her as I can possibly get it.

"You can. Just watch her IV." She points to her right hand. Fortunately, I'm sitting on her left side. "I'll be her nurse tonight, so I'll be back to check on her in a little while." She turns and walks out of the room, shutting the door behind her.

Tentatively, I pick up her hand, holding it in both of mine. "So warm," I whisper, placing my lips on the back of her hand. Lifting my head, I take a long look at her. "Bree, baby, I'm so scared," I admit. "There is so much that I want to say to you." I stop to compose myself. "I love you. I love you so damn much, it hurts. Deep inside, Bree. That's where you are. You've never been a fling, not ever. I agreed to your plan because I wanted you. I thought I would never find what I've found in you." I pause again, taking a deep breath and slowly exhale. "I never got to tell you —" My voice cracks and I lose the battle with my emotions. I don't try to hide or stop the tears that are flowing freely down my cheeks. "I was waiting for the right time, you know? I wanted it to be a moment where we were just hanging out and being us. Not when we were arguing over Jonah or making love. I wanted you to believe me."

"Please open your eyes, Bree. Please, come back to me." I hold my breath, waiting for her to do just that, but nothing happens. "I'm right here, baby. I'm not going anywhere," I tell her, resting my head beside our joined hands on the bed. "I'm not leaving here until you do."

CHAPTER Twenty Seven

BLAINE

"THANK YOU, MARIA, BUT I'M okay," I tell her for what seems like the tenth time. Jonah came through with her number, and I was able to call her Saturday morning and fill her in on everything that's going on. She's been here every day since.

"I'll be right here," she assures me. "I'll call you if there are any changes."

"I appreciate that, I do. But I'm not leaving her. Until she opens her eyes, I'm going to be here." It's Monday mid-morning and still no change. The doctors have been able to get her sugar levels regulated with insulin through her IV, but she's going to more than likely be on medication for the rest of her life.

"You need to take care of you," she tries again.

"Being here is taking care of me. She's all that I need," I say, pointing to my sleeping beauty. I just wish a simple kiss could wake her up.

"She loves you," she finally says.

I nod. "I love her too."

"You never told her." She's not accusing me; it's more of an observation.

"I was waiting for the right time." I feel like that's something I've repeated over and over too. To Bree, as she lies in this bed, I've told her countless times. To my parents, my friends, and now hers.

"At least go to the cafeteria and get something to eat, stretch your legs."

"I'm fine here. Mom brought me clothes, and I'm not hungry."

"Blaine," she says. This time there is something different in her voice. Tearing my eyes from Bree, I look at her. "Thank you. She's not had the easiest time, I'm not sure what she's told you, but it warms my heart to know that she has you and your family."

"Yeah, well, a lot of good it does if she doesn't realize she has us."

"She's a fighter. She's been through so much. This isn't going to stop her. Have faith."

"I'm trying, Maria. I really am, but it's been days and she still won't open her eyes. I just want to see them, you know?"

"I know."

Neither one of us says a word after that. We just sit in silence watching and waiting for my girl to come back to us. Maria leaves a few hours later with a promise from me to call her with any changes, no matter how big or small. Day turns into night, with my parents stopping by to visit. Kevin and the guys are getting the car ready for the Knoxville, Iowa, race this weekend, but what they don't know is that I'm not going. I can't just leave her here all alone while I go race.

"Why don't you go home, or to a hotel, and get a good night's rest?" Mom suggests.

"I'm good here," I say, patting the arm of the reclining chair I've been living in since it was brought to this room.

"Blaine—" Mom starts, but Dad cuts her off.

"Robin, let him stay. He's a grown man. He knows his limits."

"Do you need anything?" Mom asks.

"No, thanks for bringing dinner and more clothes."

"I'll take the dirties home and wash them. I'll bring them back with me tomorrow."

"Thank you." The only time I've left her side is to shower—the world's quickest I'm sure—or to use the restroom. I haven't left this room, not once since the night I walked through the door. I made her a promise, and even if she didn't hear it, I intend to keep it.

After saying goodbye to my parents, I settle into my seat. Her hand is in mine. "Night, baby," I whisper as I drift off to sleep.

I'm jolted awake by a dream. It was so real, she was squeezing my hand. Looking over at the bed, her eyes are still closed. With my free hand, I rub the sleep from my eyes. I'm just about to stand to go to the restroom and splash some cold water on my face when it happens.

She squeezes my hand.

"Bree," I choke out. I scramble from the chair and lean over her. "Open your eyes, baby. Please open your eyes." I wait and wait and wait, and nothing happens. Reaching for the call button to tell the nurse of this new discovery, I hear the sweetest sound I've heard in days. My name whispered from her lips.

"B-B-Blaine," she murmurs.

"Hey, baby. I'm right here," I assure her. "Can you open your eyes for me? Can you do that?" I wait, never blinking an eye afraid I might miss it and am rewarded by the first flutter of her eyes. "There you go. Let me see those big green eyes, Bree." Again, I wait. Her hand squeezes mine so I know she can hear me. "It's okay. Take your time. I'm right here." I don't know how much time passes, could be seconds, could be minutes, but when she finally does it, when she forces her eyes open and they land on mine, I lose it.

"I missed you," I say, wiping the tears from my eyes. I need to be able to see her. "You scared the hell out of me."

"Wh—" She tries to talk, but I'm sure her mouth is dry as hell.

"Let me call the nurse." I hit the call button twice for good measure. "You fell. Your blood sugar levels were too low. They think you hit your head, and you've been out for a few days. It's early Tuesday morning."

"Blaine," the night nurse greets me. "Oh, you're awake. That's good to see. Let me get your vitals, and we'll start with some ice chips for your dry throat. We have to start slow."

Bree nods, just slightly, but it's a nod all the same. It's a reply, one I wasn't sure I'd ever be able to see again. I stand back, letting the nurse do her thing, but never taking my eyes off her. She nods and answers questions as best as she can.

"I'm going to page the doctor, but your vitals are strong, and your glucose levels are stable. You have a lot of people on your team," the nurse tells her. "This one hasn't left your side. I'll be back with some ice chips," she says before leaving the room.

I waste no time taking my seat next to her and clasping her hand in mine, bringing it to my lips. "I was scared I'd never see those beautiful green eyes again. Did I ever tell you that? That I love your eyes?"

She nods.

"Could you hear me? When you were sleeping? Could you hear me?"

"S-somet-times," she croaks.

"Shh, don't try to talk. I'm sorry. Wait for the ice chips." The nurse walks in as soon as I say it and hands me a small plastic cup with a spoon.

"Take it slow, but if she finishes all of those and keeps it down, she can have some water."

"Let's sit you up." I press the button to slowly move her to the sitting position. "Better?" She nods. "Now, some ice," I spoon just a few small chunks and place them in her mouth. She moans and immediately opens for more. We repeat the same process a dozen or so more times before she's satisfied.

"Thank you," she says, her voice gruff from not being used.

"I need to call everyone and let them know you're awake."

"How long?"

"Friday night at the track we found you lying on the ground. It's Tuesday morning." Glancing at the clock on the wall, I see it's just a little after 5:00 a.m. "Do you remember anything?"

"I just didn't feel well. I was hot and felt... off, so I was going to go lie down. I don't remember much after that."

"You fell just between the toter home and the trailer. You hit your head when you fell. You have a nice goose egg right here." I point to the spot on her head. She runs her fingers gingerly over the spot and winces. "When we brought you in, they ran some tests and determined that your blood sugar levels were too low. They think you passed out due to that and hit your head when you did."

"I've never had issues with my blood sugar."

"That's what I told them. You'd never mentioned it. Maria later confirmed that she didn't think you had either. They say you're a diabetic now."

"What?"

"It can be controlled with medication, and they have your levels at a good number now," I assure her. "The doctor will be in soon to answer any questions you might have."

Standing from my seat, I hover over her. "I love you, Aubree." She opens her mouth, but I place my finger to her lips to stop her. "I have for a while now. Hell, probably since the first day I felt your soft skin. I wouldn't admit it even to myself not until recently. I had planned on telling you after the race. I could feel you pulling away from me, and I needed to tell you. I just never got the chance."

"Blaine," she whispers.

I cut her off by pressing my lips to hers. Just a soft featherlight kiss, but it's a kiss all the same. "I love you, baby. We're going to get you better, and then we'll decide where we go from here." I wasn't sure I would ever get to see those beautiful green eyes again. Relief washes over me. She finally knows that I love her. That I'm here for her, and there is no end date.

"What do you mean?"

"Our future, Bree. You tell me what you want, and I'll make it happen. That's how this is going to work." I'll do everything in my power to give her a life she deserves—full of love and family. The corner of my mouth lifts when I think about waking up to her every morning and going to sleep with her tucked into my side every night. No more hiding, no more sneaking around. I can shout my love for her from the rooftops.

CHAPTER Twenty Eight

Aubree

I BLINK UP AT HIM, not sure if I'm hearing him right. This causes him to throw his head back in laughter. I'm just about ready to ask him to repeat himself one more time when the door opens and a man walks in.

"Well, this is a nice surprise. Aubree, I'm Dr. Townsend. I've been treating you since you were admitted. How are you feeling?" He goes on to ask me about what I remember and then explains my new diagnosis. "You'll receive some diabetes education. Blaine and his parents and a few of your friends have already received it," he tells me.

"You did?" I ask, not able to hide the emotion in my voice.

"Of course, we did. We want to know how to help you. What signs to look for, those kinds of things."

"You're very lucky to have such a huge support system..." The doctor babbles on, but I'm stuck there. On the support system. I've never had more than Uncle Bobby growing up and Maria and Isaac after him. To think that I have Blaine and his friends and family behind me, after we've lied to them all these months. I'm shocked and so incredibly grateful.

"Do you have any questions?" Dr. Townsend asks.

"When can I go home?"

He chuckles. "We'll keep you another day or so for observation. Let's slowly get you eating some real food and see how your blood sugar reacts."

"Thank you, Doctor." Blaine reaches out and shakes his hand.

"You all did that?" I ask before the door is even shut behind the doctor.

"We did. We want to know how to help you if you start to feel bad again, the signs to look for."

"But the season is almost over," I counter.

"Baby, did you not hear anything I just said? Sure, this season is over, and then there will be next season and the one after that. I love you, Aubree. As far as I'm concerned, there is no end."

"Blaine, you don't have to—" He cuts me off once again pressing his lips to mine.

"I do," he whispers. "I do have to tell you because it's the honest truth. You're not getting rid of me that easily." He pulls back and takes his phone out of his pocket. I watch as he hits a few buttons and holds the phone out in front of him. "Hey, Maria." He grins. "I have someone you should say hi to." He turns the phone and there she is, my best friend is on the screen with tears in her eyes and her hand covering her mouth.

"Aubs," she cries. "I'm so happy to see you," she says with a teary laugh. "You gave us a scare." She motions to someone off-screen.

"Hey, there." Isaac waves. "Glad to see you're awake."

"Hi." I wave at the screen. Tears start to build. Maria has been there for me since I moved to town, and I'm so grateful to have her in my life. She encouraged me to pursue this thing with

Blaine and now… now he loves me.

"It's good to see you awake. We'll be there later today to see you," Maria says, her voice cracking.

"You don't have to come," I try to tell her, losing the battle with my emotions as the tears finally fall.

"Maybe we can get that man of yours to go grab some fresh air so we can have some girl time," Maria teases.

"Not likely. I don't leave until she does, remember?" he asks her.

"All right, you two. We'll see you soon. Love you, Aubs."

"Love you too."

Blaine hits end on his phone and dials it again. We repeat the same process with the guys at the shop, Ashley, and his parents. All of them saying the same thing that Blaine needs to get out of here and get some fresh air.

"I'm okay," I tell him after our last call. "Why don't you go grab something to eat, and uh, get some fresh air?" I end with a laugh and he playfully rolls his eyes.

"Not happening, Bree. I made a promise whether you heard me or not. I'm not leaving here until you do." My heart flips over in my chest at his confession.

"That's silly. You heard the doctor. I'm going to be fine."

"You are fine," he says. "And when you leave here, you'll be coming home with me."

"I have a place of my own."

"Yeah, we should change that."

"What? Are you feeling all right?" I ask.

"I'm good. Perfect in fact." He leans in and kisses me, and I sigh against his lips. "I missed you. I was a fool to not tell you what you meant to me before this happened. I'll never make that mistake again. If I feel it, if I want it, you'll know about it. I could have lost you, Bree."

"I'm okay." Reaching out, I place my hand on his cheek. "You really mean it, all of it, don't you?" My voice trembles as I take in a shaking breath. It's as if I woke up and all my dreams have come true.

"Every word."

"I love you too." I say the words without an ounce of hesitation. Instead, relief warms me now I'm finally able to speak them, to tell him what he means to me.

His eyes soften and a grin tilts his lips. "That's all that matters. We'll work the rest out as we go."

There are nurses and doctors in and out of my room all morning long. By lunchtime, my stomach rumbles from hunger. I'm able to convince the nurse I'm ready for solid food since I've held down my ice and water rations along with my oatmeal this morning. They bring me a piece of grilled chicken, broccoli, a roll, and some applesauce. I eat every bite. It was pretty good for hospital food. Then again, it's been a while since I've had solid food so cardboard probably would have tasted good at this point.

"Doing well, Aubree," Dr. Townsend says later in the afternoon. "Your numbers are holding strong, so if all goes well, we might let him spring you out of here tomorrow."

"Really?" I ask, hopeful.

"Yes, as long as you keep progressing."

"Thank you, Dr. Townsend."

"Glad to see you're on the road to recovery. We'll get you set up for your diabetes education. I'm not sending you home on insulin. You can try the oral medicine and diet since your levels have stabilized so well. If that's going to change, it will with the solid foods." He clicks on the computer located on a rolling cart and looks through my chart. "So far just a small spike, but that's to be expected anytime you eat. Your number is falling back to where it should be for having eaten two hours ago."

"Thanks, Doc." Blaine shakes his hand before he leaves the room. "So, what do you say we take a nap?" he asks.

As if just the thought of napping makes me sleepy, I cover a yawn. "You should go home and rest. Come back tomorrow and pick me up."

"Nope. I have a better idea." I watch him as he kicks off his shoes. "Scoot over," he says, sitting on the edge of the bed.

"What are you doing?" I ask, even though I have a pretty good idea. The idea of laying in his arms makes me giddy with excitement.

"It's been too many nights of not holding you. Too many nights of only being able to hold your hand. I just need you in my arms, just a nap, Bree."

What woman in their right mind would deny him that request? Moving over to the far side of the bed, he settles in stretching out beside me. "Now, come here." He holds open his arms and I carefully move back toward him. Once we're settled, he exhales softly and kisses the top of my head. "I love you, Aubree," he murmurs before his breathing evens out. My heart is full. Closing my eyes, I let the warmth of his body, and the security of his arms lull me to sleep.

I wake sometime later to whispers. Opening my eyes, I see Ashley and Robin sitting at the foot of the bed. Both wear matching grins. "Hi," I croak, my throat dry from sleep.

"Hey, you look comfy." Ashley winks and I can feel my face heat.

"Blaine." I shake his arm to wake him up.

"Go back to sleep, baby," he mumbles.

"Aw." Robin smiles and her eyes shimmer. "I'm so glad to see you're awake and doing well," she says.

"Yeah, the doctor says I might be able to go home tomorrow if all my numbers still stay steady."

"That's great news," Ashley chimes in. "We thought we would sit with you while the guys and Blaine talk racing."

"I'm not leaving," Blaine mumbles, nuzzling into my chest.

Robin and Ashley crack up laughing, which makes me laugh

too. This, of course, wakes him up.

"What did I miss?" he asks, groggily.

"Glad you could join us," Robin teases her son. "Your dad and Kevin are in the waiting room. We came back first."

"What happened to two at a time?" he asks.

"Apparently, now that she's awake that restriction is lifted," she says as the door opens.

"There she is." Brian smiles. He comes over to the bed and kisses me on the cheek. My heart swells with the love and support his family and friends are giving me.

"Hands off my girl, Pops." Blaine chuckles. He sits up in bed, and I do the same. However, he makes no move to climb out, so I curl up against his chest. Oddly enough, it feels natural to be with him like this, with all of them around. To be honest, that's what my heart has yearned for all along. The five of us spend the next hour chatting. Conversation simmers when they come in to read my levels, but as soon as the nurse is gone, Kevin speaks up.

"We've got the car loaded and ready to go whenever you are," he says.

"Not going," Blaine says it as if he's talking about the weather.

"What?" I look up at him. "What do you mean you're not going? It's a points race, right?" I look to Brian for confirmation and he nods.

"I'm not leaving this room until you do."

"Blaine, that's crazy. You're leading the points. You're on track to win your third championship in a row. This is what you wanted."

He shrugs nonchalantly. "Plans change."

"No. Nope, not happening, Bishop. This is your career we're talking about."

"Baby, this is you we're talking about," he says, making me blush.

I look over at his mom. "Can you talk some sense into him?"

"What if Ashley and I stay with Aubree? We'll make sure she's set up at your place, and cater to her every need."

"That's not what I meant," I grumble, and she laughs.

"No way in hell am I racing if she's still here. Even then she's going to need me."

"Blaine, I'm fine. Look, I know this was scary for you, for all of you, but I'm okay. I have this new way of living and eating, but it's not rocket science. I can do this. You can't give up your career because I'm a diabetic."

"Aubree—"

His dad cuts him off. "You said she might get released tomorrow. What if we take the car to the track? We'll leave tomorrow like we normally would. You get Aubree set up at your place, and you can fly out Friday morning. I've already checked flights. There's one that leaves here at seven in the morning on Friday, and there are plenty of seats. There is also one for Thursday night. And"—he holds up his hand to stop his son's rebuttal—"before you ask, there is a return flight home, the red-eye on Friday night. Plenty of time to get to the airport after the race and back home to Aubree early Saturday morning."

"That works for you, right? I promise I will not leave your house. I can call Maria and have her stay with me so that your mom can go." I hate that they are going through all of this trouble, but I know Blaine, and he's as stubborn as he is sexy. He has both in spades.

"We can leave the T-shirt sales for this one," Brian says.

"Definitely," Robin agrees. "No need to have Maria missing work."

"I like the sound of a girls' weekend," Ashley agrees.

"No." Blaine crosses his arms over his chest.

"Stubborn. Fine, when I get released, I'm going back to my place."

"Aubree," he warns.

"That's the deal, Checkmate. You either fly to the race and I stay with your mom and Ashley at your place or you can be bullheaded and not race, lose out on the points, and sit home alone."

"Oh, she's good." Robin laughs.

"Bree, I—"

"Please? Do this for me. I want the win, Bishop. Can you deliver?"

"Come on now, do you know who you're talking to?" he boasts.

"Then show me. Go and win this one. Bring it home for me."

"I have two conditions." He kisses my forehead as if it's just the two of us in the room. Heat touches my cheeks again.

"Let's hear them."

"You have to be out of here and settled at my place."

"Done. What else?"

"That we no longer refer to it as my place, but our place. Move in with me."

"That's your second condition? You could have asked for anything."

"All I want is you."

My heart flips over in my chest and the heart monitor goes crazy, making us all laugh. I look up into his hazel eyes and all I can see is love. All directed at me. There really is no other answer. "Looks like you've got yourself a roommate," I say with more courage than I feel.

"Yeah? We need to do something about that title, but that works for now." Excitement bubbles inside the pit of my stomach. I'm on board with whatever he has planned. Blaine Bishop owns my heart, and I never want it back.

EPILOGUE

BLAINE

"LADIES AND GENTLEMEN, I WOULD now like to introduce you to this year's points champion. This is his third year in a row winning the points, and this year's win makes him the youngest driver ever to win three back-to-back championships. He hails from Knoxville, Tennessee, Blaine 'Checkmate' Bishop!"

My peers and their families cheer as I lean over and kiss Bree before standing to take the stage. I'm stopped along the way for handshakes and congratulations. They quiet down once I reach the podium. "Thank you," I say, and they grow even quieter. "This is an incredible honor, one that I will be forever grateful for. This has been a big year for me." I point out to the crowd, to my future wife. "As some of you might know, I got engaged two weeks ago. My fiancée, Bree—" I wave to her. "—has been with me this year as well as my parents and my crew. There is no way I would be standing up here today without them. Thank you to all of you for such clean, fun racing. I'm looking forward to next year." I keep my speech short and sweet. We're a room full of late model drivers in suits and ties. We all want to go home and shed them for jeans and T-shirts. Of that I'm certain.

The crowd, which consists of racers, their families, and crew, stands and everyone starts saying their goodbyes, most of them already plotting out next season. I know this because Kevin, Rick, Jacob, Dad, and I have been doing the same thing. We have a game plan. Jonah is on for sponsorship as well as all of my other sponsors, plus a few new ones. Winning the championship helped that.

When I make it back to the table, Bree stands and wraps her arms around my neck, hugging me. "I'm so proud of you." A quick kiss to my lips and she's pulling back. "Even if I had to bribe you to race. You know, half of that trophy should be mine." She smiles.

"Baby, everything I am, everything I have is yours."

"Yeah? So, what if I said I wanted another dog? You know Camber gets lonely."

"Done."

"Hmm, too easy. What if I said I want to remodel some of the rooms in the house?"

"Done. I've already told you to go crazy."

"Really? Just like that? I need to try harder." She taps her index finger against her chin as if she's deep in thought. "What if I said that I want a destination wedding?"

"I'd say when and where?"

"All right." She nods, grinning.

"What if I said you're going to be a daddy?" She bites down on her bottom lip.

My heart pounds like a heavy bass drum in my chest. Did I hear her right? "It's loud in here, Bree. I'm going to need you to repeat that." I send up a silent prayer that I did indeed hear her correctly the first time.

"You heard me, Checkmate." Her green eyes are shining with happiness.

I'm going to be a father. Dropping to my knees, not giving a fuck who sees me, I place my hands over her belly. I hear my mom, or maybe it's Ashley, gasp. "When?" I ask, looking up at her. Emotion clogs my throat and hot tears prick my eyes.

"I just found out, so my guess is I'm only a few weeks along."

"Me too!" Ashley squeals.

"No way!" Aubree steps away from me to hug Ashley. I climb back to my feet and go to her, wrapping her in my arms as soon as they separate.

"Congrats, man," Kevin says.

"You too. Excuse us." I lace my fingers through hers and lead her out of the banquet hall down the long corridor to the corner. I need a minute, just the two of us. I need to show her what this means to me, that creating a baby with her is the most special gift, aside from her herself, that she could ever give me.

"What are you doing?" She laughs.

"This." I cup her face in my hands and kiss her. I try to pour everything I'm feeling into this one. Love, adoration, excitement, fear, all of it for her. For us. "I love you."

"I love you too."

"When can we get married?"

"I'm ready when you are. Maria and Isaac need to be there, other than that, I don't care."

"I'll take care of it." I kiss her again, this time just a quick peck on the cheek.

"Who would have thought this is where we would end up?"

The journey we traveled to get here was bumpy, but the destination is beyond worth it. I have my future wife in my arms, my hand resting over where our baby is growing inside of her. I've just won my third championship in a row. This is our life, and I wouldn't change it for a thousand championships. No, Bree and our baby, they're the grand prize, both of which I plan to cherish for the rest of my life.

"Not me." I press my lips to hers. "But I guess this is what happens when you trust the push. Best advice I've ever been given."

CONTACT Kaylee Ryan

I cannot thank you enough for taking the time to read Trust the Push. I appreciate each and every one of you. I'd love to hear from you.

Facebook: http://bit.ly/2C5DgdF

Reader Group: http://bit.ly/2O0yWDx

Goodreads: http://bit.ly/2HodJvx

BookBub: http://bit.ly/2KulVvH

Website: http://www.kayleeryan.com/

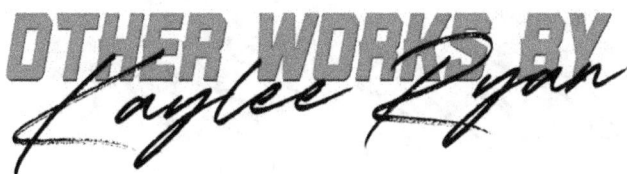

OTHER WORKS BY *Kaylee Ryan*

With You Series
Anywhere With You
More With You
Everything With You

Stand Alone Titles
Tempting Tatum
Unwrapping Tatum
Levitate
Just Say When
Unexpected Reality
I Just Want You
Reminding Avery
Hey, Whiskey
When Sparks Collide
Pull You Through
Beyond the Bases
Remedy

OTHER WORKS BY *Kaylee Ryan*

Soul Serenade Series
Emphatic
Assured
Definite
Insistent

Southern Heart Series
Southern Pleasure
Southern Desire
Southern Attraction
Southern Devotion

ACKNOWLEDGMENTS

To my readers:

Thank you! Your never-ending support is humbling. Thank you for reading and taking chance on my work.

To my family:

I'm blessed beyond measure with the support that you provide. I could not do this without you. Thank you for being my rock on this journey.

Sara Eirew:

Thank you for another cover worthy image.

Tami Integrity Formatting:

Thank you for making my words beautiful. You're amazing and I cannot thank you enough for all that you do.

Sommer Stein:

Your talent never ceases to amaze me. Thank you for yet another stunning cover. You've brought this book to life and for that I thank you.

My beta team:

Jamie, Stacy, Lauren, and Franci I would be lost without you. You read my words as much as I do, and I can't tell you what your input and all the time you give means to me. Thank you from the bottom of my heart for taking this wild ride with me.

Give Me Books:

With every release, your team works diligently to get my book in the hands of bloggers. I cannot tell you how thankful I am for your services.

Becca Manuel:

You nailed the trailer! Thank you so much for doing what you do.

Tempting Illustrations:

Thank you for everything. I would be lost without you.

Julie Deaton:

Thank you for giving this book a set of fresh final eyes.

Becky Johnson:

I could not do this without you. Thank you for pushing me, and making me work for it.

Marisa Corviesero:

Thank you for all that you do. I know I'm not the easiest client. I'm blessed to have you on this journey with me.

Kimberly Ann:

Thank you for organizing and tracking the ARC team. I couldn't do it without you.

Pam McFarland:

You won the dog naming contest in my reader group, and I love it. Camber could not be a better name for Blaine's dog. Thank you for taking part in the contest.

Bloggers:

Thank you, doesn't seem like enough. You don't get paid to do what you do. It's from the kindness of your heart and your love of reading that fuels you. Without you, without your pages, your voice, your reviews, spreading the word it would be so much harder if not impossible to get my words in reader's hands. I can't tell you how much your never-ending support means to me. Thank you for being you, thank you for all that you do.

To my Kick Ass Crew:

The name of the group speaks for itself. You ladies truly do KICK ASS! I'm honored to have you on this journey with me. Thank you for reading, sharing, commenting, suggesting, the teasers, the messages all of it. Thank you from the bottom of my heart for all that you do. Your support is everything!

With Love,

Kaylee Ryan
AUTHOR

www.ingramcontent.com/pod-product-compliance
Lightning Source LLC
Chambersburg PA
CBHW060313260626
47160CB00007B/2595